LIVE WELL DIET

The Easy Guide to Health and
Weight Management

Dr Sarita Davare
Sanjeev Kapoor

with

Rita D'Souza

Popular
Prakashan

www.popularprakashan.com

Published by
Harsha Bhatkal for
POPULAR PRAKASHAN PVT. LTD.
301, Mahalaxmi Chambers
22, Bhulabhai Desai Road
Mumbai – 400 026
www.popularprakashan.com

DISCLAIMER

The conclusions, beliefs and opinions expressed in 'The Live Well Diet: The Easy Guide to Health and Weight Management', do not aim to diagnose, treat or prevent any illness, or condition, or guarantee any kind of weight loss whatsoever. The information provided in this book is intended as a guide only, and not as a substitute for advice from a registered physician or any other qualified healthcare professional. The implementation of the diets mentioned in the book (whether in part or in whole) is entirely at your own risk and responsibility. You are advised to consult your physician before starting on The Live Well Diet.

(4346)
ISBN: 978-81-7991-787-9

Printed in India
by Saurabh Printers (P) Ltd.
Plot No. 67 A-68, Ecotech, Ext. I
Kasna, Greater Noida-201306 (U.P)

Contents

Section III

LIVE WELL DIET RECIPES

SOUPS

SALADS

SNACKS

MAIN MEAL - Chicken

MAIN MEAL - Fish

MAIN MEAL - Veg

RICE, ROTI, PASTA AND NOODLES

DAL AND KADHI

SWEETS AND DESSERTS

acknowledgements

There are many people without whose help, active support and encouragement this book would never have seen the light of day.

My family has stood by me throughout and helped me achieve my goals. I am who I am because of their love and blessings.

My entire team at the Pain and Weight Management Clinic who work tirelessly and with great dedication for the well-being of patients. I could not have done this book without their assistance, for which I am very grateful.

I thank the many doctors and medical professionals who have mentored, inspired and encouraged me with their constant advice and good wishes throughout my career.

I am particularly grateful to Dr Avinash Phadke for reading through the draft manuscript of this book and for his valuable inputs.

Over the years, many patients have become good friends and a part of my family, and my life has been enriched by their friendship, loyalty and trust. They have been at my side from the inception of this book and my appreciation for their support knows no bounds.

My yoga teacher, Jyoti Chitnis, helps me to regularly refresh and strengthen my innermost self and physical being so I can serve my patients better. I am grateful for her advice which I have included in this book.

I am deeply grateful to my patients who have given feedback about their treatment in this book. I consider every comment as a step towards excellence and perfection which I constantly endeavour to achieve.

This book would not have happened were it not for Sanjeev Kapoor, who urged me to write it so that many more people could benefit from the Live Well Diet. He has also developed recipes which will make the diet come alive in your kitchen. I offer my sincere thanks also to Harsha Bhatkal, my publisher, who has enthusiastically supported this book from the very beginning.

I am very grateful to Rita D'Souza for helping me put my knowledge and experience into words.

Dr Sarita Davare

THE BEST THING THAT'S EVER HAPPENED TO ME

I'd like to thank Dr Davare so much for everything, not only for all my weight loss, but for making me so healthy and making the entire process such a positive transformation by being so supportive through it all. This treatment is easily the best thing that's ever happened to me.

When I first joined Dr Davare's course I realised that I enjoyed it, I felt light, healthy and energetic, never starved. And I felt so fresh. The results were instant and the maintenance part of it is just as simple, if you follow it religiously, your weight loss will be permanent.

The best part about this is that, you are prescribed a diet according to your medical condition, and you are given exactly what is ideal for your body, so it's like a personalised diet, which makes it even more effective.

Dr Davare has always been comforting and full of warmth; I've always felt like I'm in safe hands with her. I'm sure that she will continue to change the lives of many, many more others like she did mine for the better.

author's note: *Dr Sarita Davare*

There are many aspects to living well in a holistic way. Eating right, exercising, managing stress, adequate sleep and good social interaction lead to a good and healthy lifestyle. On the other hand, often high stress levels or a sedentary lifestyle lead to poor eating habits and perhaps eating more than the body's requirement of food. The belief that "nothing will happen to me" leads to irresponsibility towards one's health.

Every individual is unique, with unique physical, mental and emotional attributes. Besides, the level of awareness of health issues differs in people. How much one should eat or exercise is often a mystery. Then there are stress levels, erratic routines and personal habits which add to health problems such as obesity. People often cannot find a suitable regime for total well-being.

There may be many aspects of your present lifestyle that you could be unhappy with, but one of the most common ones is excess weight which is both caused by and leads to mental and physical problems. Many people find that if they address their weight and fitness issues a number of other health and lifestyle problems are solved in the process, and vice versa – leading to a completely new life.

The common misconception about losing weight is that that it involves deprivation of your favourite foods. But that is not the case. Moderation and balance are the keys to a healthy diet and lifestyle. Because each person is unique, a weight loss programme must begin with knowledge about one's lifestyle, attitude towards health and present medical condition. More than anything else, one must also have a strong determination to undergo the programme. It begins with self-motivation to correct one's lifestyle. Therefore the diet is based on each individual's present physical and medical status and needs.

The first step towards losing weight is motivation. Years of neglect of one's health cannot be corrected in a short time. Weight loss has to be gradual and monitored very carefully. During this long process continuous support needs to be given to people so that they do not switch back to the old incorrect lifestyle.

Subsequently, when you start losing weight and feeling better, you begin to have more confidence about achieving a healthy lifestyle. "I can fit into my old dress now" itself is a great motivating feeling. People start noticing and complimenting you. That is a very euphoric feeling. All that needs to be done at this stage is to ensure that the level of motivation continues.

This is how my Live Well Diet is designed. And in this book I bring you the same advice and guidance I give to my patients in my clinic.

I get a cross-section of patients in my clinic and each one is unique with unique eating and life-style habits. Here are some examples where you will see that the approach for each patient differs, depending on age and other individual factors.

A young college student came to me with an obesity problem. She was 5 feet 7 inches tall and weighed 110 kg. She had a habit of eating fatty, junk food. Her body was getting more calories than she required, which was the main cause of her excessive weight gain. She spent a lot of time on the internet, chatting with her friends till late at night, leading to lack of sleep and midnight hunger pangs. Added to that was her craze for watching television and playing video games, which led to her sitting in one place for a long time with very little outdoor exercise. When diet control and exercise was recommended, she replied, "I have to travel to college every day and change two trains. I have to climb the stairs at the station. Is that not a form of exercise?" Often, people make the mistake of considering daily chores as a form of exercise.

I explained to her that exercise should be done with a fresh mind and adequate time with a proper daily schedule.

A few months later, the girl had corrected her lifestyle. She had learned the meaning of moderation in terms of the food that she was eating, sleep or exercise. She does not need my support any longer because she is on the right track. It was a metamorphosis which reflected in her body as well. She had achieved the right metabolic rate for her age.

The same was the case of a **middle-aged executive** who walked into my clinic one day. He weighed 120 kg. He had to do a lot of travelling, had erratic work schedules with very little sleep. Tiredness from work was leading to less exercise thereby resulting in obesity.

His zeal to come up in life and his over-ambitious attitude was creating a lot of stress. At such high stress levels, his ability to make choices about the type and quantity of food was reduced. This led to stress-induced obesity. Food was more a hobby or comfort to him than a necessity.

The habits he had formed at a young age—like smoking and drinking—led to his dependence on such vices. He had the misconception that they reduced stress levels, unaware that they were actually damaging his body.

He was afraid that a diet would force him to give up the things that he loved. My first task was to prepare him mentally by informing him of the health problems that he could have if he continued with the same lifestyle. For some people just motivation works, but with some a graphic picture of the realities of future health problems caused by an unhealthy lifestyle is required.

Eventually he has adopted a healthy lifestyle. Within a few weeks he realised that he could change his life if he wanted to. Every morning he exercises, has the right type and quantity of food. He has understood how to strike a balance between work and home, and knows how to socialise but without over-dependence on food, cigarettes or liquour. He was extremely happy when his reports showed normal cholesterol and sugar levels. He had achieved his target of

84 kg within a few months. Most importantly, he was in control of his lifestyle.

I came across a **middle-aged homemaker** in her late 40s. She met me at a function and expressed her desire to lose weight. I asked her to get the necessary medical investigations done and bring the results to me.

During our meeting I asked her what her reason was for wanting to lose weight. What she mentioned was very interesting. She had 2 children. Her daughter was married into a good family and her son had settled abroad. She was staying with her husband and in-laws. Her 25th wedding anniversary was approaching in 6 months and she wanted to surprise her husband with her new, young appearance.

I explained the diet to her and asked if she could follow it. She was confident she could.

At the end of her treatment she came to meet me with her husband. Both were very happy. Her husband told me that he had bought an entirely new wardrobe for her and thanked me for making her look as young as in their early married life. He mentioned that this was the best anniversary gift that he had ever imagined.

What he mentioned also surprised me. Due to her healthy lifestyle, the cooking styles in their kitchen had changed: the right amount of oil, more stress on fibre and a healthy diet had changed the entire household. Gone were greasy oily snacks and in came more freshly prepared, healthy food.

I thought to myself there cannot be anything more rewarding than seeing a smile and happiness on the faces of my patients.

Now, let us look at the case of an **elderly couple**. A 68 year old man came to me because his physician recommended he lose some weight. He weighed 100 kg, and suffered from diabetes and osteoarthritis. His wife was 65 years old with a weight of 86 kg. Coming from a traditional orthodox background they had some wrong information about dieting.

I asked his wife who was accompanying him, what kind of food they cooked at home. I realised that the family ate a lot of fried foods with dollops of ghee in every dish. They had fixed ideas about food habits. It was a challenging case for me, as convincing this elderly couple was a difficult task. I explained to them about the food pyramid in which ghee had to be reduced to the minimum and vegetables, fruits etc., needed to be increased.

I also explained that as one ages, one's ability to digest food or burn calories reduces. An older person cannot exercise the way young people exercise. It is therefore important to determine which foods and how much one has to eat so it can be easily metabolised by the body.

I encouraged them to make a beginning and see how they would cope. Fortunately, they agreed. They started eating right. They now eat a more healthy diet, take an early morning walk every day, and have regaled me with many amusing incidents about their morning laughter club members. They are not just feeling physically healthy but also more energetic. Gone were their complaints about knee pain and indigestion.

I was happy to see the smile on their faces when the couple's weight reduced in a few months to their target weights.

I have had many such positive cases over the years and have learned that to Live Well you need to manage your weight through the right food choices in the right proportions, exercise and have a positive attitude and determination. Many of their stories in their own words are included in this book which will bear witness to the fact that finally, it was their own resolve, perseverance and right choices that bore fruit and changed their lives for the better.

While the diet and programme described in this book is one that many patients have used successfully to bring about many positive changes in health and lifestyle, I must emphasise that as each individual is unique you will have to follow the diet as best suited to your needs and situation. This diet provides general guidelines and you are strongly advised to consult a physician before commencing it, as well as at regular intervals, so that your progress and the state of your health are monitored. As with any lifestyle change there is no single solution that will suit all individuals. Some may lose more weight in a shorter time than others, and some very little over a longer period. There are no guarantees offered as much depends on an individual's genetic make-up, age, gender, state of health, work patterns and emotional and psychological state.

I hope you will find some solutions in this book to your personal lifestyle challenges and that you will benefit from the Live Well Diet that has brought new life to countless others.

The bond between me and my patients is born of a deep concern I feel for each patient that comes to me for help. My team and I invest quality time in guiding each of our patients to discover the best and most effective path to a life of physical and mental well-being, taking into consideration all aspects of a person's life in a holistic way. This book is our way of sharing our knowledge and experience with you with the same spirit of caring and concern we show each of our patients, and I hope it will make a positive difference in your life.

Andavare

author's note: *Sanjeev Kapoor*

Living well can mean so many different things – it can mean having a 4-bedroom apartment or a farmhouse with all the latest comforts; or the latest mobile phone or iPad; for some it can mean having the means to treat oneself to a holiday now and then, and a monthly night out at the local movie theatre. For most of us living well implies financial and physical comfort. However, I would like to suggest that living well is much more than that - it has less to do with the health of one's bank balance and much more to do with the state of one's health.

To live well is to enjoy the freedom of being able to walk and even run no matter what your age, to climb a flight of stairs without getting out of breath, to eat a good meal without feeling any discomfort or ill effects; to relax into a state of peaceful calm – all tensions at bay; to sleep soundly at night and awake refreshed, ready to embrace a new day with energy and enthusiasm. The glow of one's skin and the spring in one's step is more evidence of truly living well than any manisfestation of wealth. "Health is wealth" we know, but how many of us pay attention to that tired phrase? We take good health for granted and assume our bodies will cope with all the stresses and strains we subject it to in the name of achievement and pleasure.

Being overweight is a sure sign that we are not living well. The extra weight we carry has serious and long-tem effects on our physical and mental well-being. There are solutions aplenty out there which will promise instant good health, weight reduction and even mental bliss. But there are very few that have been tried and tested and become a way of life for countless people.

The Live Well Diet is one such solution, and Alyona and I are the proof of its efficacy. We have incorporated the diet and its principles into our lives so it is no longer a diet but a way of being. We no longer have to agonise over the food choices we make as we know that we have the tools and knowledge to cope with any situation. I travel a great deal and still find it perfectly comfortable to maintain my diet within the parameters prescribed. We have learnt to be proactive and to plan, to recover from a lapse and move forward without looking back. Our exercise regimes complement our food habits and we have structured our lives to allow us to make the right choices and do what is necessary to really and truly Live Well.

Dr Sarita Davare's Live Well Diet is a holistic approach to leading a healthy life. So convinced am I about the diet as a way of life that I have developed recipes based on the principles and recommendations on which the diet is based. I offer these recipes to you so that you too can benefit from making the right choices without fear of a diet which is bland or boring.There is plenty of variety, and the options are both delicious and nutritious, so taste is not sacrificed at the altar of good health. You will find it is easy to make healthy eating a part of your life when you can always have a plate of delicious goodness in front of you.

But it all begins with wanting to make a change and to making the right choices. I hope that this book will help you on your journey towards wellness, and that the change will be liberating and full of possibility. Most of all, I wish that you truly Live Well every day of your life.

Introduction: *Dr Sarita Davare*

The fact that you are reading this implies that you are interested in changing the way you live and are curious about the path described in this book to a healthier, more balanced and more stress-free life. It implies too, that you are looking at managing your weight and weight loss as a means to achieving that healthy lifestyle.

Weight loss today is no longer viewed as merely a cosmetic issue, but one of well-being and good health, achieved by a positive outlook, an active lifestyle and appropriate food choices. Gone are the days when losing weight was only about starvation and deprivation. Today, awareness and knowledge about how our individual bodies work and the impact of lifestyle on health and fitness inform our attitudes and choices with regard to total well-being.

The LIVE WELL DIET is a holistic programme which is designed to lead you towards a more balanced and healthy life, and help you to make changes that will improve your total well-being so you can live well.

The LIVE WELL DIET emphasises some oft-quoted axioms:

There are no miracle solutions – there is only YOU!

You are responsible for the way you live – the choices you make regarding food and drink, leisure, health, and physical and mental activity.

The Live Well Diet is a plan which puts YOU at the centre and prescribes ways to optimise the most important aspects of your life – your physical and mental well-being. It is a holistic plan which takes into consideration the many factors that have an impact on your desire to live a healthy life. While it addresses health issues affecting people of all ages and lifestyles, it also emphasises that the responsibility for making those changes rests solely with you, and your personal choices and habits.

Love and value yourself

There may be many reasons why you want to change your lifestyle, but the only one that will have a long-lasting effect and help you achieve your goal is that you love and value yourself; not just the way you look or feel, but who you are as a person. How strong your belief is that you are deserving and worthy of respect will show first in how well you treat yourself. Your self-esteem and self-image is demonstrated by your own respect for your body and its care. Love is a decision – so decide to love yourself for who and how you are. Who you are and how you perceive yourself is linked very closely with your relationship to food, which is why the Live Well Diet is based on the principle that:

You are what you eat

It cannot be emphasised enough that our bodies respond directly to what we eat. As our ancient texts have described, and so much modern research has confirmed, our nutritional intake has an impact not only on the physical shape, size and composition of our bodies, but also on our emotional and mental state of health. While factors like genes and gender do play a part in our physical make-up, the food we eat plays a much larger role in our mental and emotional make-up and health. Depending on our habits and choices, food can play a positive role in our lives – it can nourish, heal, detoxify and energise our bodies. On the other hand, if not used wisely, it can deprive us of important nutrients, damage and poison our systems, affect our emotion and mental health and sap our energies. In addition to paying attention to what and how much you eat, you also need to:

Get moving

Eating right is only part of the solution to being healthy. Physical activity is another important part. Exercise activates the metabolism and tones up the body. Activities like walking, yoga, and stretching have a mood-lifting effect, which will help you stay motivated and positive while working towards your goal of Living Well. Once you get moving you will also have to learn how to:

Relax

Stress has been identified as a major cause of lifestyle diseases such as diabetes and cardio-vascular diseases. Stress and pressures, whether external or self-imposed, determine the quality of your life. Living well means enjoying a relatively stress-free life, in which you make enough time for leisure and enjoyment of your special interests. Adequate good quality sleep, meditation and relaxation are essential to live well. And you know that:

A goal is a dream with a deadline.

The first step to making your vision for yourself a reality is to specify what that reality is in terms of tangible and measureable changes you want to make. List your present health statistics – your weight and body measurements, medical reports and lifestyle habits. Identify the areas of change and set yourself challenging but achievable goals to be achieved within a reasonable time frame. Your age, gender, present weight and state of health are some of the factors that will influence your ultimate goals. But remember:

A goal without a plan is just a wish.

THE LIVE WELL DIET is a holistic, comprehensive, plan which is based on years of experience. It provides for sufficient, wholesome nutritional intake to live a healthy and energetic life, with an emphasis on foods and beverages that stimulate the metabolism, have healing properties, as well as detoxify the system. The diet also prescribes an exercise regimen which complements your diet. Relaxation and sleep techniques round off the programme.

Once familiar with the diet, you will find healthy eating has become a way of life. Recipes by Master chef Sanjeev Kapoor provide ample options to maintain the diet in a delicious and healthy way. Templates and menus for weekly diets have also been provided to help you plan your personal daily or weekly diet.

While a plan is necessary, it is also wise to remember that:

The best laid plans often go awry

The Live Well Programme is a realistic, flexible and proactive plan which takes into consideration the many individual situations and conditions that may prevent you from following a prescribed regimen. Rather than setting you up for failure, it anticipates and provides for those times when it is difficult to follow the programme to a Tee such as impromptu events, family celebrations, travel and dining out. Following the guidelines for such situations will help you to stay on the plan with minimum stress and discomfort, always keeping in mind that:

Progress has little to do with speed but much to do with direction

Change can be overwhelming and a shock to the system. Take baby steps in the direction you have chosen and celebrate each step as it becomes a habit. To help you record and evaluate your progress, we have provided you with a template of a daily record of food, beverage, exercise and sleep which will help you stay on track, and focused on achieving your ultimate goals. As enthusiastic as you may be to follow the programme, you should know that:

No pain, no gain

To turn your life around and live well you have to make changes in the way you eat, exercise and relax. Changing age-old or ingrained habits do not come easily, so it is only natural that adjusting to a new regimen will test your resolve and patience. You will have to prepare yourself mentally to go through the frustration, cravings, mood swings, bouts of self-pity and sometimes despair that accompany the diet, keeping your eye firmly on the goal - a healthier, happier you. But:

When the going gets tough, the tough get going

Determination is the key to success. The more determined you are about making the changes you need to in your lifestyle and eating habits, the closer you will get to achieving your best, healthy life. You will have to summon up every ounce of resolve to resist the temptation to reach out for those glistening gulab jamuns, that creamy dessert or those oh-so crispy fries. Walking for an hour may be the last thing you want to do on the morning after the indulgent night before. But, as you go through the programme, you will discover the inner strength that you never realised you had, and will be able to draw on it in times of crisis. Draw too on the support of family and friends who will cheer you on and will also be happy to be around the New You! But on those rare occasions, when you do fall, remember:

It's not whether you fall - it's whether you pick yourself up

Disappointing as it may be to fail in one's resolve, it is more important to get back on track, keeping one's eye always on the goal ahead. Failing is a necessary event on the road to success. It is how soon you pick yourself up when you fall, and how much you learn about yourself through the experience, that will determine how well and how soon you will succeed.

To deal with just those bumps on the road, the Live Well Diet provides you with recovery strategies from a temporary lapse, so that you do not have to beat yourself up with guilt, and can proceed towards your goal.

Don't worry. Be happy.

Finally, positivity and a sense of purpose will fuel your journey on the Live Well Diet. You will be armed with all the tools and techniques to lead a happier and healthier life. Shed your fears and greet the dawn of your new life with confidence, go ahead, have fun, and...

Just do it!

I LIKE THE 'D' FACTOR IN DR DAVARE'S PROGRAMME

Discipline

Devotion

Dedication

Detoxification

Whenever I am on the programme, I enjoy the meals and learn to respect myself...

To mentally and emotionally become a schoolgirl again,

To respect time and body,

And regenerate my energy.

Section I

Knowledge

Knowledge is love and light and vision.
— Helen Keller

1

THE LIVE WELL DIET
10 STEPS TO SUCCESSFUL HEALTH AND WEIGHT MANAGEMENT

The Live Well Diet is a prescription for a holistic change of lifestyle which involves a very effective food, exercise and relaxation regime which will have an all-round positive impact on your physical and mental health. All you need to do is follow the diets which are laid out in this book in a simple and direct manner and you are on the road to a healthy life.

THE TEN STEPS TO LIVE WELL:

1. **EAT RIGHT:** The Live Well Diet is based on foods which are essential for good health and an active metabolsim: foods that are rich in fibre, protein and essential minerals and vitamins. The diet prescribes a rotation of 3 diet plans in a specific sequence for optimum effect.

2. **EAT OFTEN:** The Live Well Diet prescribes 3 main meals and 4-6 small meals a day, including healthy beverages and snacks.

3. **EAT JUST ENOUGH:** Size does matter, so eat the recommended portions of foods in the right combination. While calories are important, do not get hung up on them but concentrate on the portion sizes which will help you regulate your diet in a practical way.

4. **DRINK PLENTY OF WATER AND BEVERAGES:** To hydrate, detoxify and nourish your system, drink at least 3 litres of water a day, in addition to antioxidant or detoxifying beverages like vegetable juices and green tea, and nutrient-rich coconut water.

5. **PAMPER YOUR TASTE BUDS:** The Live Well Diet provides you with options which are both tasty and

healthy. Besides, on 2 days in the week you are encouraged to indulge in your favourite foods with a healthy twist of course. Recipes provided by Master Chef Sanjeev Kapoor ensure you never lack for gustatory pleasure.

6. **BOOST YOUR METABOLISM:** Your metabolism plays a key role in health and weight management. An active metabolism helps to burn stored energy at a faster rate.

7. **STAY ON TRACK:** The Live Well Diet helps you to be proactive as well as to recover from a lapse. It is designed to be flexible, so you can diet 'ahead' for days when you are not able to follow the diet to a Tee. It also provides you with strategies to get back on track if you have strayed from your plan.

8. **EXERCISE:** Do some basic yoga and breathing exercises a minimum of 6 days a week, and work your way up gradually to walking at least 6 km a day (1 hour and 20 minutes), either at one stretch or in 2 or 3 segments, depending on your physical fitness and capacity. That is all the basic exercise you need to keep your metabolism revved up and ticking.

9. **RELAX AND SLEEP:** Meditation, yoga, hobbies and 7 hours of sleep every night will refresh you mentally and physically and put you in a positive frame of mind to achieve your health and weight goals.

10. **RECORD YOUR PROGRESS:** The Live Well Programme provides you with templates to record your vital statistics, weight and health status so you can assess your progress and take corrective action when necessary to achieve your goals. Regular health check-ups are an important part of the programme.

● ● ●

TELL ME MORE...

Here are answers to some concerns that have been expressed before embarking on the Live Well Diet and discovering that it has some very unique features with very successful results.

Does the diet require special foods and equipment?

No. Simplicity is the key to the success of the programme. All the ingredients recommended are easily available; no special equipment or gear is required for the exercise, and the diet and relaxation techniques are well within anyone's capabilities and means.

Is the diet suitable for everyone?

The programme has universal appeal and is suitable for all regardless of occupation, culture, age or gender. A teenager can follow the programme and benefit from it, as much as a middle-aged businessman, older woman or young homemaker. It is advisable, however, to consult a physician before you start the diet.

Many diets are very boring with a restriction on so many foods. I enjoy food so how will I cope?

Variety is a key aspect of the diet and there are options galore to suit your taste, fitness levels and lifestyle. While focussing on a few basic necessities, the variation in type and level of nutrition built into the diet ensures that you will never feel bored or tired of the same old foods. The diet encourages you to use your own preferences and creativity to produce healthy meals within the guidelines provided. Recipes by Master Chef Sanjeev Kapoor are the icing on a very delicious cake!

Many diets are impossible to follow with today's hectic lifestyle which involves juggling long hours of work, travel, entertainment and stress. Does the Live Well Diet have any solutions?

Flexibility is built into the programme, as it recognises that while discipline and motivation are essential, rigidity is the enemy of perseverance and success. The programme therefore provides for alternatives to situations where a strict diet and exercise plan may be neither possible nor productive. Proactive and recovery plans are suggested for weddings and family celebrations, vacation tours and business travel. The diet prescribes foods in portion sizes which are universally easy to understand.

It is important to note that focussing on just one aspect of the programme while ignoring the others will do you no good. The Live Well Diet is a holistic diet and you will have to commit to all aspects of it for any visible, sustained results.

● ● ●

So what is The Live Well Diet? It is as simple as ABC

The Live Well Diet is a well-designed diet based on the functioning of the body's metabolism. Briefly, your body's metabolism and the rate at which it converts food into energy determine the composition of fat and muscle in your body. Besides, your metabolism gets used to a regular pattern of either too much or too little food and reacts accordingly, either being overwhelmed by too much food and becoming sluggish, or conserving and storing energy instead of burning it when food intake is low. The Live Well Diet keeps your metabolism figuratively on its toes by rotating 3 different diet plans providing different amounts of nutritionally varied foods through the week so your metabolism is encouraged to work at optimum levels at all times. A list of essential daily foods ensures that you safeguard your basic nutritional needs.

Diet A - The **All Foods Diet** to be followed for a maximum of **2 days** in the week. The name for this plan may seem like a contradiction as the words 'all foods' and 'diet' do not often appear in the same sentence! But that is what it really is in the right proportions of course, and it is ideal for weekends, holidays and business trips when you can indulge in your favourite foods and can choose wisely from whatever food is on offer or available.

Diet B - The **Basic Diet** to be followed for at least **3 days** in the week. It is a mainly vegetarian fibre and protein-rich diet which provides you with your basic nutritional and energy needs. It is made up of common everyday foods prepared at home.

Diet C - The **Control Diet** to be followed on **2 days** in the week. The food intake prescribed is a signal for your body and metabolism to get back on track. The Control Diet is rich in protein and fibre, but simple carbohydrates are reduced to a minimum, forcing your body to burn excess fat for energy.

The Live Well Diet is flexible and there are no fixed starting points, but do try and ensure that Diet A – The All Foods Diet is always followed by Diet C - The Control Diet. You must also ensure that you treat yourself to at least 1 day (maximum of 2 days) in the week to Diet A, so you don't wind up overeating due to cravings or feelings of deprivation!

Regular meals, plenty of water and liquids, daily walking and excercise, sleep and relaxation will ensure that your body is toned your up, mind is refreshed and your metabolism is working well.

This book will take you on a journey of self-discovery and knowledge about your body and how it uses the food you eat and the many simple ways you can change your lifestyle so you will begin to live a life of well-being and satisfaction. And as a very revered, wise man once said in a different context but resonates here, 'Be the change you want to see...". In other words, that change begins with YOU.

• • •

DISCIPLINE AND MOTIVATION ARE KEY

Dr Sarita's is not just a weight-loss diet, it is a cleansing exercise. Following the programme for even one month has an effect on one's senses, mental status and physical health. It is a detoxification programme with so many additional benefits. Cholesterol and other blood levels are brought into balance.

I used to be overweight and had very undisciplined eating habits. Since going on the Live Well Diet, my life has changed.

I am motivated to stay healthy and make my health and weight a priority. Of course with my hectic travel schedules, it is not always easy. Stress also takes its toll. But I know that once I am on the diet I will detoxify my system and I will feel good again.

It is actually all a mental exercise – discipline and motivation are key.

2

THERE ARE NO MIRACLE SOLUTIONS, **THERE IS ONLY YOU!**

Our newspapers are full of advertisements offering quick weight loss, instant makeovers and miracle cures for every disease or ailment from bunions to bulimia, and hair loss to hypoglycaemia. Powders, tablets, herbs, precious stones, ointments, tonics, magnets, vibrating belts, tummy tucks and butt trims.... Like an Aladdin's lamp – rub it and a genie with a miracle will appear.

Promises, Promises!

Beware of the purveyor of instant health or life solutions-potions, procedures and products that promise you everything your heart desires and leave you with an empty wallet and a broken body. Remember, in today's world of instant everything, you would do well to pause, and take a long, hard look at what is on offer before you click on OK. Don't let your desperation for change or improvement cloud your judgment and trigger your impulsiveness.

You and You Alone (with a little help from ...)

Rome was not built in a day, and neither will the new you be fashioned with minimum time and effort. Changing habits takes patience and perseverance and that can only come from you. You have to reach deep into yourself to draw on all the positive energy you can to stay on the path to change. You have to make the choices, you have to decide, you have to work on yourself and then and only then will you be able to bask in the glow of satisfaction from achieving your goals. No external force, or rewards, no alien incentive will equal the satisfaction of a lasting, change wrought by yourself. The support of family and friends is invaluable and necessary, as is the advice of your physician and guidance from this book. The Live Well Diet is a safe and practical way of managing your weight and your health, as has been experienced by scores of happy and healthy followers of the programme.

I HAVE A NEW
LEAN LOOK

I had a very fruitful experience with Dr Davare's programme when I was preparing for the shoot of the video for the song Soona Soona for my album Classically Mild. I owe my lean look to my weight training and Dr Davare's diet and fat reduction plan.

I FEEL FRESH
AND ENERGETIC

It seems like I am always on the move. I have covered more than 9 lakh km by road and have taken more than 65 international flights. As you can imagine I lead a very hectic life. I have been on Dr Davare's programme for 7-8 years and have enjoyed every minute. I feel fresh and energetic 365 days of the year. People keep asking how I manage to look so good always. As they say your health is reflected in your face. I reply I owe it all to Dr Davare: my blood levels have been normal ever since I started her programme. I find the diet easy to manage though I travel so much. Nothing is forbidden - balance is the secret.

LOVE AND VALUE YOURSELF

Mirror, mirror on the wall.... Who goes there, friend or foe?

Is your mirror your best and most honest friend? Do you find the answers you are seeking when you stare at your reflection? Regardless of what people tell you, mirrors sometimes do lie! If you are looking for ways to change the way you look and feel, examining your reflection in a mirror is not the only way of finding out about yourself. You may actually have to engage in another type of reflection to figure out who you really are.

Your self-image or the mental portrait you paint of yourself is sometimes more honest or more distorted than any image reflected in that mirror. Apart from your perception of your physical attributes, your self-image is your perception of yourself as a person, and reveals how much you truly value yourself. Just as you focus on the tiniest blemish or the beginnings of a pimple on your otherwise flawless skin, you can also magnify your smallest faults into major flaws and begin to lose self-confidence and self-worth.

A man's own self is his friend. A man's own self is his foe.

- Bhagavad Gita

It is well known that how you see yourself affects your behaviour, attitudes towards yourself and others, and your view of the world. Your emotions are also guided by self-image and self-worth: the poorer your self-image, the more hypersensitive, diffident, or distorted your personality can be. Your relationships with others also suffer leading to an even poorer self-image and lack of self-confidence. How other people perceive you is often a reflection of how you see yourself. If you always project yourself in a poor light, the chances are other people will see you in the same way.

YOU DESERVE YOU

Living well begins with falling in love with yourself. This may sound strange, but many of us need to be reminded that we are worthy of being loved, that we have needs and aspirations that we sometimes have to put before others', and that the time and effort spent caring for yourself is necessary and well spent if you have to lead a life of good health, happiness and fulfillment.

Before you start protesting, loving yourself is not being self-absorbed or narcissistic – it is rather the recognition of your own worthiness; your desires and well being as being important enough to make the necessary changes in the way you see and treat yourself, your habits and lifestyle.

Most of us are so used to putting everything and everyone other than ourselves first – spouse, children, job, business, boss, friends, money and even fame, to name just a few—that somewhere along the way we stop thinking of ourselves as being important enough to nurture, care for, heal, pamper or even satisfy. We give off our best always to others, reserving very little for our own selves. Stress, acidity, obesity, high blood pressure notwithstanding, we somehow cannot find the time, energy or will power to listen to our hearts, minds and bodies, and the message they are giving us – value yourself, because you deserve it and you do deserve your own care of yourself.

Love yourself first and everything falls into line.

- Lucille Ball

Loving yourself means celebrating your strengths and positive attributes, and forgiving your perceived flaws and shortcomings. It also means resolving to change as many of your 'flaws' as you can, safely and naturally, and accepting and learning to live and love those you cannot. Dress yourself up in a confident and happy personality and everything else will fall into place.

Here are some simple ways to love yourself and improve your self-image:

- Keep reminding yourself that you are unique, and your uniqueness makes you special.

- List the things you love about yourself - your attributes, strengths, talents and abilities.

- Focus on one or two on the list to specially develop or improve.

- Celebrate every one of your achievements, no matter how small, in every sphere of activity.

- Try not to compare yourself to others. Come to terms with the fact that there will always be someone better than you, and therefore, you will always be better off than someone else.

- Pamper yourself – treat yourself to regular body massages, engage in a hobby or pastime that fuels your interests and passions.

- Forgive yourself – instead of beating up yourself for your faults or failures, be kind and forgiving, and resolve to improve what you can and live with what you cannot.

- Repeat this mantra coined by Virginia Satir, a reputed psychologist, several times a day:

I own me, and therefore, I can engineer me. I am me, and I am okay.

● ● ●

I FEEL LIBERATED AND LIVE LIFE TO THE FULLEST

Dr Davare's programme taught me how to maintain my health without losing out on living. The programme shows you how to manage your diet and maintain a balance. It prescribes solutions for many situations so that you need not fear that you will miss out on enjoying life. It also gives you strategies to maintain your weight loss.

I have always been a positive person but after the programme I have so much more energy. I have even taken up swimming and ballroom dancing. The compliments keep coming and my self-image has improved. I will go one step further and say – I feel liberated and now I live life to the fullest.

YOUR BODY IMAGE IS AN IMPORTANT PART OF YOUR SELF-IMAGE

How you think and feel about your physical attributes is also a reflection of your self-image. Being comfortable in one's skin, warts and all, reveals a level of self-confidence and positive self-image that few possess. Most people believe that there is always room for improvement, and they are probably right. However, a very distorted picture of one's body can lead to a number of psychological problems such as depression and eating disorders. Plastic surgery is an option that some resort to in an attempt to achieve a perfect body. Excessive physical training and muscle building are also ways people use to achieve their idea of a beautiful body. In extreme cases, dissatisfaction with one's looks can result in life-threatening disorders such as anorexia or bulimia.

Remember that perfection lies in the eye of the beholder, is highly over-rated and often just a mirage. To begin with comparisons are odious, and you do yourself no favours for indulging in wishful thinking. That size zero, perfect hour-glass figure, six-pack abs or bulging torso may look good on the other person, but you may have to settle for less. Choose health over beauty every time and find natural ways to look and feel fresh, happy and confident.

If you are having trouble feeling positive about how you look, here are some tips to help you begin to love your body:

- Accept there is a no exchange-no return policy where your body is concerned! You have only one body – so make the most of it.

- Start with the top of your head and list the things about your body that you like – your hair, eyes, shape of your nose, skin, ears, length of legs, ankles, shape of your fingers, etc.

- Look at ways of enhancing your best features and dressing to suit your body shape and size.

- List the things about your body that you would like to improve.

- Now list those improvements that are within your own control and require the intervention of a reasonable diet, or some lifestyle changes.

- Start making those changes and celebrate each step towards improving your body image.

WEIGHTY MATTERS

One of the aspects of your body image that is often within your control to improve is your body weight. Your own perception of your ideal body weight and shape plays a huge role in how you perceive yourself and your self-image. It would be important therefore to find out whether your perceptions are based on fact or wishful thinking!

Your body weight - the bare facts

When you look at yourself in the mirror you are seeing a reflection of the outer contours of your body. You may be surprised to learn that that around 60 percent of your body weight is water and fluid, which is distributed over the tissues, organs and blood.

Take away the water, and the rest of the body weight is referred to as Body Mass which is made up of Fat Mass and Lean Body Mass. The latter includes the weight of muscles, bones and organs (brain, heart, kidneys and liver etc.).

If you think you are overweight and don't like the way you look or feel, some causes may be beyond your control: your genes, the geographical environment and climate. Medication such as steroids, hormonal imbalances and psychiatric illnesses have an impact on body weight. Pregnancy, prolonged illness, or a disability are some other reasons for excess weight.

If none of those reasons apply to you, there is only one conclusion that you can arrive at: the main factor that determines your body weight is YOU.

Your diet—what you eat, the quantity, frequency, and the nutritive value of the foods you chose to eat—and your lifestyle, which may be sedentary or active, hectic or calm, regular or erratic, has an impact on your weight. The better your metabolism and the more the energy you burn through activity, the less your body weight and vice versa. Similarly, the more relaxed and stress-free your life is, the more you are able to eat and sleep at regular times, the easier it is to regulate your body weight.

In other words, all other physiological and external factors aside, YOU are solely responsible for your body weight and body image and only you can make the difference and begin to LIVE WELL.

• • •

MY STORY } Mandira Bedi
Model, Actor and TV Host

MY METABOLISM GOT A BOOST

I have benefited from Dr Davare's programme. Though I usually lead a disciplined life, eat sensibly and exercise, I needed to lose a few stubborn extra kilos that were hard to shake off particularly after my pregnancy. My weight had hit a plateau and I went to Dr Davare for help to boost my metabolism. The programme worked wonders and I was able to lose the weight. Lime water and vegetable juices hydrate the body, and the diet provides energy which is necessary after working out. The foods prescribed activate the metabolism, the effect of which lasts for a long time.

I FEEL HEALTHIER.
I FEEL HAPPIER.
I LOVE MY BODY.

My lifestyle was full of errors before I joined the programme. I used to be on a yo-yo diet, losing weight and then eating to my heart's content later; only to find that I had gained more. I was not doing any exercise at all. Sometimes, I used to starve myself. This was due to a lot of stress in my personal life. I was just gaining weight along with personal stress, particularly after my pregnancy. I was a housewife then.

The reason I began the Live Well Diet is that my son Rahul wanted to see me in western wear as all his friends' mothers were wearing those types of clothes.

Secondly, during an office training programme, I experienced severe chest pain and was really scared to death. Thankfully it was nothing serious. But it was enough to make me look seriously at my lifestyle. I felt as if God was trying to send me warning signals and nothing could stop me from becoming healthy now. The diet has changed my life totally. The overall experience is awesome. I feel great today, when I can walk into any readymade clothes shop or buy new fashion garments. It feels great when people compliment me for the change in my looks. But most of all, it feels great to be healthy. It feels great to love your body. It feels great to be totally at peace with oneself.

I have lost close to 33 kg. My health has improved significantly. I could not bend my knees earlier and now I have joined Kathak classes. I have an improved self image as I get loads of compliments from my peers. The Live Well Diet has made me love my body, and I am sure has added some healthy years to my life. The programme changes people's lives (I am one of them). It gives hope to people like me. Soon my son Rahul will see his mom in western wear!

How did I get to be this way?

Now that you know that you are mainly responsible for how you look and perhaps your other health problems, you need to figure out how it happened. Not to torture yourself with guilt, but so that you can make the changes you need to in order to Live Well.

Most natural weight gain creeps up on you. It begins with an erratic lifestyle - irregular eating habits, not enough sleep, too much socialising, or the opposite, too much work, excessive alcohol, smoking, stress, and the list goes on.

● ● ●

The Live Well Lifestyle Audit

If you want to know which factors have contributed to your excess weight, review your lifestyle with the following quiz. Answer the questions honestly, and then use your score and the questions themselves to help you evaluate your lifestyle and the changes you need to make to LIVE WELL.

Answer each of the following questions YES or NO.

Eating Habits

1. Do you eat at regular times every day?
2. Do you eat breakfast every day?
3. Do you eat 5-6 small meals instead of 2 or 3 big meals a day?
4. Do you eat a variety of foods every day in a balanced way?
5. Do you try to eat less fatty foods (pizzas, samosa, biryani)?
6. Do you make it a habit to take less salt in your food?
7. Does your daily diet contain plenty of fresh fruits and vegetables?
8. Do you eat at least one type of whole grain bread or cereal (chapati, oats, sorghum (jowar)) every day?

9. Do you consciously add less sugar in your diet through reducing or avoiding refined sugar in your beverages, sweets, snacks and desserts?

10. Do you avoid or limit your consumption of alcohol?

11. Do you drink at least 3 litres of water every day?

Physical Fitness

12. Do you do some physical exercise or activity for 30 minutes at least 5 times a week?

13. Do you do any stretching exercises such as yoga at least 3 times a week?

14. Can you climb a flight of stairs, walk up a slope or walk briskly without becoming breathless?

15. Can you bend down and touch your toes without bending your knees?

Leisure and Relaxation

16. Do you have a hobby?

17. Do you practice yoga or any other relaxation or meditation techniques?

18. Are you involved in any group or community activity?

19. Can you remain patient and calm in stressful situations such as driving in heavy traffic or multi-tasking at home?

20. Are you free of boredom most of the time?

21. Do you get at least 7 hours sleep each night?

22. Does your job or occupation have regular work hours?

23. Is the job you do and your work environment relatively stress-free?

24. Do you avoid smoking?

Health Status

25. Are you comfortable with your present weight?

26. Do you monitor your weight regularly?

27. Do you always take medications as advised by a doctor?

28. Do you take any nutritional supplements?

29. Do you have regular medical check-ups?

30. Are you free of lifestyle disease such as diabetes, coronary heart disease, high cholesterol or high blood pressure?

Give yourself one point for every YES answer. And zero point for every NO answer.

Your goal should be to score 30 points on the LIVE WELL Quiz.

23-30 points: Your have many positive habits and need to make only a few changes to LIVE WELL.

15-22 points: You have some positive lifestyle habits, but you should work on changing the others to LIVE WELL.

9-14 points: You have many poor lifestyle habits that you need to change to LIVE WELL.

8 points and below: You have very poor lifestyle habits, and you need to make many changes to improve your life and LIVE WELL.

(Quiz adapted from Assessing Your Lifestyle: Wellness Quiz www.overtoncountynews.com)

● ● ●

WHERE DO I BEGIN?

As the song goes, 'start at the very beginning - a very good place to start...'. List all the changes you have to make and begin tackling them one by one. Taking stock is the first step. Self awareness and self-examination is the next. As you go through the process of assessing your life – your appearance, your physical, mental and emotional health, you are very likely to find that your eating habits are a large part of the problem.

Tackle your eating habits and a lot of your other lifestyle problems will sort themselves out. Overeating or eating the wrong types and combinations of foods are one of the causes of excess weight, poor health and a correspondingly unsatisfactory lifestyle. Once you regulate what you eat and drink and how often, you are well on the way to Living Well.

I HAD
GIVEN UP
HOPE

Due to export business and regular travel abroad to the Middle East, UK, USA & Canada for around 60-70 days in a year; and for local sourcing travelling once a week to Pune, Gujarat etc, my lifestyle changed: during my 40s - exercise stopped, late night eating due to business, late night sleeping, stress in business... I gained 50 to 60 kg weight in the last 20 years. When I visited Dr Davare's clinic my weight was 135.5 kg.

The diet given by Dr Davare is very easy to follow with various choices of foods and clarity when it comes to what you can have and what quantity. You do not have to starve. On the diet programme, my weight started reducing day by day, week by week. The results made me more serious about my diet.

I have lost around 30 kg and my waist has reduced by 8 inches; I have lost inches all over my body; knee pain has reduced by 80%; my cholesterol level dropped to the normal range. Now I am used to Dr Davare's diet. I can control the desire to eat junk food or fried food even at social functions and parties.

Before starting the programme, I had given up hope of weight reduction without surgery, but now I am confident that I will further reduce 20 kg within 1 - 1½ years. Now I can walk for about 1 hour at a speed of 6 km/hour. Once my joint pain goes I will once again start doing Surya Namaskar which I used to do in my youth.

3

THIS IS
ME!

Your journey to LIVE WELL begins here. And just as on any journey you have to take stock of who and where you are and where you want to go. In other words map your path from this point on to your ultimate goal and destination.

Think of all the extra weight and poor habits you are carrying with you – how much you want to change, the new positive habits you want to acquire and how many negative ones you hope to shed along the way. Begin with your health and your body.

You are what your deep, driving desire is

As your desire is, so is your will

As your will is, so is your deed

As your deed is, so is your destiny

- Brihadaranyakopanishat 4.4.5

YOUR LIVE WELL NOTEBOOK

A personal diary or journal is what you need most at this point. List your goals which will act as your compass, keeping you pointed in the right direction.

Like a ship's log your journal will record your point of embarkation and then every high and low, every trough and crest on your journey to well-being.

This is one time when you do not want to trust your memory! Memory has a way of glossing over or 'losing' unpleasant facts! Get yourself a simple notebook and keep a record of all your visual observations, measurements, weight, BMI and medical reports. (page 54) Update your record on a weekly basis to keep you focussed and you will be amazed how positive and motivated you will feel when you see the numbers change as you begin to LIVE WELL!

The Way You Used To Be

Most of us have a mental picture of how we were in a past, usually happier, time. Looking at your past through rose-coloured glasses may bring back memories of a slimmer, more youthful, carefree and energetic you. You may even have moments of longing to get back to being the person you once were. If you have a photograph of yourself looking the way you want to become again, now is the time to take it out and paste it in your notebook or fix it on your mirror. Every time you see it, it will spur you on to achieving the goals you set yourself.

Take A Look At Yourself Now

If you don't have one, get yourself a full-length mirror and install it in a room where you have complete privacy. Take a long, hard look at yourself in the mirror and note down what you see. Remember, your mirror can be your best friend and will give you instant feedback!

Write down the answers to the following (Yes/No/Sort Of)

- Is your face puffy and are your cheeks very full?

- Do you have a double chin?

- Is the flesh on your upper arms flabby i.e. the skin and muscle hang soft and loose - sometimes called 'batwings' or flags?

- Is there fat build up around and behind your knees?

- Do you have cellulite - skin which is dimpled with fat - around your buttocks, thighs and/or stomach?

- Does your stomach protrude so much that if you look down you cannot see your toes?

If you have answered 'Yes' to all or most of the above you are definitely overweight. If you have answered 'No' to most, you may not be very overweight but you may want to lose some weight to live well. 'Sort Of' answers are neither here nor there and you may want to err on the side of good health and answer Yes!

Warning: Apples are more deadly than Pears

If you look round and roly-poly and are heaviest around your stomach and waist, your body is said to have an apple shape, with more belly fat. However, if you are heaviest around your thighs and buttocks your body is said to be pear-shaped. All excess fat is dangerous but belly fat is considered to be more dangerous to your health, so aim to lose as much belly fat as possible.

MY STORY } Karan Sharma *Student*

MIRACLES DO HAPPEN!

When I went to Dr Davare in Nov 2011, I used to weigh 128 kg. I had tried everything, gyming, dieting; nothing seemed to work.

At my first appointment, Dr. Davare sat me down and motivated me in a stern yet caring manner. She set me a target of 75 kg in 2 years. I actually laughed in my mind as that target seemed impossible to me at that time.

March 2013, I weigh 86 kg and am on my way to achieving the target of 75 kg before the year ends! I lost 42 kg in little over a year! My entire life has changed. I actually had to buy a whole new wardrobe. I am more confident, I have more energy and the compliments from friends and family don't seem to stop! Life is good. Believe and do as she says, miracles do happen!

MEASURE UP!

Back up your visual impression with a tape measure as you survey you body's contours in inches and centimeters.

Measure the following and note them down:

- Your chest
- Your waist
- The midsection around your navel or belly button
- Your hips

WARNING: According to the International Diabetes Foundation, if you are a woman with a waist size of more than **80 cm (31.5 inches)** or a man with a waist of more than **90 cm (35 inches)** you are medically considered to have excess belly fat and therefore your health is at risk.

Stand Tall

Also measure your height which will help you calculate whether you are overweight.

A simple way to measure your height is to stand with your back against a wall. Have someone place a ruler or book flat on top of your head so that it touches the wall and mark the spot. Measure from that point downwards and note down your height in centimeters or inches.

Weigh In

You may be the kind of person who has only ever weighed himself at a doctor's clinic or on one of those weighing-cum-fortune-telling machines at a railway station. Now is the time to invest in a personal weighing scale which will help you keep accurate track of your weight and weight loss. Electronic scales with a digital display are both accurate and easy to read, especially if you don't have your glasses on after a shower! Because the best time to weigh yourself is in the morning after your ablutions, without any, or only the lightest, clothes on. Make sure you weigh yourself at the same time and with the same clothes on each time!

Height/Weight chart for Indian Men & Women*

Height in Metres & (Feet/inches)	Men (In Kg)/Lbs	Women (In Kg)/Lbs
1.52 (5' 0")	---	50.8 to 54.4 / 112-120
1.54 (5' 1")	---	51.7 to 55.3 / 114-122
1.57 (5' 2")	56.3 to 60.3 / 124-133	53.1 to 56.7 / 117-125
1.60 (5' 3")	57.6 to 61.7 / 127-136	54.4 to 58.1 / 120-128
1.63 (5' 4")	58.9 to 63.5 / 130-140	56.3 to 59.9 / 124-132
1.65 (5' 5")	60.8 to 65.3 / 134-144	57.6 to 61.2 / 127-135
1.68 (5' 6")	62.2 to 66.7 / 137-147	58.9 to 63.5 / 130-140
1.70 (5' 7")	64.0 to 68.5 / 141-151	60.8 to 65.3 / 134-144
1.73 (5' 8")	65.8 to 70.8 / 145-156	62.2 to 66.7 / 137-147
1.75 (5' 9")	67.6 to 72.6 / 149-160	64.0 to 68.5 / 141-151
1.78 (5'10")	69.4 to 74.4 / 153-164	65.8 to 70.3 / 145-155
1.80 (5'11")	71.2 to 76.2 / 157-168	67.1 to 71.7 / 148-158
1.83 (6' 0")	73.0 to 78.5 / 161-173	68.5 to 73.9 / 151-163
1.85 (6' 1")	75.3 to 80.7 / 166-178	---
1.88 (6'2")	77.6 to 83.5 / 171-184	---
1.90 (6' 3")	79.8 to 85.7 / 176-189	---

Special Note:

Upto age of 30 Yrs. : 10% above standard is acceptable. Between 30-35 yrs: Standard is optimum weight.

Above 35 years: 10% below standard is acceptable.

*As compiled by the LIC of India and accepted as standard weight chart all over India

● ● ●

MASS EFFECT – BMI

As mentioned before, your body is made up of water, fat, bone and muscle. Almost two-third of your body is water and fluid, and the rest is bone, fat and muscle or lean body mass. If you want to know how much fat your body has in relation to lean muscle, you can use a tool called the Body Mass Index or BMI.

Your BMI is the ratio between the fat mass and lean body mass of your body. The higher the ratio between fat and lean body mass, the fatter you are.

This is where your next tool, your calculator, comes into play, for I assure you, it is not possible to do these complicated calculations in your head or on pieces of paper!
The formula used to calculate your BMI is:

BMI = weight in kilograms divided by height in metres².

Example: An adult who weighs 70 kg and whose height is 1.75 metres, will have a BMI of 22.9 (normal weight for height).
Weight (70 kg) divided by Height² (1.75 m)² = 22.9
You will also find quick and easy ways to calculate your BMI on the internet.

So what does your BMI tell you?

If you have a BMI of between 18 to 25 you are within the normal range, if between 25-30, you are overweight, and if more than 30 you are obese and your health is at risk.

Work towards achieving your ideal BMI and calculating how much weight you should lose to achieve it.

What's Up, Doc?

If you have not done so already, now would be a good time before you begin the LIVE WELL Diet to meet with your doctor and have a complete medical examination and discover your state of health. The reports may reveal health problems that may have gone undiagnosed which will have to be treated before you make the changes in your diet and exercise. Make sure you share all your concerns with your doctor and let him or her know about the lifestyle changes you plan to make.

Some basic tests will include:
- Blood pressure
- Routine Blood and Urine Tests
- Blood sugar levels (fasting and after a meal) for diabetes
- Lipid profiles – cholesterol and triglycerides
- Thyroid function tests

An annual health check up at a reputed hospital or clinic will help you to keep tabs on your health. Ideally, have the check-up at the same time each year, preferably at the same facility. The check-ups will help you keep your lifestyle on track and warn you of anything amiss. It may seem like an unnecessary expenditure for these tests, but in the long run they will prove their worth, and passing a test with flying colours will take a load off your mind.

MY HEALTH RECORD			
	READING/ LEVEL	GOAL	REMARKS
Date:			
Height in inches/cm			
Weight in inches/cm			
Bust/Chest in inches/cm			
Waist in inches/cm			
Hips in inches/cm			
BMI			
BMR			

MEDICAL TESTS - Frequency as directed by your physician			
Date			
Blood Sugar			
Cholesterol (HDL)			
Cholesterol (LDL)			
Triglycerides			
Blood Pressure			
Any Other			

A JOINT EFFORT

All my life I was obese till I met Dr Davare. I was 97 kg. I tried hard and exercised a lot to reduce my weight. I could hardly come down to 94-93 kg but my knees started paining. I was advised by my very good friend and a well wisher, who guided me to Saritaji. I joined her programme and lost 19 kg in a 4-month period. My wife too joined this programme. And I will always advise most people to join with their spouse as a change of lifestyle is a joint effort and cannot be done alone. Since then not only have we lived differently, but enjoyed our life to the fullest in its true sense.

Our pathologist, who happens to be a very close friend of mine, told me privately that he would not have believed our reports if both were not done at his lab by him in person. My physician sent his wife to this programme after seeing our improved reports and health!

FAT IS NOT FIT

Most of our favourite comedians are fat. Fat people are usually the life of a party. They laugh at themselves and make others laugh. They are often the most popular people around and the centre of attention. Fat women are cuddly and motherly – they exude care and are almost always sure to cook the best food. And how often have we given a really fat person the compliment of being 'prosperous', or a really chubby little boy of being 'healthy'?

So is there really anything wrong with being fat, overweight or obese?

The most obvious effect of obesity or being overweight is there for you to see. You look larger than you should, and your appearance may not be as attractive as it could be, or one that gives you self-confidence. Your self-image is the first casualty.

Your excess weight prevents you from leading an active life. You may tire easily and get breathless after walking fast or a short distance, or even climbing a few stairs. All in all, your excess weight restricts your movement, slows you down and makes you feel physically unfit.

Numerous studies have shown that the number one preventable cause of death is obesity or excess weight. Scared? You should be. Think about this: the excess fat you are carrying around is putting you directly on the path to some very serious, life-threatening diseases, which can cripple your life and hamper your lifestyle for the shortened time you live!

Some diseases that are caused by excess fat and weight:

Diabetes: A lifestyle related disease caused by stress, irregular eating habits, lack of physical activity and most importantly, a diet loaded with fat and sugar.

Heart Disease: Your heart is unable to cope with the stress of excess body weight and the build-up of fat within the arteries that feed the heart with blood.

Hypertension: 'The silent killer' is directly linked to being overweight or obese, and a sedentary lifestyle. Excess body fat and salt or sodium in your diet increases the pressure with which your heart needs to pump out the blood leading to hypertension.

High Cholesterol: The body produces two types of cholesterol: LDL or bad cholesterol, an excess of which leads to fat deposits within the arteries, and HDL or good cholesterol which is responsible for cleansing the bloodstream of excess fat carrying it back to the liver for disposal. Excess body weight is known to contribute to an excess of LDL or bad cholesterol.

● ● ●

Shrinking from the truth

Our society places much importance on being thin. Models that walk the ramp and film stars proudly display their oh-so-slim bodies and their washboard abs. When you feel fat, it is hard to console yourself with the thought that 'beauty lies within'. Beauty today, often rests firmly in the eye of the beholder, who would much rather behold a reed slim waif than a buxom body.

But beauty that slim comes at a price. If you are not properly guided and embark on a very restricted or starvation diet to achieve your idea of beauty, it can lead to vitamin and mineral deficiencies, anaemia, severe health problems such as osteoporosis (weakening of the bones), eating disorders such as bulimia (over-eating followed by self-induced vomiting or purging) and anorexia (total aversion to food).

Besides, being overweight can cause feelings of inadequacy and poor self-esteem, and in extreme cases, depression. Shying away from social occasions, bingeing in secret (picking on your food in public and then pigging out on everything edible within reach at home), wearing over-sized clothing to cover up your body; these are all symptoms of the psychological effects of being overweight.

The Live Well Diet helps you to become the person you want to be in a gradual and healthy way. The diets cater to your taste buds so you can continue to enjoy good food; the exercise and yoga practices put you in a state of relaxation and a positive frame of mind; and the gradual loss of weight is both motivating and rewarding.

THE FAT OF THE MATTER – All Fat is not Bad - You Need Just Enough!

Now that you have taken stock of your health and lifestyle habits and decided on your weight loss and health goals, you are ready to start the next phase which is an examination of your eating habits - the quantity, quality and frequency of what you eat and drink.

Before you launch an attack on the fat in your body you should know that all fat is not bad. Even those sylph-like women, size zero models and muscle-bound hunks have fat in their bodies, though one would be hard pressed to see where it is.

A body without fat would be like a delicate, temperature-sensitive piece of equipment without protective packaging. Fat forms a protective layer around your vital organs such as your liver, kidney and heart. Like a blanket, it provides excellent insulation against changes in external temperature, thus regulating the temperature of the body. It acts as a cushion against shocks and sudden movements, preventing friction and injury. More importantly, **fat plays the role of a battery, storing up excess energy for when the body needs it.**

However, belly fat – the excess fat that accumulates around the abdomen - is the one you need to watch out for and prevent, as that is a sure sign of danger ahead.

If you consume more starch or sugar than your body needs, the excess is also converted into fat. So beware of fat-free or low-fat but high-sugar packaged products which could do you just as much harm.

I HAVE
NEVER
FELT SO
MOTIVATED

It wasn't easy being 90 kg and to reach a point where starving to lose a little weight was not only hampering healthy life but also had an adverse effect on my personal life. I managed to get down to 87 kg, but that was all I could do by myself.

Ladies older than me fitting into jeans and clothes really upset me. Wearing these clothes were only a dream that I felt would not come true. My husband, being a doctor himself, told me that I really had to take care of my health and weight as my side of the family has a history of diabetes.

I felt the diet Dr Davare was prescribing would be difficult, but I was loyal and I realised there should be some discipline in eating also. Today I have lost 28 kg. Dr Davare would keep on reminding, "Don't worry about kilos. I will give you perfect shape - you'll lose inches." I have never felt so motivated and most importantly happy. I managed to lose weight and at the same time gained confidence.

4

METABOLISM –
A BURNING ISSUE

How What You Eat Keeps you Going

Most of what you eat or drink is transformed, miraculously and without you knowing it, into energy – the force of life that keeps you moving, thinking and feeling. That magical process of turning what you eat or drink into energy is called metabolism.

What a wonderful piece of machinery the body is! All it needs is fuel in the form of food or drink, the calories of which are combined with oxygen to release the energy that the body needs to function well. And your body needs a lot of energy to keep it humming along.

Even when you are at rest, your body needs energy for all its functions that you are not even conscious of such as breathing, circulating blood, adjusting hormone levels, and growing and repairing cells.

Metabolism comprises two processes: anabolism – the process by which with the help of the hormone insulin, excess energy is stored in the body for when it is required. Catabolism is the process by which stored energy is broken down to release it for use when required by your body.

Your body weight is the result of the excess energy stored over the energy used. The excess energy is stored either as glucose or fat. When your body needs energy, the glucose in your body is the first fuel that is burned up. If that is not enough to meet your energy needs, the stored fats are burned up to provide the necessary energy.

● ● ●

BMR (Basal Metabolic Rate)

Your Basal Metabolic Rate (BMR) is the rate at which your body, while resting, breaks down food and converts it into energy to keep your heart beating, your body temperature stable, and your vital organs functioning efficiently.

Your BMR is calculated by a complicated formula which includes among various other factors your height, weight, age and gender. Request your doctor to calculate your BMR. **The higher the BMR the better, and a BMR of above 2800 is considered excellent.**

Do you have control over your BMR? The answer is YES. The food you eat and the amount of physical activity have an impact on your BMR.

However, there are some factors beyond your control that affect your BMR such as age – the older you are the lower your BMR, and gender – men burn more energy as their bodies have more muscle and less fat.

IS YOUR METABOLISM ON SIMMER?

Symptoms of Low BMR

If you don't know what your BMR is, you can still tell if your metabolism is performing at optimum levels. A poor metabolism or low basal metabolic rate affects the overall functioning of the body and shows up in various symptoms which manifest themselves constantly, or frequently and on a regular basis. Tick the symptoms listed below if they apply to you. If you tick 5 or more of them you could be having a low BMR. If your BMR is not the problem, you will have to address the symptoms in any case as they indicate that all is not well with your health. Once again, consult your doctor about the following frequent or ever-present symptoms.

- Muscle cramps
- Constant fatigue and tiredness
- Lethargy and lack of energy
- Hyperacidity

- Bloating of the stomach
- Frequent bouts of depression or irritability
- Gradual weight gain
- Frequent body ache or headaches
- Excessive hunger
- Poor appetite

SLOW BURN AND HOW TO RAISE THE HEAT

There may be many reasons why your BMR is as sluggish as it is. Menopause, poor thyroid function, steroids and hormonal disorders are some reasons which require the attention of a physician. However there are some reasons which are within your control why your BMR may be functioning at below par. Here is a list of those causes and what you can do to rev your BMR up:

Skipping meals, starving or crash dieting: How often have you skipped a meal either because of time constraints, or because you feel you will lose weight by doing so? Wrong move! When you miss a meal or go on a crash diet, your metabolism, far from burning up calories to provide energy, actually slows down to conserve energy, as it is not sure when you will provide the next influx of energy. So instead of losing weight you often end up putting on more weight! Besides, when you skip meals or starve yourself, you often end up bingeing or overeating at your next meal or when you get off your diet.

Solution: Eat small frequent meals to keep those hunger pangs at bay and your metabolism ticking. Carry a healthy snack with you for those in-between hunger pangs.

Overeating: Those biryani and gulab jamun have a way of weakening any resolve you may have of self-control. Overeating is another sure way of slowing down your BMR. Your body goes into overdrive furiously storing all that excess energy which you have provided it and have not burned through exercise or activity. Remember, the more the fat stored, the slower your BMR.

Solution: Eat frequent, smaller, high fibre meals so your metabolism regulates itself to cope with the intake of food energy.

Late Night Snacking: Dinner is over. You've had a hard day at work, or the kids have kept you on your toes and finally you have some 'me time'. What could be better than sprawling in front of the TV with a huge bowl of ice cream and a bag of chips? Actually, what could be worse? Especially, if it becomes your secret indulgence!

Solution: Ideally, your last big meal should be two hours before you go to bed, so your metabolism gets some down time. However, if you need the comfort, sip on some soothing green tea or a glass of warm skimmed milk. Or eat a high fibre snack like an oat cookie. For more guilt-free comfort foods, check out the Live Well Diets A, B and C.

Inadequate exercise: When you consume more food energy in the form of carbohydrates, sugar or fat than you burn through activity or exercise, your metabolism gets overloaded and slows down.

Solution: Exercise and activity help to burn the excess energy that your body consumes. With a regular programme of exercise, you stimulate your metabolism, increasing your BMR so you burn more or at least as many calories as you consume.

High BMI (Body Mass Index): If your body is composed of more fat than muscle, your metabolism will slow down as body fat requires more energy to burn than muscle.

Solution: Regular exercise and eating low-fat, high protein and high fibre meals will increase your BMR.

Stress: Our lives today seem to be governed by stress – whether at work, in the home or even while driving! Walking along a crowded street can be as stressful for some as meeting important work deadlines or sitting for an examination. While sporadic stress may not be harmful, prolonged stress has a direct impact on your metabolism as it affects the digestive system – your stomach produces more acid in times of stress. In addition, for some of us, one way of soothing our nerves is to eat! Given the amount of stress most of us have, overeating and excess fat is almost a given.

Solution: To calm your nerves instead of reaching for a burger or a chocolate pastry, pour yourself a warm glass of skimmed milk – it works wonders particularly just before you go to bed. For a more long-term and non-food related solution, enroll in yoga or stress management programmes, or take up stress reducing activities like music, art, gardening or some other relaxing pastime or hobby. Exercise, especially yoga, releases all those feel-good endorphins which are mood lifting. In addition, or if all else fails, treat yourself to a relaxing body massage. A long stroll after dinner, preferably in the company of your spouse, a friend or even a pet, is refreshing and a great stress buster.

Inadequate Sleep: The quality of sleep is closely related to the amount of stress in your life, and therefore your eating habits. Lack of sleep is also known to negatively affect the production of the hormones which help to regulate hunger and appetite.

Solution: To get a good night's sleep of at least 7 hours, practice yoga, meditation or other relaxing techniques. Avoid watching TV just before you go to bed or while in bed. Once again, a warm glass of milk will also do the trick.

Dehydration: Inadequate amounts of water are known to slow down the BMR as water is essential for the metabolic process.

Solution: Drink 3-4 litres of water plus other beverages such as green tea, water, vegetable juices, soup, lime water, buttermilk or coconut water and keep your metabolism juiced up.

Poor Thyroid Function and Metabolic Disorders: These occur when the normal metabolic processes are disrupted resulting in diseases like diabetes or PCOD (poly-cystic ovarian disease).

Solution: Consult your physician who will prescribe the necessary treatment.

● ● ●

MY STORY } Swaroop Sampat
Actor and Educationist

I FEEL SO  POSITIVE NOW, I AM ON A MAJOR HIGH!

I first went to Dr Davare after I had spent 2 months in the U.S. and had put on weight with all the heavy food I was eating there. My tour was also quite hectic and I had had very little sleep. I felt overweight and out of sorts. At the same time, my husband Paresh was also overweight and had high triglyceride levels. We had heard about Dr Davare's amazing programme and both of us wanted to try it out but at Paresh's request, I offered to become the guinea pig!

I have always tried to maintain my weight and exercise regularly, so I did not find the programme difficult to follow. The vegetable juices were particularly effective and the diet just reinforced my own eating habits. I lost weight and felt healthy once again.

Paresh on the other hand, found it difficult to stomach the large quantities of vegetable juices prescribed at first, but once his triglycerides reached normal levels in a short time on the diet, and he began to feel more energetic, he too follows the programme.

I walk and jog regularly, and my BMR is so much better. I feel so much more positive now, my face glows and I am on a major high!

Other Ways to Boost your BMR

Many obesity consultants and dieticians use supplementary methods like electro-stimulation for obesity management. I prefer acupuncture as I believe it is a safe method to stimulate the digestive and metabolic processes. It also has a positive effect on the nervous and endocrine system. However, I must emphasise that electro-stimulation and acupuncture alone will not help weight loss. The treatment by an experienced practitioner must go hand in hand with diet control, exercise and stress management.

Fueling the Flames - The Thermic Effect of Food

Different foods burn or metabolise at different rates in the body using up different amounts of energy to process it. Fat from food is known to have a very low thermic rate requiring very little energy to metabolise; complex carbohydrates which are rich in fibre have a higher thermic rate as do protein-rich foods which also require more energy to process. A diet that is rich in protein and complex carbohydrates uses up more energy for metabolism and the food stays in the digestive system longer. This is also why when you eat foods like eggs, chicken, chickpeas or soya you feel full longer and are less prone to hunger pangs, whereas if you eat fatty or sugary foods you begin to feel hungry again very soon.

FOODS TO BOOST YOUR BMR

Regular exercise and appropriate food choices are the solutions to increase metabolism and your BMR. Here are some foods which are known to have a positive effect on metabolism:

- **Whole grains** such as wheat, brown rice, oats, millets (jowar, ragi), sorghum (jowar).

- **Legumes and pulses** such as chickpeas, green gram, lentils, beans.

- **Nuts and seeds** like walnuts, almonds and flaxseeds.

- **Beverages** like water, green tea, soy milk, lime water, raw vegetable juices.

- **Fruits** like amla, pomegranate, papaya, apples, lemons, limes, oranges.

- **Vegetables** like bottle gourd (lauki), cluster beans (gawar), capsicum, green tomatoes, bitter gourd (karela).

- **Herbs, spices and aromatics** like coriander, ginger, curry leaves, cumin seeds.

- **Animal products** such as egg whites, fish, chicken, skimmed milk, buttermilk and yogurt.

GOLDEN RULES TO BOOST YOUR BMR

- Eating the right foods
- Regular meals – 5 small meals a day
- Plenty of water- 3-4 litres
- Exercise – daily yoga - pranayam and walk
- Adequate sleep - 7 hours a day
- Relaxation - meditation, hobbies
- Massages – 1 or 2 per week

● ● ●

MY STORY } Priya Gupta
Media Professional

I CHANGED
MY LIFESTYLE

Being a part of the media, I lead a very erratic lifestyle. I also had very poor eating habits and no understanding of diet. Due to excessive weight, I was suffering from high blood pressure as well as was prone to diabetes due to my family history. I also travel about 15 days a month, making my food and sleep habits very erratic.

Now, I know how to manage even when I am travelling. Once you start following the diet and you see the results, you get motivated to follow it wholeheartedly. My lifestyle has changed. I no longer have high blood pressure which is remarkable. In spite of having a thyroid problem, I am able to reduce weight.

Some changes in my life: Walking throughout the year • Increased self-confidence • I have learned how to balance my diet at all times • I know the importance of sleeping for weight loss

WEIGHT LOSS IS A CHANGE IN LIFESTYLE

In Mumbai everyone lives a very hectic life and since a lot of us live in nuclear families we have to look after the kitchen, children, travelling, profession, social life, and fitness all at the same time. The lifestyle is stressful with late nights and no discipline in eating patterns; especially after 2 babies in past 5 years I had gained 25 kg during each pregnancy and had no time to look after myself.

Because of the weight gain I also had high blood pressure and after trying a few diets which helped me lose a few kilos, very soon I would gain them back.

The Live Well Diet is strict and very precise... it targets the different layers of fat... superficial, mid layer and stubborn fat, so there are a lot of liquids, veggies, soups and salads. Controlling carbs and non-veg, no sugar, oil, sweets, drink lots and lots of fresh lime water to flush out toxins and balancing your food with your daily activities.

Initially the diet is tough for the first week and then your system gets used to it, as Dr Davare says weight loss is a change in lifestyle. You have to sleep, eat, drink, on time and rest your body.

Now I eat a lot of vegetarian food, sleep on time, drink a lot more water and try to balance my meal intake.

The Live Well Diet is the most reasonable, most effective and convenient way to weight loss.

5

YOU ARE
WHAT YOU EAT

Food, Glorious Food!

Food is so central to our lives it seems that everything we do revolves around food. From the time you suckled at your mother's breast, food has been an intimate part of who you are, and often becomes the lens through which you view the world. Our closest relationships are formed by and nurtured through food. Family meals, tussles and teasing around a table, auspicious beginnings and tearful partings, packed tiffins and mithai boxes, lollipop prizes and award banquets, and every rite of passage from birth through marriage to the meal at the wake, food insinuates itself into our lives and defines our existence.

Food memories are amongst the strongest sensory memories we have - the sight or a pile of syrupy orange jalebi, the sound of pakore sizzling in a pan, the sharp hiss of kadi patta and the pungent aroma it releases as it hits the oil in a tadka, the crunch of a til laddoo or piece of chana chikki, the smell of vanilla or coffee, the feel of silky, smooth atta as you knead it gently into compliance. Memories evoked by food can whisk you back in an instant to a special time and place.

Food and religion go hand in hand. In Hinduism, devotion to Annapurna, the Goddess of food, symbolises a deep reverence for food and the role it plays in life. No religious ceremony takes place without an offering of food to the Gods. Cycles of fasting and feasting are prevalent in all religions, putting food on a central pedestal around which life and our relationship with the divine revolves.

Food nourishes and fills us with energy; it heals, cleanses and fortifies; it soothes, comforts and satisfies. But it can also hurt and harm, sully and ravage, depress and destroy. It all depends on what role you choose for it to play in your life.

• • •

MY STORY } Jitesh Gada
Businessman

FROM 30-40 ROSOGOLLAS
TO ABSOLUTELY NO SUGAR!

I used to suffer from chronic asthma and had to take 40 steroid injections a month. Since I began Dr Davare's programme I have not needed to take either tablets or injections which has been a huge achievement and change in my life! I have shared my experience with many people who visit my store and my friends who suffer from asthma. I tell them that like me they can give up their nebulisers and medication and just be on Dr Davare's programme.

I have had absolutely no difficulty with the diet; in fact I feel that the diet prescribed is in excess of what one needs. My new food habits have completely changed my life. To think I used to at one time eat 30 chapattis, or 30 dosas, or 40-50 rossogollas at one sitting! I have given up sugar completely and strangely have no craving for sweets now. Both my wife and I are on the programme which is also an advantage; she too has benefited from the programme, lost a lot of weight and is so much healthier now.

The best thing is that I can jog for 12 km without a break which is a huge achievement for an asthmatic.

DO YOU LOVE TO EAT OR LIVE TO EAT?

There are many who would agree with George Bernard Shaw, the satirist and playwright who declared, "There is no love sincerer than the love of food." One's relationship with food can be intimate and devoted, but there is a fine line between enjoying good food and being obsessed with it. Being a gourmand or lover of food is very different from being a glutton. Dr Douglas Markham, a wellness specialist, has compared food to a drug, for, as with any drug such as painkillers, one can get addicted to food. Like a drug, food has an effect on the complex biochemical workings of the body, and like a drug, food can be beneficial as well as abused.

Here are some indicators that you may be more dependent on food than you think you are or would like to be. Tick the ones that apply to you:

1. The only thing that will comfort me when I am upset is food.
2. Once I start eating I find it difficult to stop.
3. My family thinks I have an eating problem.
4. I feel guilty and ashamed every time I overeat.
5. I am obsessed with food. All I can think about is my next meal.
6. I get very agitated when I want to eat and there is no food around.
7. I pig out often on high calorie food and can wolf it down in no time at all!
8. I often eat secretly and hide food so I can eat it when nobody else is around.
9. It upsets and angers me when someone else has eaten what I have reserved for myself.
10. I am fed up of people going on at me about my diet.
11. I have tried many diets and none of them have worked.
12. I know eating excess food is bad for me but I can't stop.
13. I regularly eat even when I am not hungry and continue eating even after I am full.

14. I feel uneasy if I do not have something to eat in my bag or briefcase or close at hand at all times.
15. I have sugar cravings – only something very sweet will help.

If you have ticked only a few you obviously love food and it may be possible for you to make the necessary changes to manage that love better. If you have ticked many of the above, you may have an over-dependence on food and food may be taking over your life. You may need professional help to deal with the causes, so do consult your physician who will recommend an appropriate course of action.

Binge eating is a food disorder which may be mild if indulged in occasionally, but more serious if it becomes a pattern. Binge eating is an uncontrollable impulse to eat large amounts of food in a short span of time, followed by deep feelings of guilt, sadness and depression. Almost every person who is struggling with weight issues has at one time or another suffered a bout of binge eating, especially while trying to stay on, or soon after completing a very restricted diet. Regular binge eating needs professional help – so do consult a physician for advice.

Gluttony is an emotional escape, a sign something is eating us.

- Peter De Vries

The compulsion to eat can have many causes, but most of them are related to one's mental and emotional state. Stress is the most common cause as is low self-esteem or self-image and lack of self-confidence or a feeling of powerlessness. How good and comforting it is to eat a creamy pastry when you have been dumped by a boyfriend; how perfect that hamburger is to soothe your bruised ego when your request for a raise was turned down - again; and how happy (and defiant) do you feel as you split open that huge packet of chips as you settle in front of the TV, hoping to forget that a friend you hadn't seen for ages just told you that you had put on weight. Food is like the pacifier you give a baby to keep him from fussing – temporary oral satisfaction. Eating something, anything, you hope, will keep you from thinking or feeling too much.

On the Sugar Roller Coaster

As soon as you eat something sweet when you are depressed or stressed, your blood glucose levels rise rapidly and your body releases the feel-good chemicals - endorphins and serotonin - into your system, which lift your mood and calm your mind. But the feel-good rush is short-lived, as the levels of these chemicals fall just as fast as they rise, and in no time at all your negative feelings surface again. Beware of the sugar rush which leaves you with a roller coaster of emotions. Starchy and fatty foods such as burgers or sandwiches have a similar effect setting you off on a cycle of sadness, overeating, guilt, self-disgust, sadness and then eating again.

THE FAT PERSON'S LAMENT

CONTROL NAHIN HOTA!

I just love food – I live to eat
I eat when I am bored
I eat while I am watching TV
I eat when I am stressed
I eat when I am sad
I can't do without dessert
I must take second helpings
I can't help it – control nahin hota!

I AM
A BELIEVER

For the past 15 years, I led an extremely hectic lifestyle with frequent travel, stress, entertainment coupled with my love for food led to a drastic increase in weight.

I had tried out a couple of dietitians and gym but this did not yield results, I ended up losing weight and then immediately gaining it back. And then my wife had begun consulting Dr Davare and the results were extremely pleasing.

When I started the programme I was completely shell shocked with what at that point I thought were drastic steps. I hate dudhi and chowli with a passion, but overcame that finally treating it as medicine. The diet was a bit tough initially but managed to adhere to it thanks to my wife. Exercise, though not upto Dr Davare's standards, I was able to pick up.

The experience that began with skepticism transformed me into a believer, more from the perspective of being able to maintain the weight loss when I go back to the clinic, which is a fantastic feeling.

The changes I have made:

- Weight – total loss of 25 kg.
- Health - From no walk to be able to walk 4-5 km at least 4 times a week.
- Lifestyle changes – I avoid alcohol during the week completely; I take maybe 60 ml during the weekend; I avoid dinner after 9 p.m; I abstain from fried food and cheese etc. which was the mainstay in my diet for me earlier.
- Emotionally and mentally I am more at peace and more confident.

6

FOOD
NOURISHES

As you have read before, your body is essentially a machine which needs plenty of fuel and other inputs to keep it running well. Nutrients from the food you eat provide your body with energy, keep your body in good repair, help it to grow and keep your body functioning smoothly. Your body needs some nutrients in large quantities – called macro nutrients - which are proteins, fats and carbohydrates. Your body also needs other nutrients to help it function like minerals and vitamins, as well as plenty of water.

While food nourishes, if not taken in the right quantities or balance, food can deplete your energies and have a negative impact on your body.

PROTEINS

The main function of protein in your body is to promote growth, repair and maintenance of your body. Proteins are of particular importance in the Live Well Diet as they take longer to digest, giving one a feeling of satiety much longer than foods which are rich in carbohydrates or fat.

> **Protein- Rich Foods**
> - Meat and Poultry – Mutton, chicken
> - Seafood – Fish and shellfish
> - Eggs – Especially egg whites
> - Milk and Milk Products – Milk, yogurt, cheese, paneer
> - Legumes and Pulses – Lentils, beans, dals
> - Nuts and Seeds – Flax seeds, almonds, walnuts, sesame seeds

In addition to natural proteins from food, it is advisable to include a no-fat, no-carbohydrate protein supplement such as whey protein, particularly when one's physical activity increases. This is especially necessary if you are vegetarian as plant proteins do not contain all the essential amino acids required by the body.

FATS

Fat is essential for building your body tissue and cells, and it helps the absorption of some vitamins (A and D) in your body.

Almost all foods contain some amount of fat. You may be surprised to know that even foods we consider to be fat-free such as leafy greens and carrots contain a minute quantity of fat.

GOOD FATS

Unsaturated Fats

Unsaturated fats are called good fats because they can improve blood cholesterol levels, besides playing many other beneficial roles. They are found largely in foods from plants, such as vegetable oils, nuts, and seeds. Unsaturated fats stay liquid at room temperature.

There are two types of unsaturated fats:

Monounsaturated fats (MUFA) are found in olive oil, peanut oil, canola oil, almonds and sesame seeds (til).

Polyunsaturated fats (PUFA) are found in sunflower oil, corn oil, soy bean oil, walnuts, flax seeds and fish.

Omega-3 fats are an important type of polyunsaturated fat. The body cannot make them, so they must come from food. They are believed to reduce the risk of heart disease and boost the immune system. They are found in fish such as sardines, mackerels, king fish and Indian salmon (rawas) and fish oils such as cod liver oil.

BAD FATS

Saturated Fats

Saturated fat consists of triglycerides. Saturated fats directly raise total and LDL (bad cholesterol) levels. Foods that contain a high proportion of saturated fats include red meat; full-fat dairy products such as cheese, milk, ice cream, butter; coconut oil, palm oil and chocolate or cocoa butter. Saturated fats remain solid at room temperature.

THE UGLY OR REALLY BAD FATS

Trans Fats

Trans fats are actually unsaturated fats or vegetable oils which are synthetically made by a process of hydrogenation, turning liquid oils into solid fat. Trans fats such as margarine, vanaspati and non-dairy cream are used in processed foods to prolong their shelf life, and in cooked foods such as cakes, biscuits, pizzas, ice-creams and commercially available deep-fried foods.

The Live Well Diet recommends the consumption of small quantities of unsaturated fats and complete avoidance of both saturated and trans fats.

The Sad and Ugly Truth – the most harmful foods are often the ones that look the most appetising and taste the best – think creamy pastries, hot jalebi, buttery paranthe, etc.

● ● ●

A NEW LEASE OF LIFE

I am an architect and lead a very busy professional life with an extremely busy calendar and many social commitments. I work long hours—an average of 10-11 hours per work day. There is no fixed schedule for eating and sleeping. Before I entered the programme the level of physical activity was restricted to site visits only.

I saw amazing results in my friends, who had joined Davare's programme, it was like a miracle, their skin glowed, they looked younger and fitter and this motivated me to join Dr Davare's Clinic. I had no other health concerns before joining Dr Davare, only my pathology reports showed high triglycerides.

I was intrigued by the idea that by following her regime I would shed at least 7-8 kg in a short span of time, which otherwise would have been impossible for me to lose. The challenge I faced was remembering to drink adequate water and disciplining myself to go for a one hour walk every day.

I lost around 2.5 kg in the first week itself and this was a strong motivator for me to stick to the diet and exercise as I could see the results visibly. Eventually my weight dropped from 86 kg to 68 kg and my waist size dropped from 40 inches to 32 inches.

My experience with Dr Davare has been both exhilarating and satisfying: the weight loss with almost zero sagging skin and with the pathology reports reverting back to normal values. The transformation the programme brings about is nothing short of a miracle and when you look at yourself in the mirror after the programme you feel rejuvenated.

I have now become more aware of the importance of rightly balanced nutritious food required by the body and the positive benefits of maintaining the right diet and lifestyle. Dr Davare's programme has a positive impact at all levels, physical, mental, emotional. The weight loss literally boosts the morale and when you look good you definitely feel good.

Besides the obvious benefit of being thinner the huge hidden benefit lies in the pathological reports reverting to normal values. It's like a new lease of life.

CARBOHYDRATES

Carbohydrates are the main source of fuel for your body. They are broken down in the digestive system and enter the bloodstream as glucose. Excess glucose is stored in the form of glycogen in the liver and, in limited quantities, in the muscles.

Simple carbohydrates are easily converted into glucose and therefore provide the quickest source of energy, raising your blood sugar rapidly. They are found in the various forms of sugar and refined cereal flours.

Complex carbohydrates take longer to metabolise and convert into energy. They include starch, glycogen, and cellulose or fibre, and are found in fruit, vegetables and unrefined whole grains.

Fibre or cellulose is a form of complex carbohydrate that our bodies cannot digest. Also referred to as roughage, it provides bulk and helps the digestive system to function smoothly.

THE GLYCAEMIC INDEX

The highs and lows of carbohydrate-rich foods

All the carbohydrates in the food we eat are broken down into glucose or blood sugar by the digestive system. The more carbohydrates we eat the higher the levels of glucose or blood sugar. As blood glucose levels rise, the hormone insulin is released. Insulin helps the body's cells absorb blood sugar for energy or storage. The glucose or blood sugar levels drop as the cells absorb the blood sugar.

Carbohydrates from the foods we eat enter the bloodstream at different rates. Carbohydrates which enter the bloodstream rapidly and raise blood sugar (glucose) levels quickly are said to have a high Glycaemic Index (GI). Pizzas, sandwiches, cakes and pastries, would fall into this category and give a whole other meaning to 'fast food', describing, in effect, the speed at which the carbohydrates enter the bloodstream, raising the levels of glucose in a rapid burst.

Foods that raise blood sugar levels in a more controlled way and take longer to digest and break down have a lower glycaemic index and may be described as 'slow carbs'. Slow carbs are better for long-term health and body weight control. These foods include legumes, whole grains, fruit such as apples and pears, most vegetables and leafy greens.

White is not right: Refined flours such as maida, and sugar, and their products such as white bread and cakes, and white rice have a high glycaemic index and should be avoided.

The whole way: Whole grains have a lower glycaemic index and more fibre than refined ones. Opt for wholewheat flour (atta), brown rice, sorghum (jowar), millets (bajra, ragi).

FIBRE - Bulk up your diet

Fibre is the indigestible form of complex carbohydrates which the body cannot convert into sugar.

Being indigestible, fibre does not contain any calories. It does, however, play an important role in digestion for as it passes through the digestive system, it absorbs water helping to remove waste products smoothly and regularly from the body in the form of bowel movements.

Foods rich in fibre, because they are bulky, create a sense of fullness in the stomach, and are slow to move through the digestive tract. They also slow down the rate of absorption in the body, regulate the levels of blood sugar and reduce the levels of bad cholesterol (LDL) in the body.

The Live Well Diet is a high-fibre diet which will significantly contribute towards your weight loss and well-being. Besides, most foods which are high in fibre are also very rich in essential vitamins and minerals.

● ● ●

High-Fibre Foods

- Dark green leafy vegetables – keep the stalks on – spinach, fenugreek (methi), colocasia (arbi leaves).
- Root vegetable skins or peels – scrub carrots, knolkhol etc, instead of peeling them. Use vegetable peels ground with spices to make chutneys.
- Fruit skins – eat apples and pears with their skins on. Do not remove the thin membranes from orange segments.
- Dried fruit – figs, apricots, dates.
- Whole grains and their products – wholewheat, oats, sorghum (jowar), pearl millet (bajra), ragi (finger millet) brown rice, etc.
- Bran – add wholewheat and rice bran to your diet.
- Nuts and seeds – walnuts and unblanched almonds, flax seeds.
- Legumes and pulses – chickpeas, beans, gram, dals.

Sneak in Those Veggies

Two years ago the mother of a young patient requested me to help him change his diet and lifestyle. He obviously hated vegetables and lived mainly on potatoes! His diet at that time consisted of the following:

Breakfast: Aloo parantha with yogurt
Lunch: 2 roti with aloo sabzi and ketchup
Evening snack: Pani puri
Dinner: Dal with rice and ghee

I advised her to change his diet to include more fibre in the form of vegetables which could be introduced into his diet in delicious ways: low-fat pav bhaji, vegetable cutlets, vegetable rolls, vegetable paranthe, etc. The young man lost weight as a result and is leading a much healthier lifestyle.

MINERALS

Although minerals are found in very small quantities in every organ, tissue and cell of your body, they play a very important role in keeping your body functioning well.

A slight imbalance of these minerals can have an effect on your health. Some important minerals are calcium, iron, iodine, sodium and potassium. Of these, salt is one mineral that we tend to take for granted, not realising the impact it has on our health.

Chutki bhar namak!

In Roman times salt was such a precious commodity that wages were paid in salt (hence the word salary). Today, from a healthy-living point of view, it should also be treated as precious and used sparingly. Every nutritionist worth his or her salt (yes!) will tell you that in the case of this kitchen essential, less is more. Excess sodium in the diet can lead to water retention and oedema (swelling), and hypertension or high blood pressure.

Restrict your intake of salt to not more than 2000 mg (2 grams) sodium or approximately 1 teaspoon (6 grams) of table salt per day. Remember, that all foods contain some amount of natural sodium or salt, so literally add a pinch of salt to your food; or if you can, avoid it completely.

More importantly, beware of hidden salt in packaged foods such as biscuits, sauces, ketchup, pickles, soups, noodles, papad, snacks like namkeen (it is salty after all!), and farsan such as dhokla, where salt is used as a preservative or to enhance flavour. Avoid flavour-enhancers like MSG (monosodium glutamate) particularly in Chinese food. To find out how much salt there is in packaged foods check out the sodium content mentioned on the food label.

It is hard to control the amount of salt while eating out, but you can avoid the pickles, papad, extra grated cheese on top of the pasta, or the chutney which accompanies the dosa!

Salt and sodium do not weigh the same
1/4 tsp salt = 1.5 grams = 500 mg sodium
1/2 tsp salt = 3 grams = 1,000 mg sodium
3/4 tsp salt = 4.5 grams = 1,500 mg sodium
1 tsp salt = 6 grams = 2,000 mg sodium

I FEEL FIT AND HEALTHY FROM WITHIN

I am a complete foodie and love to gorge on sweets and Chinese food. I had zero level of exercise regime or any such activity. I used to hate going to the gym and working out. I used to eat out almost every alternate day.

I used to have a lot of knee pain due to the pressure of weight on my knees. Besides that, my reports showed hyperthyroidism.

I started the programme with a very open mind and fully charged to lose weight - to do whatever it takes. The biggest challenge is to mentally accept your diet and programme. Once you have done that, everything else is just as easy as breathing. Controlling my food and sweet tooth was the biggest challenge for me which I successfully achieved.

The programme was a bit of a new concept. But the diet and the programme are well in sync with day to day habits. And since I do not have any strict working hours, it was quite easy for me to adapt to the diet and ninety minute walk every day.

Dr Davare's weight loss programme is magical. It's a super healthy way of losing weight but it needs your 100% dedication and attention. I have lost about 12-15 kg and it's made my lifestyle much healthier than before. I am more conscious about what I eat, keeping in balance with my taste buds and how to maintain the weight loss. It is very necessary to understand the scientific repercussions bad eating has on your body versus only physical appearance and I think that's the plus point of Dr Davare's weight loss programme that you feel fit and healthy from within.

VITAMINS

Vitamins are essential organic compounds that the human body cannot make by itself and must therefore be eaten as food.

Vitamins play an important part in keeping us healthy. All fresh fruit and vegetables, especially green leafy vegetables are rich in vitamins. Milk and milk products, eggs, fish and meat, legumes and pulses are bursting with essential vitamins. Vitamin A is known to help vision, Vitamin B, particularly Vitamin B12, to help with growth, nerve and brain function, metabolism and all round health, Vitamin C to provide immunity against diseases, Vitamin E for healthy skin and Vitamin K for clotting of blood and absorption of calcium.

Vitamin D – Solar Power

Vitamin D is also called the 'sunshine vitamin' because sunlight is its main source. Most people get adequate quantities of Vitamin D from normal exposure to the sun, though some studes have shown that a majority of our population is deficient in this vital vitamin. The level of Vitamin D in the body is believed to affect weight loss: low levels of Vitamin D may increase abdominal fat, while extra Vitamin D is believed to promote weight loss on a reduced calorie diet. Howver, excess Vitamin D can also lead to toxicity which is harmful. Do have your Vitamin D levels assessed and consult your phyisician in case of Vitamin D deficiency or excess.

Vitamin and Mineral Supplements

Natural food is the best source of all vitamins, but it helps to boost one's energy and body functions to supplement one's diet with a few essential vitamins and minerals:

- Folic Acid to enhance nerve and brain function.
- Calcium to strengthen bones and teeth and prevent osteoporosis.
- Vitamin B12 to enhance metabolism.
- Vitamin C to raise your immunity.
- Vitamin E for healthy hair and skin.

FOOD HEALS AND PROTECTS

Apart from providing us with important nutrients for our bodies, food is the ultimate healer. From fighting diseases like cancer, reducing cholesterol, protecting against heart disease, food is truly the best cure, best regulator of your body's health and best medicine. The converse is also true – food can cause harm to your body if taken in excess and in the wrong proportions. The secret is to eat more foods that are beneficial to health and avoid or reduce the one's that harm.

Let food be thy medicine and medicine be thy food.

- Hippocrates

Antioxidants

Antioxidants are vitamins, minerals and enzymes that help to counteract the negative effects of oxidation of the cells in the body. Harmful molecules called free radicals produced within the body as a result of oxidation, damage the body cells and may lead to ailments such as heart disease, cancer, arthritis, and strokes.

It is possible to counteract the effect of free radicals on your system by regulating your diet, particularly with the increase of certain antioxidant vitamins and minerals -Vitamin E, Vitamin C, Beta Carotene, Selenium, Manganese and Zinc.

ANTIOXIDANTS

Foods which are rich in antioxidants help you to look younger and age better.

Vegetables: Cabbage, cauliflower, broccoli, spring onions, bottle gourd, green leafy vegetables.

Fruit: Apples, pineapple, papaya, guava, strawberries, tomatoes, amla, citrus fruits– oranges, limes.

Herbs and Spices: Mint, coriander, basil, parsley, chillies, cinnamon, cloves, turmeric, ginger.

Nuts and Seeds: Almonds, walnuts, flax seeds and sunflower seeds

Fish: Sardines, mackerels, salmon, tuna, kingfish/seer fish.

Miscellaneous: Extra-virgin olive oil, green tea.

> *The best and most efficient pharmacy is within your own system.*
> — *Robert C. Peale*

FOOD CLEANSES AND DETOXIFIES

As part of the digestive and metabolic processes our bodies produce toxins or harmful substances which need to be expelled regularly and efficiently so that the body can function in an optimum way. Sluggishness, skin problems, and gastric or digestive problems are symptoms of excess toxins in the body.

Water is the main detoxifying agent in our diets. Drinking plenty of water allows the body to flush out toxins from the system. Detoxification has a direct effect on BMR, helping to increase it and promote weight loss.

To detoxify your system:

1. Eliminate or severely restrict alcohol, smoking, refined sugar, trans fats, and other harmful foods which act as toxins in the body and are detrimental to your health.

2. Eat plenty of fibre, including whole grains, fresh fruits and vegetables. These will help flush your system of toxins through the smooth elimination of waste.

3. Drink beverages that have a detoxifying effect such as lime water, vegetable juices and green tea. Lime juice and lime water provide Vitamin C which helps digestion and cleans the body of toxins.

4. Drink at least 3-4 litres of water daily.

5. Pranayama or deep breathing exercises cleanse your system by allowing oxygen to circulate more freely.

6. Exercise ramps up your metabolism and tones up your body's systems so that they work to cleanse and eliminate toxins efficiently.

● ● ●

A TURNING POINT IN MY LIFE

I never thought that in terms of lifestyle fortunes can turn around so much. What happened to me was beyond belief. I was known as a 'foodie' and obviously gained a lot of weight over the years. Interestingly, I was very comfortable with my size and weight. But Nature had different plans for my body , mind and soul too. Type 2 diabetes came to me as a gift from my family and sleep apnea became a close companion. These two friends started living happily with me. But I was not really happy.

My friends suggested I consult Dr Sarita Davare and that suggestion proved to be a turning point in my life. When I stepped into her clinic I was sure about my goal. I was not fussy about my weight but was more worried about the two new unwelcome friends living with me. Dr Sarita understood my plight and her confidence opened up a ray of hope during our very first meeting. At that time my clinical test reports were very negative. After a few weeks of Dr Sarita's treatment I could feel the difference. At that time I was on insulin and had to regularly monitor my C-peptides. After 8 months I put away the C-peptide test kit and insulin for me has become history. The treatment changed my perspective towards life. I am more positive, more energetic and feel youthful once again. The diet truly changed me and my life.

WATER
FOR LIFE

You have seen images of parched land with a jigsaw puzzle of cracks snaking across the surface, with little or no evidence of life. That is what your skin would look like without sufficient water. Water is a major component of every cell, tissue and organ in your body. It plays an important role in almost every body function. Your blood, tears and mucus are mostly water. Water hydrates and regulates the temperature of your body. Water lubricates your joints and gives body cells their shape and stability. A lack of water causes thirst, a parched feeling, dry skin, acidity and constipation among other ailments.

The role of water in our bodies is vital and complex, and particularly so for regulating weight and living well.

• Water is essential for the fat burning process. If you are dehydrated, your metabolism slows down and your body will not be able to burn the excess fat efficiently.

• Water will flush out the toxins which are produced by an active metabolism and high BMR.

• Water prevents acidity as it dilutes the contents of the stomach and gastro-intestinal tract

• As you increase the amount of fibre in your diet, you will need the extra water to help the fibre to pass out of your body as waste. If you are not drinking sufficient amounts of water with increased fibre in your diet, you can suffer from constipation

• Dehydration causes a domino effect: when your blood volume reduces due to inadequate water, the supply of oxygen to your muscles through the blood is reduced, when there is less oxygen in your muscles you will suffer from cramps and a feeling of tiredness.

- Water is also known to prevent migraines.

- You need water to lubricate your muscles and joints as you exercise. If you do not drink enough water your muscles will be sore and your joints painful.

- With plenty of water your skin will glow and any pigmentation due to weight loss will be prevented, reduce or disappear.

- It is particularly important to drink water while on long-distance flights as dehydration can cause circulation problems such as Deep Vein Thrombosis (DVT).

To keep your body running smoothly and skin glowing, you must drink 3-4 litres of water a day in addition to other beverages.

Note: Drink lukewarm water or water at room temperature for best results.

GET WATER WISE

Here are some tips to ensure you drink enough water:

- Start the day by drinking water (see Live Well Diets).

- Carry a bottle of water with you wherever you go.

- Keep a bottle of water within reach at your work place.

- Drink water in the form of soups, coconut water, green tea, and juices.

- Do not allow yourself to get thirsty. If you feel thirsty, it means that your body is already crying out for water.

- If you are the type who is forgetful or gets too engrossed in your work, set an alarm on your mobile phone or clock to remind you to drink water.

- Measure out the amount of water you need to drink and keep drinking throughout the day till you have drunk it all.

- The Daily Food and Beverage Intake (page 192) and Essential Daily Intake (page 192) will help you keep track of the amount of water you are drinking.

CAUTION: Too much water can be dangerous because it will dilute the amount of sodium in your body. This imbalance could result in health issues. Spread your water intake through out the day and do not consume the recommended amount all at once.

HOW YOU CAN TELL IF YOU ARE DRINKING ENOUGH WATER

Your body will send out signals like thirst. But there are other ways of finding out if your water intake is sufficient.

Colour of Urine

The easiest way to tell if your body is well hydrated and your are drinking enough water or fluids is to look at the colour of your urine. If your body is getting adequate water, your urine will be clear or pale yellow. If your urine is dark yellow or almost orangey-red, assuming you are not suffering from any other symptoms, it means it is concentrated and you are not drinking enough water.

Note: Some medications, foods such as beetroot, or an illness such as Jaundice may also affect the colour of your urine.

Bowel Movements

Your bowl movements are also a good guide. If your bowel movements are soft, you have enough water in your system. Hard bowel movements or constipation can be signs that your water intake is low.

Skin Texture

If your skin looks dry and flaky, the chances are you are not drinking enough water. A well-hydrated skin glows and is firm to the touch.

● ● ●

HEALTH AND GOOD LOOKS FOREVER!

I am fond of food; love to experiment with local cuisine while I travel across the world. Though I have been conscious of health and fitness, I would often succumb to my cravings for good food and sweets. Due to hectic travel schedules and stress at work, I would binge to curb my stress resulting in the fact that I could not maintain my weight and that led to plateau of my weight which refused to move, irrespective of how hard I tried. I was doing Bollywood dancing classes to reduce my weight before I consulted Dr Davare. I tried many different things including consulting a dietician friend. The results were good, but temporary.

When I joined the programme I did not have any mental block to the regime, I was comfortable doing what I was told to do.

I started at 91 kg with Dr Davare and now I am 68 kg. With the drastic weight loss and inch loss, compliments are natural to come. I have become more disciplined in my habits and don't hesitate to say no to myself when tempted. My life is more disciplined and I manage to detox myself effortlessly when I overindulge.

It has been a tried and tested experience for weight loss. If one continues to modify the lifestyle based on Dr Davare's programme, good health and good looks are forever!

THE TRADITIONAL THALI –
A COMPLETE MEAL

Now that you have had an overview of the different foods that you should include in your diet and their benefits, it is time to see what your Live Well Diet plate should look like.

We are fortunate in India to have a centuries-old tradition of eating a variety of foods all on the same plate – the thali. If you look closely at the food traditions we have taken for granted, or replaced with newer fusion or foreign ones, you will see that much of what has been described in the preceding pages resembles the diet of our forefathers.

The thali comprised a variety of nutritious foods, each one having some nutritional benefit. It included a vegetable dish made from a seasonal, locally grown vegetable, a dish of leafy vegetables, a fresh salad (kachumber/koshimbir), a dish of whole legumes or pulses, a lentil dish (dal), a cereal – rice or wholewheat bread (roti), a small bowl of yogurt or glass of buttermilk, a wedge of lemon and a dollop of pickle to stimulate the appetite. For non-vegetarians, a piece of fish and occasionally a few pieces of chicken or meat appeared on the thali.

The thali was the epitome of variety and balance. Many Indians continue to eat that way, but for many, especially in the urban areas, exposure to new food trends and flavours and a hectic lifestyle, have led to an overhaul of our eating habits and the complexion of the food on our plates. We do less physical work than our forbears and therefore our diets have to be regulated accordingly.

In addition, the thali made provision for perfect portion size. Each katori contained just the right amount of food for a single, nutrition-rich serving. The science of counting calories was unknown – the homemaker knew by instinct honed by tradition which size of katori was appropriate for which dish.

The Live Well Diet is based on these ancient traditions where fresh, seasonal, natural foods are served in the right proportion to make a nutritionally balanced meal.

PLATES AND PALATES

Apart from balancing nutrients, our age-old traditions place great emphasis on balance in the textures and flavours of food. A meal should have all of the six tastes or flavours represented on a plate or thali, which stimulate the appetite as well as provide adequate nutrition.

A PALATE OF FLAVOURS

Taste	Foods	Benefits
Sweet	Natural sugar, honey, fruit, cereals, milk and milk products	Satisfies, soothes the nerves, nourishes the body
Sour	Citrus fruits, yogurt, fermented foods such as vinegar, salad dressings and pickles	Stimulates the appetite, boosts immunity, aids digestion, detoxifies
Salty	Salt, sauces especially soy sauce, pickles and preserves, snacks, especially salted foods	Stimulates the appetite, enhances flavour of food, aids digestion, maintains mineral balance
Pungent	Spices, aromatics and herbs: chillies, cumin, pepper, ginger, garlic, onion, coriander, mint	Stimulates the appetite, aids digestion, activates metabolism; detoxifies
Bitter	Green leafy vegetables, bitter gourd, fenugreek seeds	Purifiy the blood, antibiotic and antiseptic functions, reduces inflammation, detoxifies tissues
Astringent	Apples, legumes and pulses, raw fruit and vegetables, tea and coffee	Heals tissues, absorbs water and dries out fat

A Balancing Act

Whatever the diet or combination of foods, the keys to eating well for health are balance and moderation. Make sure you eat enough of those foods that nourish you and provide you with energy, build your strength and immunity and keep all your systems humming along at optimum levels.

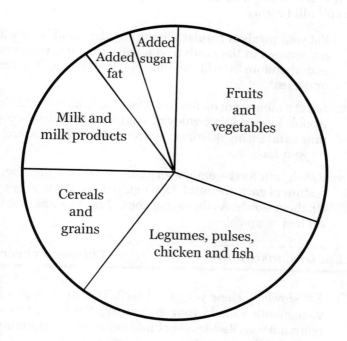

The above diagram describes the proportion of the different food groups to give you a nutrition-rich meal to Live Well

SAVOUR THIS

The Pleasures of Mindful Eating

Mindful eating is the practice of eating with thoughtfulness and pleasure. The focus is on choosing the right foods, enjoying your meal to the fullest and leaving each meal with a sense of satisfaction.

Here are some habits that will help you cultivate the practice of mindful eating:

1. Eat your meals at regular times every day. Your body will get attuned to the rhythm, you will rarely feel ravenous and therefore it will be unlikely that you will binge or overeat.

2. Eat at a table – not on the run. Make the time and take the trouble to spend time enjoying your food. It is also a good time to take a break from everything else and concentrate on your food.

3. Relish your food – enjoy every bite, savour the tastes and texture of each spoonful. Don't gulp down those juices – sip them slowly. As the saying goes, 'Take twice as long to eat half as much'.

Eat less, taste more.   *– Chinese Proverb*

---

4. Eat slowly – chew your food well. Digestion begins in your mouth so help your system to process food in an optimum way. Besides your brain needs about 20 minutes to receive the signal that you are satisfied.

5. Eat small portions and eat till you are satisfied – not till you feel full. Stop eating while your stomach is still a little empty.

6. Balance is essential. Make sure that you have all the nutrients, tastes and textures represented on your plate for complete satisfaction and benefit.

7. Eat fresh and natural foods — always the healthiest option. Avoid packaged or processed foods as they are usually full of additives and preservatives.

8. Double the pleasure — eat with a friend or your family. Meals are more relaxing and enjoyable when shared with someone you love.

• • •

MY STORY } Jackky Bhagnani
Actor

I FEEL SO GOOD!

Can you believe I used to weigh around 130 kg at one time! Now I have lost around 60 kg and I am feeling so good. I was so unhappy with my weight that I was a serial dieter. As an actor it was important for me to look good. I had been a victim of so much ridicule, I used to get depressed.

Once I started Dr Davare's programme my whole life changed. I realised that working out and eating right is all a matter of discipline – like getting up each day and gong to work. I had to learn about losing and maintaining my weight by eating every 2-3 hours; how to make the right choices of food. The programme gives you all the tools to achieve success.

The difficulty I experienced was with the reduced portions. I had to resist the temptation to eat a lot and remind myself how badly I wanted to look good. When I go to restaurants I no longer order biryani, my favourite food, or desserts. I am satisfied now with just a small piece of cake and I have stopped drinking 6 cups of tea!

My diet diary helps me to stay on track and serves as a reality check. It is a reaffirmation of how much progress I have made. Now that I have lost the weight I feel so much confident and my self-image has improved. My waist which used to measure 44 inches is now 29-30 inches. I feel so good I am unstoppable!

SUMMARY

EAT LESS:

- Simple carbohydrates: refined sugar, refined flour, sugary foods
- Starchy foods: potatoes, sweet potatoes
- Fatty foods: butter, ghee, oil, cream, cheese, coconut, red meat

EAT MORE:

- Complex carbohydrates which also provide fibre: Vegetables, whole grains, legumes and pulses, and some fruits.
- Protein rich foods: Legumes and pulses, skimmed milk, egg white, fish and chicken.
- Good fats: Olive oil, rice bran oil, canola oil, fish oils (Omega-3 fatty acids)

DRINK LESS:

- Sugary beverages
- Whole milk and creamy beverages

DRINK MORE:

- Water with a few drops of lime juice
- Skimmed milk and buttermilk
- Antioxidant beverages: coconut water, fresh vegetable juices, green tea

AVOID:

- Trans-fats: Hydrogenated vegetable fats, Vanaspati, Margarine
- Smoking
- Alcohol

● ● ●

SOLUTION,
IN GOOD TIME

I belong to a simple well-to-do Maharashtrian family and my daily routine was like any other boy brought up in such a family. I used to go regularly for a swim or morning walk before leaving for office after breakfast. Office work took up 10-12 hours of my time interspersed with a normal lunch and tea in the evening. Dinner was a family affair after returning from office. Although I am in my office for long hours, my work also involves frequent travel out of Mumbai and even abroad.

Unless I am travelling, my daily diet is a typical Maharashtrian diet consisting of chapati, bhaji, rice, dal and maybe some curd. Daily routine involved moderate physical activity and I have never been too overindulgent with food. Yet, I was obese. Perhaps it is in my ancestral genes.

Until a few years ago, I was always overweight although I am over 6 feet tall. Even as a schoolboy, I was easily the tallest and the fattest, and a foodie. I loved food and liked to eat all varieties of food. In those days a chubby roly-poly child was considered a healthy child. At that age, you do not understand the implications of being fat and I was quite happy being fat till I grew up a little and started getting teased by my friends for being a 'fatty'. Not that I was physically inactive. I was a regular swimmer, used to go for walks and was active in sports. My bulk or weight was never a hindrance for me and I led a normal active life. But, I stayed fat and never managed to lose weight.

I tried all possible remedies – exercise, gyms, diet, anything and everything I could. But the end result was the same. I lost weight, but put it on again. I tried other diets and even set up a small gym in my office and engaged a fitness trainer. I used to work out for about two hours every evening. I also used to diet, but the results hardly showed.

I often read that being overweight leads to many health problems, but became even more serious about losing weight after crossing 40, as most health problems start manifesting themselves after this age. In fact, I recently read that doctors now advise people above 30 to have regular health and cardiac check-ups because the present stress filled and irregular lifestyle of people is resulting in early onset of heart and other health problems. Moreover, both my parents are diabetic. Diabetes, it is said, is an open invitation for all future health complications, and I needed to guard against it. That combined with obesity is a lethal combination.

When I was in my early 40s, I was still groping in the dark about how to shed my excess weight and get fitter. I had heard about Dr Davare and signed up for her programme. I religiously followed Dr Davare's regimen. Diet and exercise were not new to me and it was not difficult. After just one week, I was amazed to see that I had lost 2½ kg. Wow! That was an achievement after trying all possible solutions in the past. It was unbelievable, a great morale booster and motivator.

Then there was no looking back. In the first month, I lost 10 kg. Besides, based on various pathological tests, a candidate is evaluated on a scale of 0-10 before starting the programme. I scored between 8-10 on various parameters at the start of the programme, but after the first month, I dramatically came down to less than 5! That was too good to be true.

Then it was just a question of maintaining my weight. What was once a strict regimen is now an intrinsic part of my lifestyle. Now, it never even occurs to me that I should have anything other than something very light like fruits for dinner. Dinner does not feature in my daily routine at all. What is truly effective about this programme is that after a point of time, it becomes a way of life with you. Therefore, maintenance is no problem at all. It is not that I cannot eat what I like all the time. I do eat in limits sometimes, but I also know what needs to be done to maintain my weight when this happens.

So after years of quest of finding a satisfactory solution for my excess weight, I have finally found one, and in good time too.

● ● ●

GET MOVING TO
LIVE WELL

'No pain no gain' applies as much to exercise and physical movement as to diet. MOVE is a key mantra in the Live Well Diet. And move you must if you want to lead a more energetic life, have a calmer and more relaxed disposition, have all the systems in your body, especially the cardio-vascular system, working at optimum levels, and above all if you want to shed all that excess weight.

So what does exercise really do for you?

The most obvious benefit is weight loss. The more you exercise the more calories or energy you burn which aids in reduction of excess fat in the body. Regular physical activity also helps blood circulation and prevents diseases like cardio-vascular disease. Fitness and toning of muscles is another benefit which is immediately noticeable after regular exercise. There are however some other benefits that may be less visible or obvious:

It will lift your spirits: Sustained activity causes your brain to release feel-good chemicals called endorphins which fill you with feelings of positivity and well-being. Your self-image will be the first to benefit from the activity as positive feelings will help you look at yourself in a new light. The more you exercise and the fitter you begin to look, the better you will feel about yourself.

It will reduce your stress: There is no more effective way of reducing stress instantly than a quick run up and down a flight of stairs or a short brisk walk. Skipping or a few jumping jacks will also do the trick. The endorphins will kick in, the stress will drain out of you in a flash and you will feel relaxed and able to cope with life once again. Regular exercise will reduce the overall stress in your life and equip you with the strength of spirit to deal with whatever is thrown at you in a more positive way.

It will boost your energy: Regular exercise has an overall effect of making you feel more energetic. Watch how your sluggishness will disappear within a few days of starting an exercise programme. There will be a new spring in your step which will only make you want to exercise even more!

It will clean out the cobwebs from your mind: Exercise will give a boost of energy to your brain, releasing chemicals which will help you concentrate and think more clearly. Every nerve cell will be jogged into action – you will feel mentally and physically more alive and responsive to everything around you. Your senses and intuition will sharpen and just like after you have cleaned your cloudy glasses with a tissue, you will be able to see things more clearly and in sharper focus again!

While it does matter how much you move, it also matters how and when. So many words are bandied about by fitness experts – aerobics, anaerobics, strength training, power walks, body sculpture, pilates and so on. It can all be very confusing. But like in everything else simplicity and practicality are the keys to success.

And what can be simpler, more practical (and inexpensive!) than getting back to basics in the Live Well Diet exercise plan which includes:

• Pranayam
• Suryanamaskar
• Walking
• Body Massages

Once your body systems are up and running and you feel you can take on more, you can embark on a more ambitious programme at your nearest gym involving treadmills, stationary cycles, elliptical and cross trainers, steps and so on.

MIND STRONG  KARKE ANA!

We all love food in our family. I could say we are a food-centric family. We eat 4 non-vegetarian meals a day and enjoy every one of them. In addition to my love of food, as a result of my pregnancies I became overweight. My life was often chaotic and with 2 small children, I found I was getting very moody and tired.

I weighed 83 kg after the birth of my first child and managed to lose some weight quite easily. My weight stabilised at 77 kg and after enrolling in Dr Sarita's programme the first time, I gradually lost just 6 kg in weight but lost inches all over my body.

I persevered with the programme and am now 57 kg. How did I do it? I first worked on my self-discipline. Being in awe of Dr Davare helped! She used to say, 'Mind strong karke ana'! I hate cardio so I was happy to walk for exercise.

I am so fit now I can run for 50 minutes without tiring. I have made several lifestyle changes and eat healthier food as prescribed by the diet. I supplement my diet with vitamins and a protein supplement.

PRANAYAMA—The Breath of Life

Pranayama has been around in India for centuries. It is the most fundamental principle of Yoga – one of India's gifts to the world of health and fitness. As described in the Yoga Sutras by the sage Patanjali, pranayama is the art and practice of breath control. Prana in Sanskrit is breath or vital energy which is the life force, and ayam means control. With pranayama one can control the flow of energy through the body to achieve the holistic well-being of body, mind and spirit.

According to **Yoga instructor Jyoti Chitnis**, there are four types of Pranayama which you should practice in sequence according to your abilities and fitness levels:

- **Shuddhi Kriya:** (Cleansing the Air Passages) minimum 1 set of 10 and maximum 3 sets of 10.

- **Anuloma Viloma Pranayama:** (Breathing through Alternate Nostrils) Start with 3 cycles, and gradually work your way up a minimum of 10 cycles and a maximum of 30 cycles.

- **Kapalbhati Pranayama (Deep Inhalation and Forceful Exhalation):** 120 sets of kapalbhati rechaka and pooraka in 1 minute. Start slowly and work your way up to a minimum of 300 sets for a low level of fitness, 500 sets for a moderate level and 1000 and over at an advanced level of fitness.

- **Bhastrika Pranayama:** (Deep Breathing) Perform a minimum of 1 set (10) and a maximum of 3 sets (30).

SURYA NAMASKAR

Surya Namaskar is a form of stretching exercise which uses and strengthens almost every muscle in the body while assuming the 12 asanas or postures that make up the sequence, leading to overall flexibility. It has a favourable impact on blood circulation and stimulates the cardio-vascular and nervous systems in the body. After performing Surya Namaskar one feels fresh, calm and at peace.

Perform minimum of 11, moderate - 21; maximum 50 +

SIMHASANA

The Roaring Lion Posture or Simhasana gets its name from the fierce look one assumes while stretching the facial muscles and sticking the tongue out in a yogic grimace. This is one exercise that can be performed by people of all ages and levels of fitness as it involves little other than the facial muscles.

Simhasana tones up the facial and neck muscles and causes the facial skin to glow. It is believed to have a positive effect on the sinuses, respiratory system and thyroid glands.

Perform 3 sets – 3 times

Note: You must consult a trained yoga therapist before starting on any of the exercises described.

• • •

MY STORY } *Sheetal Davalkar*

A DREAM  COME TRUE

I came to know about Dr Sarita from my daughter Sandhya who had lost about 20 kg while on the programme. In November 2009 I weighed 94 kg but today after being on the programme my weight is 62 kg. I feel so fresh, young, active and confident. I am so happy that now I can wear any style of clothes. The lower back pain I used to have has vanished. At the start I was apprehensive about following the programme strictly, but I soon got used to it. Now I walk 6 km every day and eat healthy food. I feel I have got new life and it is a dream come true!

WALKING - NOT JUST LEG WORK

Walking is the best way to get a total body workout. All you need is a pair of comfortable shoes, some loose clothing, a strong will and good weather. The last is not within your control, but the shoes and clothing are easy to arrange. You may actually have the most trouble with the strong will.

If you have been leading a sedentary life in which the most exercise you get is walking to your car and back, or moving your cell phone from table or pocket to ear, you will need to do more than just make resolutions. Remember that not doing any physical exercise will only sabotage your plan to Live Well.

THE PLAINT OF THE COUCH POTATO

MAN HI NAHI LAGTA

I don't have the time to exercise, there is no space
I don't have the energy, I'm depressed
I'm too old, I'm too weak
I'm too fat, I sweat profusely
I have a headache, it's that time of month
I hate to exercise, it's so boring
It's raining; it's too hot
It's too dark; it's too sunny
I've just eaten; I feel faint
After I exercise I eat more
I'd rather die!
Kya kare! Man hi nahi lagta!

GET GOING!

Stop the whining and excuses and start putting one foot in front of the other and walk! A few tips to help you get the most out of your walk:

- Get yourself comfortable walking footwear.
- Wear loose comfortable clothing made of absorbent fabric like cotton.
- The best time to walk is the early morning when your energy levels are high and the sun is just rising.
- Get yourself a walking companion – your spouse or a friend. Support and companionship can be crucial to your resolve and motivation.
- Listen to music while you walk – it will help the time pass quickly and before you know it you will be home for breakfast.
- Do some simple warm up exercises before you begin walking and cool down exercises after your walk. Limbering up with a few stretches, bends, ankle rotations and jogging in place will warm up your joints and muscles and make walking more comfortable. Cooling down with a few simple moves helps your heart rate to come back to normal and your body to get back to its pre-exercise state.
- Start slowly and gradually – walk for about 5 minutes at a normal pace to warm your body up. Then increase the speed and walk briskly at a smooth rhythmic pace for as long as you can and then pause. Start again, walk briskly and slow down after a while.
- Do not allow yourself to get uncomfortably breathless or put too much of a strain on your muscles.
- Drink plenty of water (preferably not cold) before and after your walk. Carry a bottle of water with you to rehydrate yourself as walking is a thirsty business.
- If time or energy is a constraint, break up your walk into 2 sessions, which you can do at any time of the day.

You must walk at least five days a week for maximum benefit.

EXERCISE PLANS TO LIVE WELL

The Live Well Diet recommends 2 Exercise Plans - A and B. Make sure you follow any one diet consistently for a whole week. Do not mix and match the activities from both plans. For variety and to prevent boredom from setting in, you may follow Exercise Plan A for a week followed by Exercise Plan B for the next and alternate the weekly plans.

At the outset it is important to know that the plans can be individualised according to your age and ability. How much you exercise, the speed at which you walk and for how long will depend on many factors. If you have never exercised before or are physically not very fit or have any health problems, start slow and work your way up to an optimum level for yourself. Most of the exercises do not require any special equipment so you should be able to get in enough physical activity without much investment in anything other than your time!

It is normal that during summer, we feel fatigue very soon while walking. During extreme weather conditions do not exert yourself. In such conditions you may do spot jogging, pranayama or yoga at home. Remember that your exercise should be enjoyable, should not be monotonous and should not increase your heart rate rapidly. Always consult a trained physical trainer as also a physician before taking up exercise if you are not accustomed to it.

● ● ●

EXERCISE PLAN A	
Pranayam	Daily, minimum three to four times a week
Suryanamaskar or stretching exercises	Three to five times a week
Walking	4-6 km (1 hour 20 minutes) a day (6 days a week)
OR Treadmill (no incline)	1 hour 10 minutes at 4-5 speed (6 days a week)
OR Yogasana	40 minutes + walk 40 minutes (6 days a week)
OR Dance/ Aerobics/Floor Exercises	40 minutes + Walk 40 minutes
Body Massage	twice a week
Take a protein supplement twice a week	

If you are a regular at a gym and are accustomed to exercise, the following Live Well Exercise Plan B will benefit you:

EXERCISE PLAN B	
Pranayam	Daily, minimum 3-4 times a week
Suryanamaskar or stretching exercises	3-5 times a week
Gym training	Treadmill, Cross Trainer, Stationary Cycle, Elliptical Trainer – 60-80 minutes daily (3 days a week)
Body Massage	Twice a week
Protein Supplement (zero carbs, no sugar)	Three times a week, especially after weight training

Note: You can also do weight training 3 times a week, in which case make sure you follow Plan A or Plan B on those days. Also make sure you take a protein supplement on those days, provided your uric acid levels are normal. Do check with your physician.

MAKING SMALL MOVES: (or how to start slow and slip some exercise into your daily routine)

No matter how motivated you are, it may not be possible for you to exercise every day. There may be days when you just cannot do the walk – it is raining, you are in a rush, you woke up late, your child is sick and you just can't leave the house, it is the morning after the night before etc. Don't panic or beat yourself up with guilt. Here are a few ways you can get your body moving in short bursts of activity.

These exercises are also good to get you warmed up if you have not exercised a lot before, or if you are an older person who is easing into an exercise routine, have difficulty following the programme prescribed, or have trouble leaving home.

1. **Lift those legs:** Use the stairs instead of a lift to climb at least a few floors.

2. **Get down from your car, cab or bus some distance away from your destination:** Office, meeting place, restaurant, residence, supermarket - and walk the rest of the way.

3. **Walk briskly whenever you walk**: In the office, in the mall, up the stairs, through the corridors. Do not dawdle or amble – speed it up.

4. **Move more than your eyeballs**: Do some form of physical activity while watching TV – stretches, sit-ups cycling on a stationary bike, simple calisthenics (PT exercises). The commercial breaks are ideal for this – get up off the sofa and move!

5. **Immobilise your mobiles and mobilise yourself:** For at least one hour in the day, place your mobile phone at a distance so you have to move to get to it; do the same with your TV remote so you have to get up every time you want to change channels! Stop carting that cordless telephone around. Place it in its cradle and get up to answer it every time it rings.

6. **Desk yoga or exercises:** These are great to loosen and tone up your static muscles and give yourself a burst

of energy while at work. Stretch while seated, simple squats and dips using your chair as a prop, vertical crunches with your hands behind your head while seated and twisted crunches when you bring your elbow to the opposite knee. Do 5 minutes of these exercises every few hours and you will feel refreshed.

7. **PT 101:** Remember those physical training periods in school and the calisthenics we performed as kids to the loud counts or blasts of a whistle by a PT master or mistress? They are perfectly good for you even today at your age! The arm and leg exercises, jumping jacks, lunges, sit-ups, crunches, push-ups, stretches, etc. are perfect for those days when the weather is bad and you have to stay indoors. Do the exercises in front of a mirror if possible. Add some weights in the form of two full bottles of water to tone up your arm muscles.

8. **Dance:** Yes, you heard right! Put on your favourite music and let yourself go! Release your inner rock star and shimmy and shake to the vigorous strains of some heart pumping music for at least 5 minutes. Your endorphins will get a great work out and you will feel liberated and on top of the world.

9. **Give your house help some time off:** House work - making beds, sweeping, dusting and washing clothes by hand – is an excellent way of giving yourself a workout and demonstrating how the job must be done!

10. **Workout with an exercise or yoga video:** There are many videos and DVDs available that you can use at home to exercise along with. You can pace yourself and stop and start as you please so you are not pressured to perform as you would be in a class. Tai chi, yoga and fitness programmes abound on the internet which you can download for free, or purchase at any music store. Find one that has been produced by a reputed organisation or expert, and one which is suitable for your age and fitness level.

● ● ●

10

RELAX

It seems strange that today, in what is believed to be a 'chilled out' time we have to learn how to chill! Relaxation has become an art which one has to practice and make a conscious effort to incorporate into daily life. Busy-ness is the hallmark of our times whether you are slaving on the job, treadmill or pedalling furiously on the eternal cycle of managing home and family. Time never seems to stop long enough for you to catch your breath, leave alone to stop and stare, or for that matter, to smell the roses.

But relax or chill you must if you want to add quality and quantity to your life. No pills or potions will provide you with the long-term relief that changes to your lifestyle will. Buckle down and take a long hard look at your life and what you can do to introduce some fun, relaxation and the luxury of a good night's sleep into your daily routine.

Numerous studies have shown that stress plays an important role in our lives and has an impact on one's health and quality of life. The hormone cortisol is released during times of stress which is why it is called the 'stress hormone'. Prolonged bouts of stress result in excess cortisol which affects the entire system and can lead to heart disease, depression, skin conditions such as eczema, obesity, digestive problems, sleep disorders and so on.

No matter how much pressure you feel at work, if you could find ways to relax for at least five minutes every hour, you'd be more productive.

- Dr Joyce Brothers

STRESS BUSTERS

Food to relax by:

Weight gain can be directly linked with stress: When stressed, the hormones cortisol and insulin that are involved in metabolism are affected, resulting in a low BMR (Basal Metabolic Rate). In general, foods that are high in magnesium, Vitamin C and B Complex are known to reduce stress, so increase your intake of foods that are rich in these nutrients.

To counteract stress increase the intake of the following:

- **Happy Food:** Foods that increase production of serotonin, a brain chemical that creates positive feelings of optimism, relaxation, security, comfort and well-being. Protein rich food such as chicken, fish and eggs are rich in amino-acids which stimulate the production of soothing brain chemicals.

- **Calming Food:** Herbal teas are soothing and provide comfort and relaxation to strained nerves. A glass of milk which contains tryptophan, a soothing nutrient, is also helpful.

- **Comfort Food:** Avoid sugary and fatty foods which are the universal go-tos for stress and treat yourself to a piece of dark chocolate, munch on a sugar-free whole grain cereal-nut bar, or eat a couple of dried dates or figs.

BUT - Beware of foods that increase stress such as refined sugars, simple carbohydrates and fatty foods.

Those who eat too much or eat too little, who sleep too much or sleep too little, will not succeed in meditation. But those who are temperate in eating and sleeping, work and recreation, will come to the end of sorrow through meditation.

- Bhagavad Gita

THE PROGRAMME HAS CHANGED OUR LIVES

We decided as a family to enroll in Dr Davare's programme. My wife Parul and I have one son, Pranay who is 17 years old. My mother also lives with us.

I used to suffer from many health problems- my cholesterol and SGPT levels were high. My liver was not functioning well - I was lethargic and had no energy. I weighed 94 kg.

We decided that if we wanted to change our lifestyle and eating habits, all of us should be on the same programme. My wife Parul cooked all the food recommended for the programme and we enjoyed the tasty but healthy food she cooked. The recipes for the bhindi sabzi, palak matar sabzi, pani puri pani, and palak soup are very good. The diet helped to clean out the toxins from our systems especially the liver. On the whole we felt lighter and cooler, more refreshed. I lost 17 kg on the programme and my health is better. My cholesterol and SGPT levels are normal and I feel I have new energy.

Pranay has taken a little longer to get used to the new way of life. He is a typical teenager who loves food and does not like to do much exercise. But he is now motivated to walk and this together with the diet has helped him to lose 5 kg in two and a half weeks. He feels more alert and his concentration while studying has improved.

The programme has made a big difference in our lives.

REGULAR BODY MASSAGES - EVERYBODY KNEADS SOME

We can all do with a little pampering now and then, but the benefits of body massage go far beyond the feel-good factor.

Massages are an integral part of the Live Well Diet, as they lead to a toned, shapelier body and a sense of wellness, so make sure you make the time and schedule body massages for yourself at least twice a week. Ayurveda speaks of Abhayanga and its restorative and therapeutic effects on the body which are essential for your well-being.

Why do we pay for psychotherapy when massages cost half as much?
— Jason Love

A good massage will help you to LIVE WELL in several ways as it

- **Relieves stress:** Stress is one of the key causes of overeating and therefore gaining weight. Massages are known to reduce the levels of cortisol, a stress hormone, which causes anxiety and depression.

- **Stimulates the release of endorphins:** 'Brain chemicals' produced by the nervous system, which promote a feeling of well-being as well as control the harmful effects of eating disorders.

- **Relaxes your muscles** especially those unused ones that have been put into action with the Live Well exercise plan, and increases flexibility.

- **Helps you to sleep** better as your mind and body are in a state of relaxation.

- **Makes your skin glow** as it stimulates the nerve endings on the surface of the skin.

- **Increases circulation of blood** and oxygen through the body, thus rejuvenating your body tissues.

- **Boosts immunity:** Some studies have shown that massages increase the production of white blood cells which fight diseases in the body.

- **Increases the circulation of lymph** (fluids in the tissues) throughout the body thus preventing fluid retention, which is also a cause of excess weight.

- **Fights build-up of fat** in the form of cellulite, which you can see around your thighs, stomach and buttocks as clusters of dimpled skin. A good, deep massage helps to soften and loosen cellulite or fat deposits which are trapped under the skin, so they can be excreted.

● ● ●

MY STORY } Rupal Mehta

A TOTAL SOLUTION TO FITNESS

I am a housewife with a daughter, Aayushi. Both of us have been on Dr Davare's programme.

Dr Davare's programme is a total solution to fitness – not just weight loss.

If there is one thing I have gained from Dr Davare's programme it is self-confidence. Since I lost weight (I used to be 75 kg and now I am 64 kg) I feel confident enough to handle family pressures and day to day problems without any stress. I used to suffer from acidity and hormonal imbalances, which made it difficult to cope with stressful situations. I am now calm and energetic and can face situations in a better frame of mind.

My daughter, Aayushi is very overweight – at 13 years she weighs 87 kg. As my husband suffers from diabetes and there is a family history of the disease, I am worried that she too may become diabetic. She is also, naturally, very self-conscious. After being on the programme, she has made many changes in her diet and lifestyle and has lost 15 kg. This has made her more self-confident and sure of herself and motivated her to continue with the programme, which is a godsend to all of us.

SLEEP

When you sleep, your muscles relax, your breathing and heart rate slow down and your body temperature drops. While you sleep many physiological changes that help the immune system take place in your body. Sleep also enhances learning and memory, and mental and emotional well-being. While you sleep, those parts of your brain that control emotions and social interactions are in a state of rest.

Lack of sleep affects the levels of stress hormones leading to emotional and mental distress.

A good laugh and a long sleep are the best cures in the doctor's book.   *– Irish Proverb*

Some studies have shown that there is a connection between lack of sleep and fat accumulation, and a good night's sleep and weight loss and this has been borne out by the experiences of many of those who have experienced the Live Well Diet.

Lack of sleep reduces the levels of the hormone leptin that controls the appetite and lets the body know when it has had enough food. This leads to overeating, poor insulin resistance and a higher risk of developing Type 2 Diabetes. Less sleep also affects levels of ghrelin, the hormone that sends hunger signals from the stomach to the brain. Other studies have shown a direct correlation between less sleep and a higher BMI.

Give it a rest

- Follow a consistent sleep routine.

- Prepare your body for sleep by using relaxation techniques like deep breathing, meditation, taking a warm shower, listening to soothing music, reading a few s of a book.

- Eat your last meal at least 2 hours before you go to bed. Give your system time to digest your meal and your body to relax.

- If you have to have foods that interfere with sleep, like those which contain caffeine and pungent spices—do so at least 3-4 hours before going to bed.

- Exercise at least 5-6 hours before your bedtime.

- Drink a warm glass of milk or eat a couple of Marie or digestive biscuits before going to bed.

- Shut off the TV, your mobile phone and computer and give them some rest as well!

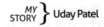

MY STORY } Uday Patel

I HAVE A NEW LIFE

I lead a retired life with very few physical activities. Though on a vegetarian diet, with little sugar, I had health problems. I was prescribed medication for high triglycerides. While on the programme I enjoyed the planned and restricted diet as prescribed by Dr Davare. Her recipes are tasty and manageable. With a planned diet and a regular 80-minute walk, I got excellent results. My energy levels increased and I did not need to take the prescribed medication. The experience which was mind blowing, resulting into a 'New Life'.

A GOAL IS A DREAM WITH A DEADLINE

Now that you have gone through all the various aspects of healthy living you should be ready to decide the changes you need to make to Live Well and by when. While it is unreasonable to expect that you will overhaul your life overnight, there are small changes that you can begin with right away. Refer to the Lifestyle Audit you took on page 44 List the changes you need to make and set a rough deadline against each one. Unreasonable or unachievable goals in very short deadlines will only lead to failure and frustration. Tackle one or two or even 3 habits a week and set a time frame within you feel you can master the change. As long as you don't set yourself a deadline, your desire will remain just that - a happy thought in your head!

Add the following to your health record so you can record your progress and the promises to yourself you have been able to keep.

	PRESENT LEVEL	GOAL	REMARKS
PHYSICAL ACTIVITY			
Yoga			
Walking			
Other			
RELAXATION			
Sleep			
Hobbies			
Body Massage			
Any other			

NOTHING  IS IMPOSSIBLE!

Before I joined the programme, I weighed 102 kg. I had tried almost every other weight loss diet available and was unable to find any programme which managed to keep off the initial weight loss experienced in any diet.

I was resigned to being overweight. One day a friend of mine mentioned Dr Sarita Davare's programme and gave me a few examples of some very overweight people who had lost weight in a relatively short span of time. Something triggered me.

I guess in every weight loss situation, you have to have the drive and the determination within yourself. I knew that this was my chance to prove to myself that I can do it. I decided to dedicate one month to the programme and do everything I was asked to in order to get the desired results. At the end of my first session, I was surprised to see that I was 11 kg lighter on the scale. What was more exciting to me was that my weight loss was so dramatic and proportionate in terms of inch loss.

After the weight loss in the first session, the compliments started pouring in. It added to my belief and self confidence Today, I have lost a total of 40 kg and I have never felt healthier and better in my entire life. Also, being a fashion designer, the weight loss has added to my self confidence as it is a profession in which appearances do count.

I have made it a point to adapt my lifestyle now based on Dr Davare's teachings. I walk regularly for an hour. I also avoid fried foods and sweets and make it a point to have a light and early dinner. These simple measures help me to maintain my weight loss.

The programme has proved to me that nothing is impossible.

Section II

The Live Well Diet

*All you need is the plan, the road map, and
the courage to press on to your destination.*

– Earl Nightingale

11

THE LIVE WELL DIET –
EATING FOR YOUR LIFE

A goal without a plan is just a wish

The Live Well Diet offers you all the tools to make your desire to change your lifestyle a reality. In the previous section you have been armed with all the knowledge to help you identify those lifestyle habits you need to change and set your goals. Wishful thinking and good intentions will only take you so far. It is now time to buckle down and map out a plan of action. In this section, The Live Well Diet provides you with just such a plan which will help you on your journey to Live Well.

The ABC OF THE LIVE WELL DIET

The Live Well Diet is a unique diet plan based on eating the right foods in a weekly cycle that promotes an efficient metabolism.

To elaborate further, the uniqueness of the Live Well Diet lies in the fact that it is actually made up of 3 diets: Diet A – The All Foods Diet, Diet B – The Basic Diet and Diet C – the Control Diet.

The diets are so planned as to enable you to lose weight by varying the daily intake of foods in terms of quantity and nutrition so your metabolism works more efficiently.

The principle behind the varying diets is that when your body gets nutrition in different amounts, your metabolism is forced to take notice and respond accordingly.

Providing your body with a basic amount of high fibre and high protein food, which provide both nutrition and energy, and alternating it with a day of pleasurable indulgence in favourite foods (in moderation), followed by a day of controlled food intake, keeps your metabolism on its toes and encourages it to function better.

A sustained diet programme that incorporates the 3 different diets is one that I have found to work the best. Rigid diets with too many restricted foods are known to fail.

The flexibility of the Live Well ABC Diets is what provides nutrition as well as for unusual circumstances, while catering to one's need for variety and the body's need for stimulation of the metabolic processes.

The ABC Diets cater to your taste buds, by allowing you delicious foods every day and a day of delicious indulgence at least once a week.

The Live Well Diet A – The All Foods Diet: 1-2 days a week

This is the fun plan which encourages you to indulge in your favourite foods, cater to your cravings and satisfy your taste buds, all in moderation of course. Diet A is ideal for weekends when you can relax your diet, especially if you have to attend social functions, as most people do on weekends, or for when you travel.

The Live Well Diet B – The Basic Diet: Minimum 3 days a week

This is the backbone of the diet and provides the strength and sustenance that will keep you going through the week. A largely vegetarian plan, it provides you with protein, complex carbohydrate and fibre-rich foods on at least 3 days of the week. The high amount of fibre and proteins in the diet will fire up your metabolism.

The Live Well Diet C – The Control Diet: Maximum 2 days a week

This diet helps your body to burn the excess fat stored in the body. The diet has a detoxifying effect and should ideally follow Diet A, which is richer in nutrients. As far as possible do not follow Diet C on 2 consecutive days. Diet C is your friend in need—a rescue plan which helps you recover from any lapses or excesses.

As you will see, the Live Well Diet provides plenty of protein, complex carbohydrates and fibre, with fewer simple carbohydrates and minimal added fat.

This has been found to be the most effective combination of nutrients for sustained weight loss, as it activates your metabolism. Of all the nutrients, fibre and protein from food are known to provide satisfaction and keep hunger at bay.

The diet provides animal protein in the form of eggs, milk, yogurt, chicken and fish and vegetable or plant protein in the form of soya, legumes and pulses and whole grains. Complex carbohydrates contain fibre which is also slow to digest, leaving one feeling satiated and full.

The Live Well Diet is fortified with mineral, vitamin and protein supplements which will ensure fitness and provide for any deficiencies in your diet. These include Vitamin B12, Folic Acid, Calcium and Vitamin E.

As mentioned before, unlike many popular diets you can tailor-make the sequence of your diets to suit your schedule and requirements as long as you broadly follow the sequence of plans.

CAUTION: Do not reduce the combinations of foods recommended in the plans. In your enthusiasm to lose more weight, you may decide to skip meals or omit certain foods prescribed. The Live Well ABC Diets have been designed to give you all the essential nutrients in the required amount. If you must reduce the quantity of a particular food do so, but as far as possible do not omit the prescribed food or beverage itself.

• • •

MY STORY } Aditya Kalyanpur
Musician

CONSCIOUSNESS.
CHOICE. DISCIPLINE.

I am a musician and play the tabla and because of my performances all over the country my eating habits and lifestyle are very erratic. I used to eat my dinner very late at night and eat a lot of junk food as it is more easily available. While I was not very overweight, I was not comfortable with my fitness and overall health.

I managed to lose 12-15 kg on Dr Sarita's programme and bring my weight to normal. I have now made many changes in my life so I can maintain my health and weight.

To begin with I am more conscious about my health and my food choices. I am mentally prepared to follow the programme to the best of my ability and try to be disciplined.

I avoid junk food and try not to overeat on my trips. I follow the proactive diets while travelling so I compensate for the different foods I eat. I exercise every day and walk 6 km a day.

The key aspects of Dr Sarita's programme:

- Consciousness - becoming aware of one's health and fitness
- Choice – making the right choices of foods and exercise
- Discipline – sticking to the programme and new way of life

I must also state that none of this is possible without family support and encouragement.

● ● ●

LIFELINES TO THE RESCUE

You would be an exceptional person if you managed to strictly follow all the recommendations of the Live Well Diet. You will constantly face circumstances and situations which threaten to derail your plans and challenge your resolve.

The Live Well Diet is a proactive and flexible plan which provides you with options for special occasions such as family celebrations, travel and eating out.

For example, if you are going to travel for 8 days follow The All Foods Diet (A) alternately with the Control Diet (C) for all those 8 days. On your return, follow the Basic Diet (B) and the Control Diet (C) alternately for the next 8 days. This will help balance your diet and keep your metabolism functioning at optimum levels.

Do not despair if you have had an occasional lapse – the Diet will provide you with recovery strategies so you can get back on track. You can also have recourse to Lifeline foods for those hard-to-control hunger pangs or cravings.

LOG IN

If you want to celebrate your progress, record your weight on a weekly basis and maintain a detailed food and exercise log or diary.

These help to motivate you and/or analyse the reasons for the rate and success of your weight loss. A sample record has been provided on page 192.

RECIPES

A diet is just a plan till you have the tools to make it happen. Armed with over 140 delicious recipes that promote weight loss specially provided for you by Sanjeev Kapoor, India's leading chef , you should have no trouble at all cooking well-balanced, tasty meals for yourself and your family.

There are recipes for every course based on the LIVE WELL DIET. Sample menus help you get started so you will have no trouble figuring out what to cook.

A bonus - the recipes will serve four persons so the whole family can enjoy the same healthy tasty fare and benefit from it. However, do note the size of the portion prescribed for you while you are on the Live Well Diet.

● ● ●

WONDERFUL
EXPERIENCE

Being a teacher, I have to reach school early in the morning. I used to leave with a cup of tea and drive to Santacruz (Northwest Mumbai) from Malad (North Mumbai). Then at around 9.00 a.m. the staff shared tiffins and practically stuffed our stomachs with everything there on the table. At 1.30 p.m., on reaching home again I used to have lunch and go to sleep as I felt very tired handling 15 year-olds. Evenings passed working out rigorously in a gym. Inspite of this, I did not lose any weight, convincing me somewhere, something was wrong: I had low stamina and was suffering from hypothyroidism and water retention.

I tried many diets and visited the gym regularly. My stamina improved but weight loss though minimal, was not permanent. The bigger challenge was to be on a strict diet while maintaining the same energy level at school as well as at home.

I was highly motivated to achieve my goal with Dr Davare's programme. She suggested that I never leave home without a bottle of water. The recipes given are very good and tasty and easy to follow.

I have lost 13 kg since I started the programme. My energy levels have improved. Headaches and acidity have gone! Emotionally I have become strong. I love it when people compliment me. Most important, mentally I have become very calm and I have a lot of positivity. The food and the programme have removed all the toxicity from my body. I can say I have got more connected with myself and it's a wonderful experience. I missed my own company for all these years, and now I am at ease with MYSELF, thanks to Dr Davare!

YOUR DAY ON THE LIVE WELL DIET

The Live Well Diet provides you with a nutritionally healthy diet which will keep your metabolism active throughout the day. It provides foods that are rich in complex-carbohydrate fibre and protein which are known to boost the metabolism.

It also prescribes plenty of essential liquids in the form of water, lime water, coconut water, buttermilk, green tea, and vegetable juices which detoxify the system while providing it with essential nutrients. Make sure you spread the intake of these liquids right through the day – they make for perfect snacks and fillers between meals and pick-me-ups for flagging energies.

The diet also ensures you eat 3 main meals and several small meals a day which keep your metabolism functioning well. It also provides you with options to assuage those cravings or hunger pangs.

Exercise is an essential part of your daily diet as is good sleep and relaxation. This comprehensive plan takes care of your health in a holistic way, leading to an all-round improvement in your well-being.

When you wake

Hopefully you have had a good night's rest of at least 7 hours sleep and are ready to take on a new day. Try and rise early so you can ease into the day, giving yourself enough time to put into practice all the healthy habits that you need to Live Well.

Instead of reaching out for that cup of tea or coffee as many of us are used to, begin by drinking a lot of fluids (lime water, green tea, and detoxifying vegetable juice) which will hydrate your body, get your metabolism going and flush out the toxins which have accumulated overnight in your system.

Start your day with 2 glasses of warm water laced with the juice of a quarter lime (*nimboo*).

Lime juice or *nimboo ka rus* helps the body regulate its metabolism, thus helping you to lose weight. Limes are rich in citric acid before consumption but turn into an alkali as soon as it is metabolised. When you drink lime juice in plain warm water first thing in the morning, you introduce a healthy natural digestive aid into your stomach.

The lime juice interacts with the acids and enzymes in your digestive tract, creating a detoxifying effect which leads to healthy digestion.

Drink green tea which also acts as an antioxidant. Then drink any of the detoxifying vegetable juices which will cleanse your body and flush out the toxins that have accumulated overnight.

Get Active

Having cleansed your body of all the residue toxins, it is now time to greet the day with a few deep breathing exercises – Pranayam, followed by Simhasana and Suryanamaskar.

The yoga exercises will limber you up for your walk. You will feel energetic and lighter and your mood will be more positive as the breathing exercises will have put you in a relaxed and positive state of mind.

Enjoy your walk at a brisk pace, listening to music if you prefer. Do some warm ups before you walk and cool down exercises after. Don't forget to take a bottle of water along. Make sure you do not get too out of breath, and that you vary your pace so you get your metabolism revved up.

If you prefer to go to a gym this would be a good time to get a work out. While exercising or physical activity at any time of the day is beneficial, early morning exercise is particularly so.

To begin with you are well rested and have the energy to devote to serious physical activity. Exercise in the morning jumpstarts your metabolism and gets it into high gear so that it will function well through the day.

Besides the endorphins or feel-good hormones released by exercise make you feel upbeat, positive and energetic. Many people feel more alert and energised after exercise. If you exercise early in the morning you are less likely to be disturbed by colleagues or work demands. You can indulge in some serious 'me time' knowing you are living well. If you feel you need the energy before your walk or exercise, eat a piece of fruit to give yourself an energy boost.

Morning Tea

Walking or working out can make you ravenous, but don't head straight for the breakfast table where you overload your system with food. Wind down with a quick shower and a relaxing cup of tea or coffee, and a couple of khakras or biscuits. Catch up on the news in your favourite newspaper or on TV before you head for a good breakfast.

The snack will infuse energy gradually into your system and your body will have a chance to slow down and relax. Marie or digestive biscuits are perfect as they are less sweet than other biscuits and digestive biscuits have added fibre. Khakras, particularly of the diet kind provide just the right touch of spice with which to begin the day, particularly if you are used to munching on some farsan or nasta with your cup of tea!

Breakfast

Everybody knows that breakfast is the most important meal of the day and yet so many of us skip it entirely or eat it on the run, grabbing whatever is at hand, which is most often not the healthiest food. Breakfast is when you should provide your body with the boost it needs for the day. Breakfasts should be nutritious, providing you with energy and sustenance and help to activate your metabolism more vigorously.

The Live Well Diet provides you options which are rich in complex carbohydrates, fibre and protein which will be both nourishing and satisfying. The foods will take longer to digest giving you a sense of fullness which will last longer and ward off those hunger pangs. On no account should you skip breakfast, as the long gap between your last meal the previous night and your next one will put your metabolism into starvation mode, preserving the fat and excess stored energy instead of burning it.

Mid-Morning

If you have had a good breakfast, you may not need a snack till lunch time. However, should you feel hungry and you are sure it is not thirst you are feeling, use one of the lifelines or snacks that will come to your rescue. A cup of green tea or a glass of buttermilk may do the trick or if not at hand, a couple of almonds, walnuts or dates will help.

An apple, pear or orange will give you some oral satisfaction especially if you are used to munching something every few hours. The snack will also keep your metabolism ticking. This would also be a good time to consume one of the two glasses of coconut water that are mandatory on the diet. Just make sure you stay away from sugary or fat laden snacks – chocolate or wafers are a definite no-no!

Lunch

If you are at work, the chances are you may not have a fixed lunch break. If you have a delayed lunch, stave off hunger by munching on one of the mid-morning options mentioned above. As far as possible carry lunch from home or if you are in Mumbai, have a dabba with a home-cooked meal delivered to you at work. You can then choose the right foods to maintain your diet.

The options provided are many and varied, including several non-vegetarian choices so you do not have to feel restricted or deprived. The recipes in the recipe section provide you with tasty meals which are good for everyone in the family, so you need not have special meals cooked for yourself. If you are the type of person who cannot function properly on a heavy stomach, you can interchange the lunch and dinner options so you eat a lighter meal in the afternoon and a heavier meal at night. Just remember to eat at least 2 hours before you go to bed.

The Afternoon Slump

Mid-afternoon can be one of the most difficult times of the day to get through. It is a time when your system seems to shut down and you feel lethargic, yawning every few minutes. This is natural – dictated largely by our circadian rhythms whereby there is a natural drop in energy midway through the day.

This is more or less avoided if you have had a fibre or protein rich meal at lunch time. Taking into account this natural flagging of energy, the Live Well Diet provides you with just the right pick-me-up: a cup of tea or coffee and a piece of fruit. In no time at all you will feel perky enough to finish your work day productively. Some other tips to deal with the afternoon slump: do a few simple stretches, drink a glass of cold water (you have 3-4 litres to go through remember!), take a short walk or splash some water on your face.

Evening Snack

Yes, there is also provision for a tasty evening snack! Evenings are meant for chit-chat, reliving the highlights of the day, or catching up with friends on facebook or on the phone. Serve yourself some dhokla or khandvi, some steamed momos or spring rolls; or wash away the cares of the day with a cold glass of buttermilk.

If you have not completed your exercise quota this would be a good time to walk or visit the gym. While you may not feel as energetic as at the beginning of the day, some physical activity is better than none, so do complete your exercise regime and tick it off your list. Do not exercise too close to bed time as you will find it harder to relax your body and sleep well.

Dinner

Your metabolism has been active all day and is in need of some rest. It is time to taper off your food intake so you can sleep well on a not-too full stomach. The meals suggested are light meals of soups and salads or vegetables. Drink the last of your daily quota of milk at the end of dinner or just before you go to bed. It will have a soothing effect on your system. Avoid yogurt with your night meal.

Make sure you do not go to bed immediately after dinner. Though it may be very difficult for you if you work late every day, give yourself at least 30 minutes before you retire.

Winding down

A warm shower, some soft music, a few minutes spent in meditation or prayer are the perfect ways to end a busy day.

If you have followed your diet and done enough exercise, sleep will come naturally, and you will awaken refreshed to a brand new day.

Your Day on the Live Well Diet	
ON WAKING	2 glasses lemon water + black or green tea + vegetable juice
PRE-BREAKFAST	Beverage and biscuits /khakra
Exercise and Walk *	
BREAKFAST	As recommended
MID MORNING	Fruit, Beverage or light snack
LUNCH	Veg or non-veg options as prescribed
MID-AFTERNOON	Beverage and a piece of fruit
EVENING	Beverage and light snack
Exercise and Walk *	
DINNER	As recommended
Sleep 7 hours	
*Exercise and walk either in the morning or evening, or in 2 sessions, at least 30 minutes before next meal.	

● ● ●

A BETTER BODY, MIND AND SOUL

When I first heard about Dr Davare's programme I was a bit apprehensive about being able to follow it. My profession as an actor demands that I travel a lot. The irregular working hours and diet made me feel unfit and lethargic. However, it is important in my profession to always be energetic and healthy and look good.

I am a disciplined person and have followed some kind of diet all my life. I do not binge. I was happy to see that Dr Davare's diet provides nutrition for a better body, mind and the soul. I feel energetic and my skin glows- I have never looked so pretty! I feel so confident and happy. After the programme my metabolism is so much more active - I burn what I eat. I exercise regularly and have no cellulite or excess fat.

The programme focuses on the self and I learned how important it is to invest in one's health. It is all about working out an individual health management plan, and making a decision to stick to it.

I had tried so many other diets and used to jog a lot, but did not have much success at maintaining my weight and appearance. Dr Sarita's programme with the combination of diet and exercise helps me to maintain my weight. Walking actually helps to maintain a lean, curvy body.

135

THE LIVE WELL FOOD GUIDE

Here is a list of foods that you should eat and those you should, as far as possible, avoid. This will help you make the right food choices and act as a ready reference when in doubt

Food	Eat/Drink	Avoid
Beverages	Tea, especially green or black tea, hot skimmed milk shakes, coconut water, vegetable and fruit juices, buttermilk, vegetable soups Control: Coffee in moderation	Aerated drinks, alcohol, sweetened fruit juices
Bread	2 whole grain (jowar, bajra, wholewheat), roti or chapatti or 2 slices multi-grain bread per day	White bread, buns, croissants, naan, sheermal, roomali roti etc.
Cereals and grains	Wholewheat flour, sorghum (jowar), millets (bajra, ragi), oats, corn and wheat flakes. Control: Rice - only twice a week, small quantities of eggless wholewheat noodles and pasta occasionally. Sago (sabudana) occasionally	Refined flour and cornflour. Pizzas, cakes and pastries
Chicken (for non-vegetarians)	Chicken without skin and fat; chicken salami or sausages	Chicken fat and skin, chicken liver
Dried fruit and nuts	2 pieces of any 2 per day: walnuts, almonds, dates	Cashew nuts, peanuts, raisins,
Eggs (for non-vegetarians)	Egg whites	Egg yolks
Fruit	Papaya, pineapple, watermelon, pear, guava, apple, jamun, cherries, strawberries, oranges, mosambi, lemons	Mangoes, chikoos, grapes, bananas, custard apple (sitaphal), coconut

Food	Eat/Drink	Avoid
Legumes and lentils	All legumes and pulses; restrict use of gram flour- mix it with moong dal flour	
Meat (for non-vegetarians)	Mutton: Occasionally	Red meat and pork
Milk	Only low-fat or skimmed cow's milk. Total consumption per day – 2½ cups including yogurt	Buffalo milk
Milk Products	Skimmed milk yogurt; buttermilk; yogurt should not exceed 1 katori per day; paneer max 5-6 cubes, twice a week (reduce milk intake accordingly); unsweetened fruit yogurt	Cheese, butter, ghee, cream
Oil	3 teaspoons per day essential. Preferably olive oil, rice bran oil, sunflower oil, canola oil	Margarine, hydrogenated vegetable fat (vanaspati), palm oil, coconut oil, mayonnaise
Root Vegetables	Yam, suran, potatoes, etc. occassionally	
Salt	Maximum 1 teaspoon per day	Namkeen, pickles, papads and snacks
Seafood	Fresh fish	Shellfish and prawns
Soya products	Soya flour, chunks, granules, milk, tofu	All soya products if suffering from thyroid problems
Spices and aromatics	Unlimited onion, ginger, garlic, herbs and spices	

Food	Eat/Drink	Avoid
Sugar/ Sweeteners	Maximum 5 sachets or tablets sugar substitute per day; eat max 1-inch cube of jaggery per day; eat max 1 piece chikki occasionally; eat max 2 teaspoons honey per week	Sugar
Vegetables	Eat all - especially leafy vegetables and salads; mushrooms	
Water	Drink total 3-4 litres of water every day including 1 litre lime (nimboo) water made with juice of ¼ lime, 1 glass (200 ml) coconut water	

SOME IMPORTANT FOODS FOR YOUR DIET

Food	Benefits
Almonds	Rich in minerals and Vitamin E, good for the skin, regulates blood pressure and cholesterol
Amla	Rich in minerals and Vitamin C; antioxidant
Canola oil	Contains healthy Omega-3 fatty acids
Chicken	Rich in protein
Dates	Provides energy, aids digestion, rich in potassium helps nervous system
Egg whites	Rich in protein minus cholesterol or fat
Fish	Rich in protein and heart healthy Omega-3 fatty acids
Flaxseeds	Rich in ALA- alpha-linolenic acid that improves brain function
Fruits	Rich in vitamin, minerals and fibre; antioxidants
Garlic	Natural antibiotic, blood thinner and lowers cholesterol and blood pressure
Ginger	Aids digestion, anti-inflammatory and antioxidant
Herbs and spices	Boost immunity and have healing properties

Legumes and pulses	Rich in protein, vitamins, minerals, fibre; aid digeston
Oats	Rich in fibre aids digestion, lowers cholesterol, controls blood sugar and blood pressure
Olive oil	High in mono-unsaturated heart-healthy fat, antioxidant
Rice bran oil	High in mono-unsaturated heart-healthy fat, antioxidant and rich in Vitatmin E
Skimmed cow's milk	Rich in Calcium, whey protein, Vitamins B2 and B12 improve the nervous system
Skimmed milk yogurt	Rich in Calcium, protein and B Vitamin
Vegetables	Rich in vitamin, minerals and fibre; antioxidants
Walnuts	Contain healthy Omega -3 fatty acids, antioxidants and amino acids necessary for heart health
Whole grains	Rich in magnesium which helps regulate fat metabolism; aids digestion

DRINK TO YOUR HEALTH:

These natural beverages provide you with nutrients, fibre, hydrate your body, activate your metabolism and help to heal or detoxify your system. They are an important part of the Live Well Diet so do include them as recommended.

Detoxifying Vegetable Juice

Raw, uncooked vegetables are a natural way of detoxifying the system as well as providing the body with essential nutrients. Raw vegetables preserve all their nutrients which are lost through cooking. The juice is particularly beneficial at the start of the day as it contains natural fibre which will kick start your digestive system and help evacuate your bowels. It also mobilises the fatty tissue which is essential for weight loss.

Bottle Gourd (Dudhi) Juice

The humble bottle gourd may seem like a vapid apology for a vegetable but it packs a hefty nutritional and healing punch. Make sure you use only tender, seedless bottle gourd. It is a diuretic which helps remove excess water from the system and prevents flatulence, indigestion and acidity.

Lime Water (Nimboo Pani)

Lime water helps you lose weight naturally, and helps your body improve its immunity and digestion as a bonus. It is an antioxidant, reduces skin pigmentation, stops hair fall and delays graying of hair and makes your skin glow. It also reduces leg cramps and improves blood circulation. A note of caution: avoid lime juice if you have a sore throat as it will aggravate it.

Green Tea

Besides having a soothing and calming effect, green tea is known to have several health benefits especially for weight loss. Add a squeeze of lime and it becomes that much more beneficial. Green tea is an antioxidant which prevents damage to the body's cells. It also prevents oxidation of bad cholesterol (LDL), and promotes the production of good cholesterol (HDL) and is an appetite suppressant.

Wheatgrass Juice

Wheatgrass is nothing but the tender shoots of the wheat plant. It is easy to grow at home in tiny pots on your window sill or in a warm, sunny place. Sow wheat grains in soil and sprinkle lightly with water every day. Tender shoots of wheat grass will begin to emerge and by the seventh or eighth day will be ready to harvest. Use only the top parts of the grass. Wash well grind with water and strain to make a nutritious drink.

Wheatgrass juice has many health benefits and should be included in your Live Well Diet. It contains beneficial enzymes, lowers blood pressure and purifies the blood, increasing red blood cells.

Aloe Vera Juice

Aloe vera is a succulent plant which has been used to improve the skin and hair and cure skin problems including burns. But it is also a healthy food supplement with many positive effects on the functioning of the body. It improves digestion, has a detoxifying effect and promotes healthy cell growth particularly of the skin. It has a mood lifting and soothing effect which is a good antidote to stress.

Coconut Water

Coconut water is a refreshing, natural nutrient booster and is an essential part of the Live Well Diet It is rich in minerals and vitamins and low in fats. It is an excellent and tasty way of hydrating the system without any adverse effects. It is a natural isotonic beverage which rehydrates the body and provides it with essential salts particularly after exercise. Rich in potassium it prevents cramps. It also reduces pigmentation of the skin that may accompany weight loss.

Buttermilk (Chaas)

Buttermilk is perfect for a weight loss diet as it is rich in calcium and protein while low in fat. To add more value to buttermilk, add ginger and cumin seeds which are known to have healing properties. The good bacteria and enzymes present in buttermilk have a pro-biotic effect which aid in digestion (it is more easily digested than milk) and boost the immune system.

● ● ●

ENOUGH IS AS GOOD AS A FEAST!

The importance of portion sizes

Sticking to a diet which provides for variety and flavour can be a challenge because you can cook and eat tasty foods but have to restrict yourself to just the recommended quantity! No piled up plates and second helpings, please! The portion sizes have been recommended keeping in mind the right quantities and balance of essential nutrients.

To help you with the diets and figure out how much you should eat at each meal a table of measures has been provided below. It would be helpful to get yourself a set of measuring cups and spoons, but the homely chamach and katori will also do.

Equivalents			
Measures	**Volume/Size**	**Measures**	**Volume/Size**
1 tablespoon	15 ml	⅓ cup	65 ml
2 teaspoons	10 ml	½ cup/ 1 small katori	100 ml
1 teaspoon	5 ml	1 teacup/ ¾ cup/ ¾ katori	150 ml
½ teaspoon	2.5 ml	1 cup/1 katori /1 glass	200ml
¼ teaspoon	1.25 ml	1 bowl/ 1½ katori	300 ml
¼ cup	50 ml	1 plate	6 inches diameter

12

THE LIVE WELL DIETS – A, B AND C

The Live Well Diet would be just an idea till it is put into action. Given below are details of the many options that you can avail of on all 3 diets whether you are at home or travelling so you can maintain your diet with the least amount of discomfort or disruption.

Most of the foods suggested are everyday easily available foods and there is enough variety to keep your palate happy for a lifetime. Once you familiarise yourself with the proportions and kinds of food choices within each diet, you will find it has become a way of life for you and you will effortlessly and instinctively make the right food choices, suited to the occasion.

You may even feel that there are too many meals and too much on offer, but do remember that the diet is meant to provide you with the right nutrition in the right balance, keeping in mind the best way of keeping your metabolism always at its optimum levels.

Remember the sequence of Diets A, B and C and try to follow them as closely as possible.

I am sure you will discover that far from being very restricitive diets, your Live Well diet will enable you to live both fully and really well!

● ● ●

LIVE WELL DIET A - THE ALL FOODS DIET

Vegetarian and Non-Vegetarian Diet - Maximum 2 days of the week

ON WAKING	2 glasses warm water + juice of ¼ lemon
PLUS	1 cup black/green tea + a drop of lemon juice
PLUS	1 glass health juice
PRE-BREAKFAST	1 cup coffee with skimmed milk. No sugar. May use sugar substitute
OR	1 cup regular/ginger/masala tea with skimmed milk. No sugar. May use sugar substitute
PLUS	2 Marie or Digestive biscuits or 1 glucose or 1 cream cracker biscuit or 2 Khakra (page 259) or a few pieces of dried fruit or nuts (almonds, walnuts, dates)
BREAKFAST	1 bowl cereal [cornflakes, wheatflakes, broken wheat (dalia) or oats] with 1 cup milk
OR	1 bowl spiced cereal (upma/poha) with chutney
OR	2 plain or vegetable rawa idli/2 medium oil-free dosa/1 medium uttapam + 1 bowl sambhar
OR	2 oil-free paranthe + 1 katori yogurt
OR	1 (2 triangles) wholewheat/multigrain bread vegetable or chicken sandwich
OR	2 boiled egg whites/2 egg white omelette with 2 slices wholewheat/multigrain bread or toast
LUNCH	VEG. & NON-VEG. OPTIONS
	1 bowl vegetable soup
PLUS	1½ six-inch roti + 2 katori cooked vegetables + 1 katori raita + 1 bowl dal
OR	1 katori steamed rice + 1 bowl kadhi or 1 bowl dal + 1 bowl cooked vegetable
OR	1 bowl moong khichdi + 1 bowl kadhi + 2 katori cooked vegetable + 1 or 2 roasted papad (optional)
OR	1 bowl vegetable or chicken fried rice/vegetable, chicken or fish pulao or biryani
OR	1 six-inch thalipeeth + 1 katori yogurt + oil-free lime pickle + 1 six-inch plate salad
OR	2 stuffed vegetable paranthe + 1½ katori vegetable raita + 1 bowl chole/rajma/other legume

OR	2 six-inch stuffed aloo paranthe + 1 katori raita + 1 katori legume + 1 roasted papad
OR	2 medium oil-free uttapam/masala dosa/2 Idli + 1 bowl sambhar
OR	Pav Bhaji: 2-3 wholewheat pav or 1-2 regular pav + 1 bowl bhaji - no butter
OR	1½ tandoori roti + 1 bowl dal tadka/1 bowl vegetable curry + 1 plate salad + 1 roasted papad (optional)
OR	1 bowl vegetable pulao + 1 katori raita + 1 bowl low-oil vegetable curry + 1 roasted papad (optional)
OR	1 bowl vegetable biryani + 1 katori raita + 1 plate salad + 1 roasted papad
OR	1 bowl fada ni khichdi + 1 katori yogurt
OR	1 bowl low-oil undhiyu + 2 medium roti + 1 katori dal + 1 plate salad
OR	5-6 pieces vegetarian/chicken/fish appetisers + 1 roomali roti + 1 bowl dal
OR	1 vegetable or chicken frankie
OR	Bread omelette made with 4 slices brown bread + 2 egg white omelette
OR	6 pani puri + 1 plate bhel
OR	1 plate of 6 dahi puri + 2 idli
OR	1 plate dahi vada (4 vade) + 1 plate dosa
OR	1 bowl chole + 1 roti + 1 roasted papad + 1 katori raita
OR	6 pieces low-oil kadai paneer/1 bowl paneer dish (6 pieces paneer) + 1 tandoori roti + 1 plate salad or spinach soup
OR	1 diet sandwich + 1 glass fresh unsweetened fruit juice
OR	6 vegetable/chicken steamed wontons/spring rolls + 1 bowl clear vegetable or chicken soup + 1 bowl noodles with vegetables, chicken or fish + 1 bowl Chinese salad
OR	1 bowl Chinese bhel with 1 plate steamed vegetable/chicken momos
OR	1 chicken/vegetable Subway sandwich without mayonnaise + 1 glass fresh unsweetened fruit juice

OR	1 vegetable, chicken or fish burger without cheese + 1 fresh unsweetened fruit juice
OR	3-5 pieces grilled chicken + 1 bowl vegetable + 1 bowl salad
OR	1 whole or 1 large piece grilled fish (eg. mackerel, surmai, bhetki, rawas) + 1 bowl vegetable + 1 bowl salad or 1 bowl vegetable or chicken soup
MID-AFTERNOON	1 cup tea/coffee
EVENING	1 bowl chana kurmura/bhel puri/moong jor garam
OR	1 glass buttermilk
OR	2 small diet khakra
OR	4-5 steamed wontons/spring rolls
OR	2-3 pieces khandvi/dhokla/patra
OR	4 oil-free vegetable cutlets
OR	1 katori chanu gur (1 katori chana + 1 inch jaggery) 2-3 pieces corn tikki, corn cutlets or steamed corn
DINNER	3 or 4 katori/whole fruits (eg. apples, pears, oranges, sweet lime, guava, papaya)
OR	1 bowl vegetable soup + 1 bowl salad
OR	1 bowl stir-fried or steamed vegetables
NOTE: Keep an hour's interval between fruit, soup and salad	
NOTE: Lunch and dinner options may be interchanged	
LIFELINES/ SNACKS*	1 glass buttermilk
OR	1 glass coconut water
OR	1 glass cold coffee with skimmed milk and sugar substitute
OR	2 citrus fruits (mosambis/oranges)/2 guavas/ 1 katori strawberries/1 apple/1 pear
OR	2-3 pieces of any one: date/almond/walnut
* Any 2 per day in addition to essential daily intake	

● ● ●

LIVE WELL DIET B - THE BASIC DIET	
Vegetarian Diet* - 3 days of the week	
ON WAKING	2 glasses warm water + juice of ¼ lemon
	1 cup black/green tea + a drop of lemon juice
	1 glass any 1 health juice
PRE-BREAKFAST	1 cup coffee with skimmed milk. No sugar. May use sugar substitute
OR	1 cup regular/ginger/masala tea with skimmed milk. No sugar. May use sugar substitute
PLUS (optional)	2 soya/ragi/jowar/bajra khakra or 2 oat biscuits
BREAKFAST	2 egg white omelette/scramble
OR	1 bowl oats with 1 cup milk
OR	1 bowl jowar/bajra/oat upma with chutney
OR	1 bhajnee thalipeeth with yogurt
OR	1 bowl bajra/jowar vegetable khichdi
OR	2 moong dal cheele with chutney
LUNCH	1 wholegrain flour roti (soya, jowar, ragi, bajra) + 1 katori leafy vegetables + 1 bowl dal or 2 egg white omelette + 1 plate salad
OR	2 egg white omelette + 1 bajra roti + 1 plate salad + 1 bowl cooked vegetables
OR	2 egg white omelette + 1 bowl spinach soup + 1 plate salad + 1 bajra roti
MID - AFTERNOON	1 cup tea/coffee
EVENING	1 glass buttermilk
OR	1 katori soya nuggets or 3-4 pieces soya toast
OR	2-3 bajra/jowar/ragi biscuits
OR	3-4 pieces moong dal dhokla
OR	2 medium moong dal cheela or thepla or ragi paranthe
DINNER	1 bowl legume salad

OR	1 bowl lentils with greens
OR	1 bowl veg soup with 2 jowar/bajra/soya/ragi soup sticks
OR	2 egg white omelette/scramble with vegetables
OR	1 bowl lightly spiced/boiled or steamed vegetables + 1 Jawari Bhakri (page 308)
OR	1 bowl jowar/bajra khichdi
OR	1 bowl stir-fried vegetable 6 pieces paneer tikki or any vegetable starter with 1 bowl salad
NOTE: Lunch and dinner options may be interchanged	
LIFELINES/ SNACKS**	2 pieces soya/bajra/jowar/ oat/oil-free and sugar-free snacks (chakli, khakra, biscuits)
Plus (any 2)	1 glass buttermilk
OR	1 glass coconut water
OR	1 glass cold coffee with skimmed milk and sugar substitute
OR	2 mosambis/2 oranges/1 pear/1 guava/ a few cherries/a few jamuns
OR	2 pieces of any one: date/almond/walnut
OR	1 piece chikki or 1 small piece jaggery
* Except for egg whites which are optional, this is a vegetarian diet	
** Over and above essential daily intake	

● ● ●

LIVE WELL DIET C - THE CONTROL DIET	
Vegetarian and Non-Vegetarian Diet - 2 days of the week	
ON WAKING	2 glasses warm water + juice of ¼ lemon 1 cup black/green tea + a drop of lemon juice
PRE-BREAKFAST	1 cup coffee with skimmed milk. No sugar. May use sugar substitute
OR	1 cup regular/ginger/masala tea with skimmed milk. No sugar. May use sugar substitute
BREAKFAST	1 glass health juice
LUNCH	1 bowl vegetable soup
PLUS	1 bowl cooked vegetables
OR	1 bowl stir-fried vegetables
OR	5-6 pieces vegetable or chicken seekh kababs
OR	5-6 mixed vegetable cutlets
OR	1 bowl fruit salad
OR	5-6 paneer/chicken/fish tikka
OR	1 glass strawberry/papaya/apple/dried fruit milkshake
OR	1 bowl fruit yogurt
OR	1 bowl chicken salad without mayonnaise
MID-AFTERNOON	1 glass buttermilk or 2-3 pieces dried fruit or 1 piece steamed corn
EVENING	1 or 2 katori/whole fruit
OR	2 moong dal cheele
MID EVENING	1 bowl chicken or vegetable salad or vegetable soup or chicken soup
DINNER	1 katori moong or rajma salad + 1 bowl vegetables
OR	1 bowl masoor dal/Sambhar (page 322)/rasam + 1 bowl vegetables
OR	1 katori chole or matki usal
OR	2 egg white omelette/1 bowl chicken/fish + 1 bowl vegetable or salad

OR	2 medium green moong dosa/cheela with mint chutney + 1 bowl vegetable/chicken soup or salad
OR	4 pieces green gram dal dhokla + 1 bowl chicken/vegetable soup or salad
LIFELINES/ SNACKS	2 pieces soya/bajra/jowar/oat/oil-free and sugar-free snacks (chakli, khakra, biscuits)
Plus (any 2)	1 glass buttermilk
OR	1 glass coconut water
OR	1 glass cold coffee with skimmed milk and sugar substitute
OR	2 mosambis/2 oranges/1 pear/1 guava/a few cherries/a few jamuns
OR	2 pieces of any one: date/almond/walnut
OR	1 piece chikki or small piece of jaggery

NOTE: Include chicken or fish only once a day either for lunch or dinner.

IMPORTANT: There may be times you will not feel like eating all that is prescribed. While you may cut down on the quantity, DO NOT OMIT THE FOOD PRESCRIBED, as it contains essential nutrients for your well being.

● ● ●

I FEEL
REBORN!

Being a singer by profession, I perform and tour a lot and over the years had developed very irregular eating habits. Late nights and fried foods had led me to put on a lot of weight. I felt uneasy all the time. My legs used to swell. I tried many diets, enrolled in gyms but to my surprise, my weight increased further! I stopped going to parties and developed a complex about my obesity.

I had other health problems as well – my cholesterol, triglyceride and homocysteine levels were very high; I suffered from high blood pressure. A good friend introduced me to Dr Sarita's programme. I was determined to make a success of it. After the first few days on the programme, I lost 2-3 kg and that motivated me. I became determined to stay on the programme and to extend my walking beyond the target. My wife too has started the programme so it was much easier for both of us.

Instead of outside food, I began to carry home-made salads, juices and milk shakes with me. The dried fruits I started carrying with me gave a boost of energy while rehearsing.

Today my cholesterol and other blood levels are normal. So normal, that even my family doctor is surprised! And best of all, I lost 33 kg in 1 year!

The programme has changed my whole life. I am so much more disciplined now. I could never resist gajar halwa and would eat a bowlful. But now I eat just a spoonful for the taste. I am so much more energetic now – even my performances have improved. I have a new wardrobe to suit my new look and I feel young and self-confident again.

I honestly feel reborn. I have a new life!

13

LIVE WELL DIET MENUS

This is a 2-week menu planned especially for you, which will enable you to plan and prepare your meals and food and liquid intake. You will find recipes for most of the dishes in Section III-Recipes, especially developed for you by chef Sanjeev Kapoor. As you will see there is plenty of choice and variety which will provide you with both taste and nutrition. Your diet will soon become a way of life and you will find that you can repeat the menus and interchange the dishes within each diet to provide yourself with endless combinations that will please your palate in a very healthy way. Do remember to stick to the portions recommended, though if you are unable to consume the foods in the prescribed quantities, you must not avoid any of the foods prescribed to get the right nutritional balance.

The menu is based on a weekly plan of 7 days: 2 days of Diet A – All Foods Diet, 2 days of Diet C – the Control Diet, and 3 days of Diet B – The Basic Diet. Do remember too that Diet A should be followed by Diet C, and that you should not exceed more than 2 days of Diets A or C in a week. You can however, continue Diet B for more than 3 days in the week, depending on the circumstances.

SOME SUGGESTIONS FOR WEEKLY PLANS						
Day 1	Day 2	Day 3	Day 4	Day 5	Day 6	Day 7
Diet A	Diet C	Diet B	Diet B	Diet A	Diet C	Diet B
Diet B	Diet C	Diet B	Diet B	Diet B	Diet A	Diet C
Diet B	Diet A	Diet C	Diet B	Diet A	Diet C	Diet B
Diet C	Diet B	Diet A	Diet C	Diet B	Diet B	Diet B
Diet C	Diet A	Diet C	Diet B	Diet B	Diet B	Diet B

DIET A – THE ALL FOODS DIET

DIET A MENU 1		
7:00 AM	ON WAKING	2 glasses warm water + juice of ¼ lemon
	+	1 cup black or green tea with a drop of lemon juice
	+	1 glass Mixed Vegetable Juice (page 203)
7.30 am	PRE-BREAKFAST	1 cup sugarless coffee or tea with skimmed milk
	+	2 Marie or Digestive biscuits
9.00 am	BREAKFAST	1 bowl cereal [cornflakes, wheatflakes, broken wheat (dalia) or oats] with 2 chopped dates or almonds + 1 cup skimmed milk
	OR	2 Tomato Egg Cups (page 225) + 2 slices wholewheat or multigrain bread or toast
	+	1 whole fruit (apple, orange, pear, etc)
11.00 am	MID-MORNING	1 glass coconut water
1.00 pm	LUNCH	1 bowl Palak Soup (page 230)
	+	1 tandoori roti
	+	1 bowl Chole Dhania Masala (page 320) or Chicken Dhansak (page 275) or Pudina Kali Mirch Rawas Tikka (page 278)
	+	1 bowl Masaledar Kaddu (page 291)
	+	1 bowl kachumber
3.00 pm	MID-AFTERNOON	1 cup sugarless coffee or tea with skimmed milk
	+	1 whole fruit (apple, orange, pear, etc)
5.30- 6.00 pm	EVENING	1 glass buttermilk

	+	1 bowl Healthy Cornflakes Bhel (page 255) or 2 small diet khakra
8-9.00 pm	DINNER	1 bowl Clear Vegetable Soup (page 240) + 1 plate mixed vegetable salad
	OR	2 bowls chopped mixed fruit
	+	1 cup green tea

● ● ●

DIET A MENU 2		
7:00 AM	ON WAKING	2 glasses warm water + juice of ¼ lemon
	+	1 cup black or green tea with a drop of lemon juice
	+	1 glass Doodhi Juice (page 200)
7.30 am	PRE-BREAKFAST	1 cup sugarless coffee or tea with skimmed milk
	+	1 Glucose or Cream Cracker or Marie biscuit
9.00 am	BREAKFAST	1 bowl Green Pea and Carrot Dalia (page 211)
	OR	1 Steamed Egg Katori (page 224) with 2 slices wholewheat or multigrain bread or toast
11.00 am	MID-MORNING	1 glass buttermilk
	+	1 whole fruit (apple, orange, pear, etc)
1.00 pm	LUNCH	1 bowl Mushroom Soup with Light Soy (page 235)
	+	1 bowl Chicken Tetrazini (page 310) or Oodles of Noodles (page 312) or Masala Pomfret (page 280)
	+	1 bowl Slimmers' Salad with No-Oil Dressing (page 246)

3.00 pm	MID-AFTERNOON	1 cup sugarless coffee or tea with skimmed milk
	+	1 whole fruit (apple, orange, pear, etc)
5.30- 6.00 pm	EVENING	1 glass coconut water
	+	2 Thepla (page 309)
8-9.00 pm	DINNER	1 bowl Mixed Vegetable Soup (page 234)
	+	1 bowl Lapsi aur Shimla Mirch Salad (page 244)
	+	1 cup green tea

• • •

DIET A MENU 3		
7:00 AM	ON WAKING	2 glasses warm water + juice of ¼ lemon
	+	1 cup black or green tea with a drop of lemon juice
	+	1 glass Aloe Vera Juice (page 199)
7.30 am	PRE-BREAKFAST	1 cup sugarless coffee or tea with skimmed milk
	+	2 diet khakra
9.00 am	BREAKFAST	Scrambled Eggs on Toast (page 223) (2 slices of toast with 1-2 egg whites)
	OR	1 bowl Fruity Yogurt with Cereal Topping (page 212)
11.00 am	MID-MORNING	1 glass coconut water
1.00 pm	LUNCH	1 bowl Red Pumpkin Soup (page 231)
	+	1 bowl Char Dal ni Khichdi (page 299) with 1 bowl Bhinda ni Kadhi (page 318)

	OR	1 bowl Chicken Haleem (page 274) with 1 tandoori roti
	+	1 bowl Spring Onion-Tomato Koshimbir (page 251)
	+	1 whole fruit (apple, orange, pear, etc)
3.00 pm	MID-AFTERNOON	1 cup sugarless coffee or tea with skimmed milk
5.30- 6.00 pm	EVENING	1 glass buttermilk
	+	2 Baked Vegetable Samosa (page 254)
8-9.00 pm	DINNER	1 bowl Thai Hot and Sour Vegetable Soup (page 236)
	+	1 katori Fruit Sorbet (page 328)
	+	1 cup green tea

• • •

DIET A MENU 4		
7:00 AM	ON WAKING	2 glasses warm water + juice of ¼ lemon
	+	1 cup black or green tea with a drop of lemon juice
	+	1 glass Amla Juice (page 199)
7.30 am	PRE-BREAKFAST	1 cup sugarless coffee or tea with skimmed milk
	+	1 Glucose or Bourbon or Cream Cracker biscuit
9.00 am	BREAKFAST	2 Egg White Omelette - any variation (page 209) with 2 slices multigrain or wholewheat bread or toast
	OR	1 or 2 medium Moong Dal Uttapam (page 214)
	+	1 small katori Chocolate Yogurt (page 326)

11.00 am	MID-MORNING	1 glass coconut water
1.00 pm	LUNCH	1 bowl Tomato Egg Drop Soup (page 237) or Clear Vegetable Soup (page 240)
	+	1 bowl Clay Pot Rice (page 300) + 1 bowl Eight Jewel Vegetables (page 282)
	OR	1 bowl Green Fried Rice (page 301) + 1 bowl Bean Curd with French Beans and Hot Hoisin Sauce (page 283)
	+	1 bowl Som Tam (page 250)
	+	1 katori Watermelon and Strawberry Granita (page 333)
3.00 pm	MID-AFTERNOON	1 cup tea or coffee or 1 glass cold coffee
5.30-6.00 pm	EVENING	1 glass Vaghareli Chaas (page 206)
	+	1 bowl Egg Chaat (page 256) or 1 bowl Green Chana Chaat (page 257)
8-9.00 pm	DINNER	1 bowl Masoor, Gajar aur Pumpkin Soup (page 233)
	+	1 whole fruit
	+	1 cup green tea

● ● ●

DIET B – THE BASIC DIET

DIET B MENU 1		
7:00 AM	ON WAKING	2 glasses warm water + juice of ¼ lemon
	+	1 cup black or green tea + a drop of lemon juice
	+	1 glass Carrot Juice (page 201)
7.30 AM	PRE-BREAKFAST	1 cup sugarless coffee or tea with skimmed milk

	+	2 Methi Khakra (page 259) or 2 Oat Biscuits
9.00 am	BREAKFAST	2 Egg White Omelette - any variation (page 209)
	OR	1 bowl Kande Pohe with Oats (page 221)
11.00 am	MID-MORNING	1 glass coconut water
	+	1 whole fruit (apple, orange, pear, etc)
1.00 pm	LUNCH	1 Jawari Bhakri (page 308)
	+	1 bowl Maathachi Bhaji (page 284)
	+	1 bowl Keoti Dal (page 316)
	+	1 whole fruit (apple, orange, pear, etc)
3.00 pm	MID-AFTERNOON	1 cup sugarless coffee or tea with skimmed milk
5.30-6.00pm	EVENING	1 glass buttermilk
	+	2 Moong ke Cheele (page 261)
8-9.00 pm	DINNER	1 bowl Palakwali Dal (page 317)
	OR	2 Egg White Omelette with Spinach (page 209)
	+	1 portion (1 katori) Apple Crumble (page 325)

● ● ●

DIET B MENU 2		
7:00 AM	ON WAKING	2 glasses warm water + juice of ¼ lemon
	+	1 cup black or green tea + a drop of lemon juice
	+	1 glass Beet Juice (page 200)
7.30 AM	PRE-BREAKFAST	1 cup sugarless coffee or tea with skimmed milk
	+	2 soya/ragi/jowar/bajra khakra or 2 oat biscuits
9.00 am	BREAKFAST	1-1½ Anda Parantha (page 302)

		OR	1 Bhajnee Thalipeeth (page 208)
		+	1 whole fruit (apple, orange, pear, etc)
11.00 am	MID-MORNING		1 glass coconut water
		+	1 whole fruit (apple, orange, pear, etc)
1.00 pm	LUNCH		1 bowl Tomato Soup (page 238)
		+	1 bowl Khatte Moong (page 323)
		+	2 roti
		+	1 whole fruit (apple, orange, pear, etc)
3.00 pm	MID-AFTERNOON		1 cup sugarless coffee or tea with skimmed milk
5.30- 6.00 pm	EVENING		1 glass buttermilk
		+	1 bowl Mixed Sprout Ussal (page 260)
8-9.00 pm	DINNER		1½ Spinach and Cabbage Parantha (page 304)
		+	1 bowl Kakdi Raita (page 244)
		+	¾ katori Doodhi Halwa (page 327)

● ● ●

DIET B MENU 3		
7:00 AM	ON WAKING	2 glasses warm water + juice of ¼ lemon
	+	1 cup black or green tea + a drop of lemon juice
	+	1 glass Cucumber Juice (page 201)
7.30 AM	PRE-BREAKFAST	1 cup sugarless coffee or tea with skimmed milk
	+	2 soya/ragi/jowar/bajra khakra or 2 oat biscuits
9.00 am	BREAKFAST	1 Steamed Egg Katori (page 224)
	OR	1 Mooli-Bajra Roti (page 306)
	+	1 whole fruit (apple, orange, pear, etc)

11.00 am	MID-MORNING	1 glass coconut water
	+	1 whole fruit (apple, orange, pear, etc)
1.00 pm	LUNCH	1 bowl Masoor Dal Soup (page 229)
	+	1 bowl Chakvatachi Bhaji (page 286)
	+	1 bowl Vegetable Raita (page 251)
	+	1 whole fruit (apple, orange, pear, etc)
3.00 pm	MID-AFTERNOON	1 cup sugarless coffee or tea with skimmed milk
5.30- 6.00 pm	EVENING	1 glass buttermilk
	+	Pav Bhaji (2 pav and 1 bowl bhaji) (page 263)
8-9.00 pm	DINNER	1½ Dhania Pudina Parantha (page 303)
	+	1 bowl Lauki Chana Dal (page 288)
	+	1 whole fruit (apple, orange, pear, etc)

● ● ●

DIET B MENU 4		
7:00 AM	ON WAKING	2 glasses warm water + juice of ¼ lemon
	+	1 cup black or green tea + a drop of lemon juice
	+	1 glass Tomato Juice (page 205)
7.30 AM	PRE-BREAKFAST	1 cup sugarless coffee or tea with skimmed milk
	+	2 soya/ragi/jowar/bajra khakra or 2 oat biscuits
9.00 am	BREAKFAST	1 masala omelette
	OR	1½ Wholemeal, Oat and Cinnamon Pancakes (page 219)
	+	1 whole fruit (apple, orange, pear, etc)

0 am	MID-MORNING	1 glass coconut water
	+	1 whole fruit (apple, orange, pear, etc)
.00 pm	LUNCH	1 bowl Makai Palak (page 289)
	+	1 bowl Red Pumpkin Raita (page 245)
	+	1 Paushtik Bajre ki Roti (page 307)
	+	1 whole fruit (apple, orange, pear, etc)
3.00 pm	MID-AFTERNOON	1 cup sugarless coffee or tea with skimmed milk
5.30- 6.00 pm	EVENING	1 glass buttermilk
	+	4 Nutritious Soya Kababs (page 262)
8-9.00 pm	DINNER	1 bowl Tomato Beet and Carrot Soup (page 239)
	+	1 bowl Moth and Moong Sprout Salad (page 248)
	+	¾ katori Mixed Fruit Custard (page 329)

DIET B MENU 5		
7:00 AM	ON WAKING	2 glasses warm water + juice of ¼ lemon
	+	1 cup black or green tea + a drop of lemon juice
	+	1 glass Palak Juice (page 204)
7.30 AM	PRE-BREAKFAST	1 cup sugarless coffee or tea with skimmed milk
	+	2 soya/ragi/jowar/bajra khakra or 2 oat biscuits
9.00 am	BREAKFAST	1 Tomato Egg Cups (page 225)
	OR	2 small Oat and Mixed Flour Onion Cheela (page 220)
	+	1 whole fruit (apple, orange, pear, etc)

11.00 am	MID-MORNING	1 glass coconut water
	+	1 whole fruit (apple, orange, pear, etc)
1.00 pm	LUNCH	1 bowl Dal Dhokli (page 313)
	+	1 bowl Mooli Saag (page 294)
	+	1 whole fruit (apple, orange, pear, etc)
3.00 pm	MID-AFTERNOON	1 cup sugarless coffee or tea with skimmed milk
5.30- 6.00 pm	EVENING	1 glass buttermilk
	+	1 portion Moong Toast (page 216)
8-9.00 pm	DINNER	Bean and Vegetable Soup (page 226)
	+	2 soya soup sticks
	+	2-3 Oat and Nut Cookies (page 330)

● ● ●

DIET B MENU 6		
7:00 AM	ON WAKING	2 glasses warm water + juice of ¼ lemon
	+	1 cup black or green tea + a drop of lemon juice
	+	1 glass Mixed Vegetable Juice (page 203)
7.30 AM	PRE-BREAKFAST	1 cup sugarless coffee or tea with skimmed milk
	+	2 soya/ragi/jowar/bajra khakra or 2 oat biscuits
9.00 am	BREAKFAST	1 katori Oats with Dried Fruit (page 331)
	+	1 whole fruit (apple, orange, pear, etc)
11.00 am	MID-MORNING	1 glass coconut water
	+	1 whole fruit (apple, orange, pear, etc)

1.00 pm	LUNCH	1 bowl Dhingri Matar (page 287)
	+	1 bajra/Jawari Bhakri (page 308)
	+	1 bowl Tzatziki (page 252)
	+	1 whole fruit (apple, orange, pear, etc)
3.00 pm	MID-AFTERNOON	1 cup sugarless coffee or tea with skimmed milk
5.30- 6.00 pm	EVENING	1 glass buttermilk
	+	1 Energy Dosa (page 210) with Chutney
8-9.00 pm	DINNER	1 bowl Spinach and Tofu Soup (page 241)
	+	2 soya soup sticks
	+	1 small katori Saeb aur Sooji Halwa (page 332)

● ● ●

DIET C – THE CONTROL DIET

DIET C MENU 1		
7:00 AM	ON WAKING	2 glasses warm water + juice of ¼ lemon
	+	1 cup black or green tea + a drop of lemon juice
7.30 AM	PRE-BREAKFAST	1 cup sugarless coffee or tea with skimmed milk
9.00 am	BREAKFAST	1 glass Carrot Juice (page 201)
	+	1 whole fruit (apple, orange, pear, etc)
11.00 am	MID-MORNING	1 glass coconut water
1.00 pm	LUNCH	1 bowl Palak Soup (page 230)
	+	1 bowl Peshawari Chana (page 295)
	+	1 bowl Baingan Bharta (page 281)
	+	1 whole fruit (apple, orange, pear, etc)

3.00 pm	MID-AFTERNOON	1 cup sugarless coffee or tea with skimmed milk
5.30- 6.00 pm	EVENING	1 glass buttermilk
8-9.00 pm	DINNER	2 Vegetable Seekh Kababs (page 268)
	OR	4 Grilled Fish Fingers (page 258)
	+	Chilled Melon Ball Salad (page 242)

• • •

DIET C MENU 2		
7:00 AM	ON WAKING	2 glasses warm water + juice of ¼ lemon
	+	1 cup black or green tea + a drop of lemon juice
7.30 AM	PRE-BREAKFAST	1 cup sugarless coffee or tea with skimmed milk
9.00 am	BREAKFAST	1 glass Palak Juice (page 204)
	+	1 whole fruit (apple, orange, pear, etc)
11.00 am	MID-MORNING	1 glass coconut water
1.00 pm	LUNCH	1 bowl Mixed Vegetable Soup (page 234)
	+	1 bowl Poached Fish and Dill Salad (page 249) or 5 pieces Saunfia Paneer Tikka (page 264)
	+	1 whole fruit (apple, orange, pear, etc)
3.00 pm	MID-AFTERNOON	1 cup sugarless coffee or tea with skimmed milk
5.30- 6.00 pm	EVENING	1 glass buttermilk
	+	2-3 pieces dried fruit or 1 piece boiled sweet corn
8-9.00 pm	DINNER	1 bowl Sour and Spicy Chicken Soup (page 232) or 1 bowl Masoor, Gajar aur Pumpkin Soup (page 233)

	OR	1 bowl Vegetable Shashlik (page 298)
	+	1 medium katori Pineapple Yogurt Fool (page 331)

● ● ●

DIET C MENU 3		
7:00 AM	ON WAKING	2 glasses warm water + juice of ¼ lemon
	+	1 cup black or green tea + a drop of lemon juice
7.30 AM	PRE-BREAKFAST	1 cup sugarless coffee or tea with skimmed milk
9.00 am	BREAKFAST	1 glass Amla Juice (page 199)
	+	1 whole fruit (apple, orange, pear, etc)
11.00 am	MID-MORNING	1 glass coconut water
1.00 pm	LUNCH	1 bowl Clear Vegetable Soup (page 240)
	+	1 bowl Shanghai Stir-fried Vegetables (page 297)
	+	1 whole fruit (apple, orange, pear, etc)
3.00 pm	MID-AFTERNOON	1 cup sugarless coffee or tea with skimmed milk
5.30- 6.00 pm	EVENING	1 glass buttermilk
	+	2-3 pieces dried fruit or 1 piece boiled sweet corn
8-9.00 pm	DINNER	1 bowl Middle-Eastern Vegetable Stew (page 292) or 1 bowl Steamed Fish (page 279) or 1 bowl Chicken Stew (page 270)
	+	1 bowl Citrus Cucumber Salad (page 243)

● ● ●

DIET C MENU 4		
7:00 AM	ON WAKING	2 glasses warm water + juice of ¼ lemon
	+	1 cup black or green tea + a drop of lemon juice
7.30 AM	PRE-BREAKFAST	1 cup sugarless coffee or tea with skimmed milk
9.00 am	BREAKFAST	1 glass Doodhi Juice (page 200)
	+	1 whole fruit (apple, orange, pear, etc)
11.00 am	MID-MORNING	1 glass coconut water
1.00 pm	LUNCH	1 bowl Chilled Cucumber and Buttermilk Soup (page 228)
	+	1 bowl Masala Khumb (page 290) or 6-8 cubes Pudina Kali Mirch Rawas Tikka (page 278) or 1 bowl Quick Jeera Chicken (page 269)
	+	1 whole fruit (apple, orange, pear, etc)
3.00 pm	MID-AFTERNOON	1 cup sugarless coffee or tea with skimmed milk
5.30- 6.00 pm	EVENING	1 glass buttermilk
	+	2-3 pieces dried fruit or 1 piece boiled sweet corn
8-9.00 pm	DINNER	1 bowl Ratatouille (page 293) or Hot and Fragrant Fish (½ pomfret) (page 276) or 1 bowl Spicy Salsa Chicken (page 273)
	+	1 bowl Microwaved Celery-Corn Medley (page 285)

NOTE: Pullout of Weekly Diet Chart available next to page 160.

THE MOST
EFFECTIVE
DIET

There is only one word to describe Dr Davare's programme –
Magic! So committed am I to her programme that I make it a
point to instruct the chefs at whichever hotel I am staying about
my diet for the day – and they invariably oblige. I exercise on the
treadmill every day. I have suffered no ill effects or hair loss. I
can say without hesitation that this is the most effective diet I
have ever come across.

14

THE BEST LAID PLANS
OFTEN GO AWRY....

LIFELINES TO THE RESCUE

No matter how firm your resolve, being on any kind of controlled regime is bound to be fraught with pitfalls and temptation. Motivation will keep you on your chosen path but situations will arise when for one reason or another you are not able to follow the diet and exercise plans as you would wish.

The Live Well Programme has made provision for such situations and offers you solutions to the very real problems of hunger and craving.

FOOD CRAVINGS

Cravings, especially for something sweet, are a very real problem for most people on a diet. The lifelines offered by the Live Well Diet will satisfy your longing in a flash. Only don't overdo it. Eat just the amount recommended!

- 2 dates or dried figs
- 1-inch square of chikki made with jaggery and gram (chana) or sesame seeds
- A few gur-chana
- 1 kurmura laddoo
- 1 mosambi or orange

To help with the persistent problem of cravings try the following as well:

- **Distract yourself** – taking your mind off the food in question can help.

- **Give in just a bit** – take a small piece of the desired food. Just tasting it will satisfy your desire for it. In the case of craving – **taste everything – eat nothing!**

- **Substitute a healthier version** of the food which may do the trick, eg bitter chocolate for milk chocolate.

- **Chew some sugarless chewing gum** – keeping your jaw active and the mint taste should help.

- **Brush your teeth** - yes you read right. Brushing your teeth can leave your mouth feeling refreshed and the sweet minty taste will satisfy your craving.

HUNGER MANAGEMENT

Hunger can strike you at any time threatening your resolve and putting all your good intentions and weight loss efforts at risk.

Appease those hunger pangs with a maximum of **any 2** per day of the following foods:
- 1 glass (200 ml) buttermilk
- 1 glass (200 ml) coconut water
- 1 glass (200 ml) cold coffee
- 2 mosambi/oranges
- 2 almonds/walnut kernels
- 2 dates/dried figs
- 1 small katori (100 ml) of roasted chana or moong dal, chana jor garam
- 2-3 teaspoons flaxseeds
- Chewing on a piece of sugar-free chewing gum also helps

ADJUSTING TO THE LIVE WELL DIET

The Live Well Diet is a balanced and practical way of eating the right foods in the right proportion in the right sequence. If followed correctly and with the support and advice of your physician you should not suffer any ill effects.

However, as you begin the diet you may notice some changes in your body which may alarm you. These are natural and you need not worry – as they are all temporary while your body adjusts to the new eating regime. However, do consult your physician if you have any severe symptoms and suspend the diet till you get the problem correctly diagnosed and treated.

BE PROACTIVE TO STAY ON THE DIET

The Travel Plan

How to maintain your diet while travelling can be a challenge. But the Live Well Diet is designed to be flexible so you can travel without stress and still stay on track. The diets also provide you with ample choices so that there will always be something you can eat without jeopardising your diet.

Follow this schedule and you should be fine:

Day 1 - Diet A
Day 2 - Diet C

Follow Plans A and C alternately till your travels end and you are back home.

The Wedding and Celebration Plan

Weddings and other family celebrations can be trying times for everyone. In addition to the preparations, shopping and parties, which are stressful enough, staying away from all the good food can be a real challenge. Don't panic. Be proactive!

- 2 days before the fun begins, switch your diet to Diet C.
- On the day of the celebration, eat a hearty breakfast of idli-sambhar, or any one of the breakfast options.
- For lunch, eat a simple meal of dal-roti and a simple salad.
- At the dinner reception, opt for the grilled starters and salads (no mayonnaise, please). Avoid vegetables which are deep-fried, grilled in butter, or coated in white sauce. Give the rice and breads a go-by and steer clear of the desserts. But if your host twists your arm, serve yourself a spoonful of one dessert. Remember the mantra – taste everything, eat nothing!

- Exercise may not be an option on days of such hectic activity, so make up for it by walking the next 2 days without fail.

The Busy Work Day Plan

Hectic work schedules can upset your diet, leaving you drained of energy. If you have no time to eat a proper meal during the day, make sure you eat a proper breakfast which will keep your energy levels up and your mind and body functioning well.

- Carry a piece of fruit or a light snack with you if possible which you can munch on at around lunch time.
- Drink a glass of coconut water, which will boost your energy through the afternoon.
- A few almonds or walnuts will keep hunger pangs at bay.
- Drink plenty of green or black tea which will trick your stomach into feeling full.
- When you get home, eat dinner as specified in your diet for the day.

The Ramzan Fasting Plan

It would seem almost impossible to maintain a diet while on a fast especially one as rigorous as the Ramzan fast which prohibits the intake of any solids or liquids for most of the day. But do not fear. The Live Well Diet is flexible enough to accommodate those on such a fast. Here is what you do:

At Sehri which is the daily early breakfast meal before the fast, consume the following which will fortify you for the rest of the day and provide you with enough liquid nourishment:

- 1 glass dried fruit milkshake
- 4 glasses water
- 1 cup black tea
- 2 moong dal cheele

At Iftaar when you break your fast consume the following:

- 2 dates
- 1 glass thick buttermilk or fruit juice

- 1 litre of water
- Any one of the dinner menus depending on the A, B or C diet for the day

Note: Do take a safe protein supplement while on a fast to compensate for the lack of sufficient protein.

●●●

It isn't how often you fall, it is whether you pick yourself up!

OOPS! I DID IT AGAIN! – FALLING OFF THE LIVE WELL DIET AND HOW TO GET BACK ON!

Here are some situations that we come across regularly in our clinic. Ditch the guilt and hand-wringing and get right back on track. Remember it isn't how often you fall but how quickly you pick yourself up!

I binged on a whole piece of rich chocolate cake at a birthday party. How can I make up for it?

Don't beat yourself up and despair. Get back on track by doing the following for the next day (24 hours):

- Switch to Diet C - The Control Diet
- Add more proteins in the form of legumes or egg white
- Reduce your milk intake to 1 cup
- Drink 1 glass of Amla Juice (page 199)
- Avoid any dried fruit and fresh fruit
- Do not drink coconut water on that day

I went out with friends to a fast food joint and after virtuously ordering a salad, I ate a plateful of French fries. And then I ate almost half my friend's chicken burger, though all I wanted was just one bite. I just could not help myself. I feel so guilty now, but can I remedy the situation?

This is going to happen from time to time. And I am glad you did not avoid going to the fast food restaurant. It would only increase your cravings. Your resolve is bound to weaken when you are having a good time in the company of your friends. But do not waste your time and energy in guilt. Pick yourself up, be positive and follow this plan for the next 24 hours:

- Switch to Diet C – the Control Plan

- Increase proteins in the form of legumes, or egg white

- Do not use oil in any of the recipes

- Avoid indulging in any of the Lifelines

And then the next time you are planning to go out with your friends, be proactive! Fill yourself up with a thick vegetable soup, or a piece of fruit and a bowl of salad, which will curb your appetite. If you feel full, the chances are the French fries may not be that appealing after all.

● ● ●

FREQUENTLY ASKED QUESTIONS

Will I put on weight when I stop the diet?

If you continue to eat according to the principles of the Live Well Diet and your BMR continues to be high, you should be able to maintain your body weight.

The Live Well Diet is a diet that will help you to live a healthy life whether you need to lose weight or not. A positive attitude and strong personal motivation will help to control your eating habits and ensure you will stay on the path to good health. Remember to:

- Eat 4-5 small meals every day instead of 2-3 large meals.
- Eat plenty of dietary fibre and protein, and a smaller quantity of simple carbohydrates.
- Avoid foods which are high in fat and sugar.

- Drink plenty of water.
- Make sure you exercise at least 5 days a week.

What should I do if my weight stabilises at a point and I have not yet reached my goal?

What you are describing is a 'plateau'. Almost everyone on a diet reaches this stage at some time. Your body gets used to a certain pattern of eating and your metabolism adjusts to the diet. What you need to do is mix things up a bit. Increase your exercise and vary your work out. Speed up your walking pace in short bursts. Add an extra day of Diet C in your weekly diet and reduce the number of days you avail of Diet A.

I have a sweet tooth and find it difficult to give up sweets and desserts. Also I find it hard to drink black tea or coffee without any sugar. Can I use sugar substitutes instead?

Sugar substitutes do help you cope with the absence of sugar. However, I recommend that you restrict your intake to 5 pellets (each pellet equal to 1 teaspoon of sugar), or the equivalent in sachets per day. The idea is to wean you off your cravings, which can lead you to even more temptation for the real thing.

How long can I continue on this diet?

The Live Well Diet is a holistic programme which can be followed by any healthy individual for an indefinite period of time. However, it is always wise to consult your physician and monitor your health regularly while you are on any diet and exercise programme.

I suffer from diabetes. Will this diet harm me in any way? What about the medication that has been prescribed by my doctor?

Several individuals have benefited from the diet and have brought their blood sugar levels under control by following this diet. However, your physician will be the best person to guide you.

My doctor has prescribed strong painkillers for my back problem. Will the diet provide me with enough nutrition?

Yes the diet is nutritionally sound and will withstand the effect of painkillers. However, you may need to take antacids which your physician will prescribe.

I am 35 years old and am overweight but have no other health problems. I am active, can run to catch a bus or train, and all my blood reports are normal i.e. I do not have any diabetes or high cholesterol. But my wife insists I diet and lose weight. Do I really need to?

While you feel fit and fine at the moment, your weight can cause problems for you in the future. The excess fat you are carrying around is like a slow poison which is harming your system. You are on the direct path to heart disease, diabetes and other life-threatening conditions. Be proactive and act now! As good as you feel now, you will be surprised how much better you will feel after a few months on the diet!

I am only a few kilograms overweight. My main problem is that my thighs and arms look heavy. Will the Live Well Diet help me to reduce the weight in just these two places?

There are many diets and exercises that offer you spot reduction. The truth is that fat loss happens evenly all over the body. It may appear that fat loss begins first on our cheeks, neck, hands and calves. This is because there is a thinner layer of fat in these places. Spot reduction can only happen with special treatments and not with a general diet and exercise plan.

Every time I go on a diet I begin to look tired and haggard with dark circles around my eyes. My friends have the same problem and we feel that losing weight may not be worth it if we look like hags. Will the Live Well diet have the same effect?

The Live Well Diet is a well-rounded holistic plan which provides you with adequate nutrition to be active and healthy. Far from feeling tired you will feel energised and lighter in body and spirit. The various vegetable juices not only hydrate your skin but remove the toxins from your system, causing your skin to glow. Make sure you get enough of sleep as well as that can also be a cause of dark circles.

My son is 12 years old and is quite obese. He loves his food, snacks a lot and somehow we cannot seem to tear him away from his computer or video games. Is the Live Well Diet suitable for my son?

The Live Well Diet is suitable for everyone. Whole families have followed the programme successfully and benefited as individuals. Your son may not always relish the foods prescribed eg he may refuse to drink the dudhi juice. Be creative with the foods recommended and give it to him in different, more palatable forms eg cutlets or soup or in a dal. The recipes by Master chef Sanjeev Kapoor will show you fun ways of getting all that nutrition into him without him suspecting it! You will also have to encourage him to do some physical activity. Joining a sports club or a gym may help or just playing games in the building compound or nearby park will lure him away from his sedentary activities.

I am 28 years old, married with 2 children and live with my husband and in-laws. I run the kitchen in our home. I would love to go on the LIVE WELL Diet as I put on weight after my daughter was born four years ago. But I do not know how I will manage to follow all the diet rules and cook separately for myself, and then other meals for the rest of the family who will not want to eat 'diet food'.

The Live Well Diet is a diet suited to the whole family. Check out the options for eah day and you will see the variety of dishes you can eat and enjoy. Recipes by Master chef Sanjeev Kapoor give you even more options which will surely please any palate. Other than the special juices, nobody need even know that you are on the diet as the food you will cook will be deliciously healthy!

I travel abroad on work and sometimes on holiday. How will I maintain my diet?

Today many restaurants abroad cater to the desire for healthy options. Steamed vegetables, salads, and soups are easily available. For non-vegetarians steamed and grilled options are aplenty. But to be on the safe side, pack some non-perishable ready-to-eat or ready-to-cook foods which you can feast on at a moment's notice. Thepla, soya soup sticks and toast, khakra, diet bhel and other snacks are readily available. If you have the luxury of access to a kitchen in which you can prepare your own meals, carry packets of upma, idli and wholegrain dosa mixes.

I fast at least one day a week. Which foods can I eat while I am on a fast?

As you will be avoiding grains and cereals, you can replace them with pseudo cereals such as amaranth (rajgira), samo (vari tandul), and water chestnut flour (singhada atta). To provide you with energy, increase your intake of fruit, especially pineapple, and milk, yogurt (cucumber raita), buttermilk and coconut water.

I suffer from pre-menstrual syndrome and have a miserable time just before and during my periods. I fear I may not be able to maintain the prescribed diet as I get irritable and stressed out.

Monthly periods and the time that leads up to them are a trying time for many women. Here are some foods that you can eat that will see you through those stressful days:

- **Dried Fruit Mix:** Mix together 10 chopped seedless dates, 10 chopped figs, 5 chopped almonds and 5 chopped walnuts kernels. Eat this mixture through the day.

- **Fruit Salads:** Pomegranate and Sweet Lime (mosambi) salads are particularly helpful. Mixed fruit and vegetable salads also help.

- **Milk Shakes:** Apple milk shake and dried fruit milk shake provide some relief.
- **Sweet Something:** 1 bowl of jaggery coated chickpeas (chana gud), amaranth (rajgira) chikki or laddoo and a glass of coconut water will trigger those feel-good hormones and lift your spirits.

● ● ●

MY STORY } **Paramjit Ghai**
Hotelier

I HAVE DISCOVERED THE FOUNTAIN OF YOUTH

The best thing about Dr Davare's programme is that it is a holistic programme. It is a natural programme without any shortcuts. It demands discipline and self-control. I could say it is almost like a religion based on nature without any side effects.

It involves detoxification and cleansing of the body and a holistic plan which results in total regeneration – I feel like a changed person. Besides the diet, the programme teaches you techniques to maintain good health, yoga, exercise and massages. It also emphasises the importance of sleep and relaxation.

I am in the hotel business and you can imagine how difficult it is to run restaurants and maintain a healthy life. The working hours are also erratic. I was overweight and had several health problems.

After being on the programme, my weight dropped from 101 kg to 83 kg. My triglyceride and cholesterol levels came down. I feel so energetic, with a bounce in my step that I feel I have discovered the fountain of youth! And best of all there are no side effects.

15

EATING OUT AND
HOME COOKING

Eating out is one of the pleasures of modern life. Some years ago dining in a restaurant was a treat that one indulged in on special occasions. Today, eating food that is cooked outside the home – in restaurants, cafes, street food stalls, dhabas etc, is almost a way of life. For many, especially single men and women, it has become a daily routine. Calling friends over for a home-cooked meal is now a rarity as many people prefer to entertain at restaurants. It is therefore a challenge for anyone who wants to regulate diet and food choices as it is almost impossible to control the amount of fat and refined carbohydrates in the food.

Some restaurants, happily, do offer healthy options as demand has gone up for leaner food choices. Do ask your waiter to suggest ways you can make your favourite dish lighter.

Eating out while you are on the Live Well Diet need not be the bugbear you imagine. There are plenty of dishes out there which are both healthy and flavourful so go for it and indulge in those dishes that will give you pleasure, keeping in mind a few tips given below.

HOW TO EAT YOUR CAKE AND HAVE IT TOO!

Snack before you dine out: Never enter a restaurant 'starving'! You will definitely order more, especially calorie-laden dishes on an empty stomach! Eat an apple or drink a glass of skimmed milk before you set out for the restaurant.

Bypass the bread! Treat the bread bowl as your enemy and give it a wide berth. Or better still, if none of your dining companions objects, have it removed from the table. Butter only adds insult to injury so stay clear of it as well.

Try and resist the pickled onions, chutneys and pickles in the condiment bowls. They are loaded with sodium.

Split it: Halve the amount of a dish by splitting it with someone else, thus consuming only half the amount you normally would have. Or, you can ask for the other half to be packed and take it home.

Words to order by: Chose dishes on the menu which are described with the words steamed, grilled, poached, stewed, light, clear, fresh, natural. Avoid dishes which say deep-fried, pan-fried, crumb-fried, batter-fried, smoked (high in sodium), au gratin (smothered in cheese sauce).

Cut it out or swap it: Request the waiter to leave out certain no-no items from your dish e.g. French fries, mashed potato, cheese or mayonnaise on a salad; or cream or ice cream with a dessert. Many restaurants will gladly replace them with steamed or boiled vegetables; or a salad with a light dressing. You can also ask for the cheese, dressing, sauce and cream on the side so you can serve yourself a small portion.

Beware the 'F' and 'S' words: The two most deadly words in the menu 'fried' and 'sauce'. These two words are a deadly combination and play havoc with our resolve to eat better. F and S also stand for Fat and Sodium, both of which are taboo for a healthy diet so do avoid items on the menu that contain excess fat or salt which includes fried foods and sauces!

Load up: Start by ordering a light soup or salad that will fill you up so you will need to order less of the main course. Drink plenty of water which will also make you feel full.

Enough is as good as a feast: Order just enough to keep you satisfied without making you feel full. Think twice before you order a dish for every course. Sometimes just ordering a variety of starters or appetisers is enough to make the event special and you can sample many different flavours and textures.

Spread yourself thin: At buffets, pile up your plate with salads (not the creamy ones). Steer clear of the baked dishes and ones with rich gravies. Choose the steamed or grilled fish, vegetables or chicken, or kababs. Serve yourself the roti and a dal, provided it is not a creamy one and give the rice or pulao a miss. Bhajjias and fried papads are a definite no-no! Do not make dessert your main dish! Go to the dessert table only if you know there is fresh fruit on offer, or else stay far from it so you are not tempted!

Drink to your health: Fresh lime soda without sugar and a pinch of salt is perfect. Fresh fruit juices with no sugar added or zero calorie aerated drinks taken occasionally are refreshing.

● ● ●

MASTER CHEF RECOMMENDS

Here are some tips to help you order foods that will help you stay on track.

INDIAN

Order: Plain dal, plain roti, vegetables without coconut, steamed or gravied pulses, tandoori chicken, paneer, vegetable or fish kababs (mop up the excess oil or ghee with a paper napkin), idli and other steamed dishes, fruit chaat.

Avoid: Deep-fried snacks (samosa, kachori), naan and other rich Indian breads, rich cashew nut, almond, khoya or cream-based gravies, tadka dal, butter chicken, payasam and kheer, kulfi, halwa, jalebi.

CONTINENTAL

Order: Grilled or steamed fish or chicken with steamed or boiled vegetables, fish, chicken or vegetable sizzlers (sauce on the side), baked potato without cheese, water ices, sorbets and fresh fruit desserts.

Avoid: Garlic bread, baked dishes in white or cheese sauce, deep- fried fish and chips, chicken kiev, chicken or fish pies, crumb or batter-fried chicken, quiche, caramel custard, soufflés and mousses, cheesecakes.

CHINESE

Order: Clear soups, steamed or stir-fried fish, chicken, tofu or vegetables, steamed rice, steamed wholewheat noodles with vegetables, fish or chicken, steamed momos. Choose lychees and fresh fruit for dessert – minus the ice cream.

Avoid: Spring rolls, fried wontons, thread paneer, sweet corn soups, sweet and sour dishes, fried noodles and fried rice, honey-fried noodles and date pancakes.

ITALIAN

Order: Wholewheat pasta, Italian tomato sauce, minestrone (soup), roasted or grilled vegetables with olive oil and herbs, grilled fish and chicken, thin-crust wholewheat pizzas with vegetables, fish or chicken toppings with minimum cheese, 1 or 2 wholewheat biscotti.

Avoid: Bruschetta, creamy or cheesy pasta sauces, cheese-filled pastas, pesto sauce, tiramisù, panna cotta.

THAI

Order: Hot and sour soups, som tam – green papaya salad, satay chicken, fish or vegetables without the peanut sauce, lettuce wraps stuffed with chicken, fish or vegetables.

Avoid: Thick creamy soups and curries with coconut milk, pad thai (stir-fried rice noodles), refined flour or rice flour wraps, dishes with plenty of peanuts.

MEDITERRANEAN/MIDDLE-EASTERN

Order: Mezze platters with pitta bread, hummus (chickpea dip), baba ganouj (eggplant dip), tabouleh (burghul salad), tzatkiki (cucumber and yogurt dip) fish or chicken shawarma in wholewheat pita, chicken or fish cooked in fresh tomato and herb sauce.

Avoid: Falafels (fried lentil patties), moussaka (baked mince and aubergine dish), baklava (sweet pastry) harissa (ground meat and wheat), maqlooba (chicken and rice).

HOME COOKING

Whatever the delights of eating out, you will have to admit there is nothing like good old ghar ka khana. Especially when you are trying to control what and how much you eat. While restaurant food is tasty and different from what you may normally eat at home, and require some amount of special skill and equipment to prepare, think of the advantages of eating healthy and hygienic food prepared at home. Not only can you control the amount of fat and sugar that goes into the food, you can choose the right combination of ingredients that will provide variety and flavour at a fraction of the cost.

One way of weaning yourself away from restaurant food is to cook it yourself in your kitchen. Master chef Sanjeev Kapoor has provided recipes for a number of restaurant quality dishes that can be replicated in your own kitchen. He has also suggested creative alternatives to give your favourites a makeover. The feeling of satisfaction you will experience will only motivate you to take charge of your own health and well being.

COOK SMART

Now that you have acquainted yourself with the principles of the diet and armed yourself with the Live Well Diets, it is time you put it all into practice. Here are some tips to optimise the nutritive value of what you choose to eat:

1. Do not peel the skins of fruit like apples and pears, and vegetables like cucumbers and tender gourds. They add fibre to your diet.

2. Add plenty of herbs and spices – you will hardly notice the absence of oil in your food.

3. Spray the pan with oil instead of pouring it in for shallow-frying.

4. Replace the fat in baked goods with apple purée or yogurt.

5. To thicken soups and gravies, purée cooked vegetables (especially bottle gourd or cauliflower), or lentils.

6. Seasoning (tadka): Use a small non-stick pan and use just a drop of oil if at all. Add the spices and stir them till they are coated with the oil and begin to roast and change colour.

7. To sauté (bhunao), grate or purée the onions, ginger and garlic and cook them without any oil in a non-stick pan till almost dry. Add a teaspoon of oil and brown the paste to remove the raw smell. Continue cooking as required.

8. Remove the skin and excess fat from chicken.

9. Use methods that require little oil and preserve the nutrients in the food such as steaming, poaching, grilling, stir-frying and microwave cooking.

MEAL MAKEOVERS

In addition to the recipes provided in the following pages, you can also make small changes to your regular home cooking to make it healthier.

Meal Makeovers	
Your Recipe	**Live Well Makeover**
Snacks	
Aloo Parantha	Replace potato with mooli, cabbage or cauliflower
Batata Poha	Replace potato with mixed vegetables and beaten rice with oats
Mayonnaise based dip with chips	Replace mayonnaise with yogurt and chips with raw vegetables
Plain rice idli/ upma	Replace rice with oats or other whole grains and add vegetables or leafy vegetables
Sev Puri	Moong chaat on roasted mini papad
Roti Wraps	Lettuce or cabbage leaf wraps

Sauces and Accompaniments	
Coriander and Coconut Chutney	Coriander and mint chutney
French Dressing	Omit the oil and use sugar substitute
Mayonnaise	Skimmed milk yogurt flavoured with mustard, sugar substitute, lime juice, salt and pepper. Add garlic to make aioli (garlic mayonnaise)
Fried Papad	Roasted or microwaved papad
White Sauce	Skimmed milk and puréed cauliflower
Sweet Sauces for desserts	Apple purée with vanilla or cinnamon
Mashed Potato	Replace most of the potato with cauliflower or pumpkin purée, omit butter, increase skimmed milk
Main Dishes	
Paneer Palak/ Matar Paneer	Replace paneer with soya nuggets or tofu
Chicken Curry	Add spinach, fenugreek (methi) or dill (suva) leaves to the gravy for a more nutritious meal
Chicken or Vegetable Stew	Thicken stew with puréed cauliflower
Fried chicken	Grilled or roast chicken
Mutton Kheema/ cubes	Soya granules/ chunks

EXCUSE ME!

So you have now reached the stage where you are about to begin to change your life. You are all pumped up and determined to focus on yourself – your health and lifestyle and to take charge of your well-being, keeping in mind all that has been discussed earlier.

There is just one last thing I want to share with you, and that is that every person who has entered the clinic has been filled with resolve and determination and well-motivated to begin with, and then poof! One day it all comes tumbling down!

Of course it takes courage and even more determination to pick oneself up again. And with encouragement and support they almost always do. But I thought I would share with you some of the reasons or excuses I have heard over these many years for giving up or stumbling, just so you can take heart, and at the same time prevent yourself from falling into the same trap!

I am stressed out:

This one is as old as the hills and as mentioned before can be the reason for any bad behaviour! Just know that the cream puff that you just ate will leave you feeling great for about half an hour and you will crash back again and begin to beat yourself up all over again.

Solution: If you are stressed out take a deep breath, do a few pranayams or drink some green or black tea while you listen to some soothing music. You will feel calmer and more relaxed and best of all you will still stay on the diet wagon!

I have PMS:

Pre-menstrual syndrome is another excuse often used to justify a binge, but overeating can only exacerbate the bloated feeling.

Solution: Some TLC – or tender love and care which, if nobody is around to provide, you can treat yourself to a hot shower, a hot water bottle, some soothing music which will comfort you. Refer to Frequently Asked Questions (page 173) for more solutions.

I have been so good what's the harm if I pig out this once?

It is hard to stay on a rigorous plan which provides you with little choice or variety. But, you should have no problem with The Live Well Diet as it allows two days a week when you can eat all the foods you enjoy in moderation. And, should you fail, the diet provides for recovery and course correction. Also beware of rewarding yourself with food – it could become a habit that is self-defeating.

Solution: Enjoy and indulge yourself on Plan A and, should you trip up, make a quick recovery by following Plan C the very next day. And reward yourself for your 'good behaviour' with a membership in a gym, a visit to a spa, or that fitness equipment or outfit you have had your eye on.

I have already messed up my diet for the day, so what is the point of continuing? I may as well forget about it for the rest of the day or even week!

Following any plan is bound to have pitfalls and stumbles. Remember it is not whether you fall but if you pick yourself up. The fact is that you have come so far, you have shown you care enough about yourself and want to LIVE WELL. Just because you have eaten that plate of biryani doesn't mean you have to eat the gulab jamun and ice cream and the phirni too!

Solution: Stop yourself from falling further. Repeat the Live Well Diet C—the Control Diet the next day to make up for the biryani!

I have only one life to live – so why should I spend it giving up all the things I love?

The fact is you do have only one life to live and so why would you want to shorten or ruin the quality of your life by neglecting your health and asking for trouble? Living well is not living a life of deprivation, but allowing yourself to enjoy it to the fullest by making a few changes in your lifestyle and food choices. You will not only live better and longer, you will also free yourself of stress, look better, have increased self-confidence, and the good health to show it all off!

Solution: Make the wise choices that the Live Well Diet offers and lead a long and happy, healthy and fulfilled life!

I hate to waste food:

I find it difficult to stay on my diet as I invariably eat up what the kids have left on their plates. Besides, as others are not on the diet there is always so much food left over so how can I throw it away? I have to cook especially for myself and it seems to be such a waste.

Solution: Try and get your family to eat the food that is suggested by the Live Well Diet. There are so many options available and the recipes are for a family of four. You will be able to provide healthy and tasty meals for everyone and you will not feel left out. Even while you are on the diet resist the temptation to finish up leftovers and keep in mind that in the end the price you will pay in terms of poor health will be much higher than the few scraps that you have filled yourself up with!

I have done half an hour extra of exercise so I have earned that burger!

That is a good excuse to use once in a while but it can soon become a habit and you will find yourself on the slippery slope to your old self!

Solution: Try to stay clear of fatty and sugary foods as they are addictive and you can soon become hooked again!

I hardly eat anything and I am not losing any weight. I might as well give up the diet. The chances are you are not really following the diet as prescribed. We sometimes have a mistaken perception of what and how much we eat. Fill in your food diary and record every day. It will give you a good idea of where you are going wrong and what you need to do to stay on course. You may even have reached a plateau, which means your weight has remained steady at a certain level.

Solution: Faithfully and accurately fill in your food diary and if you have reached a plateau, vary your diet and increase your physical activity to kick start your stalled metabolism once again. (see Frequently Asked Questions (page 173))

I CAN is 100 times more important than IQ.

— unknown

NO PAIN NO GAIN!

While you are on the Live Well Programme you will find many reasons to feel sorry for yourself. The absence of your favourite foods can send you into a depression! You watch other people filling up their plates at a buffet and feel deprived. You begin to hate birthday parties as there will definitely be chocolate cake and other goodies that you simply cannot resist.

Stop whining and playing the victim. The Live Well Diet offers you so many choices and alternatives, and so many solutions to every possible challenge that you are well armed to cope with any and every situation. All the excuses to not-diet or exercise have been properly dealt with so with the Live Well Diet you no longer have a reason to put on a long face and feel sorry for yourself. The proactive and flexible programme lends itself easily to sensible adaptation, so you need never feel the pain of deprivation. In any case, no pain, no gain. A little discomfort will only help you appreciate the new you!

It IS about YOU

Finally it comes down to this – YOU are in charge of your own health and well-being and you should not surrender that power to anything or anyone else. In this book, you have the knowledge, you have the tools, and you have the real life testimony of many who have benefited from the diet which has given them better health, self-confidence, peace of mind and a new vision of their own best life. You can be there too if you decide to make your well-being the focus of your attention and care.

Positive thinking, motivation, resolve... call it what you will – draw on your inner strengths and **Just Do It!** Seize the opportunity and make a promise to yourself that you will love and value yourself enough to make the changes you need to really LIVE WELL.

● ● ●

THE LIVE WELL PLEDGE

*I **Love** Myself*

*I Want To **Improve** The Way I Look and Feel*

*I **Value** My Health and My Well-Being*

*I **Eat** Foods that Nourish and Heal My Body*

*I Drink **Water** And Liquids that Refresh and
Cleanse My System*

*I **Exercise** to be Fit and Active*

*I Make Time for **Leisure** and Relaxation*

*I Embrace **Life** and Live Well*

● ● ●

MY STORY } Kiran Bagchandka
Homemaker

IF I CAN, ANYONE CAN!

I have always suffered from health issues. I moved to Mumbai from Kolkata after marriage 15 years ago. I used to suffer from severe osteoporosis and was even bed-ridden for 3 years. For 10 years I was treated with allopathic medicines without any real relief. I also suffered from thyroid problems and was treated by an endocrinologist.

The steroids prescribed increased my weight to 93 kg! I was very bloated and could not do any exercise. I tried several weight loss programmes but could not get any relief or success. I used to feel very depressed as I had tried so many ways to lose weight

I then heard about Dr Davare's programme. On my first attempt at following the diet and exercise plan I lost 13 kg and my weight came down to 83 kg. Unfortunately I did not maintain the diet and once again I went back to 93 kg. I was so disheartened.

I tried the diet again and this time I was determined to lose the weight and to stay on the programme. If I had lost weight once, I could do it again.

My perseverance paid off and after two and a half years on the diet my weight has gradually reduced to 56 kg! These two and a half years have been a beautiful journey for me, especially as I kept steadily losing weight. I now maintain a weight of around 62 kg.

I try to be as disciplined as possible even when I travel, and if I put on a few kg I am not happy until I lose them and get back to normal. I follow the programme religiously and exercise regularly. I walk every day for 1 hour 10 minutes. I started by walking 4 km then slowly increased it to 5 km and now I walk 6-8 km without any effort.

The best part of the whole programme is that my skin does not sag and my body is toned up and firm. I put this down to my regular eating habits, eating the right foods and exercise. Before, I used to eat any and everything and at any time; today I chose what is best for my body and health. Seeing how I benefited, my family too has become conscious of their food choices and habits.

I also feel so happy and liberated now that I can wear trendy clothes. I had stopped wearing jeans and used to hide myself under a stole; now I wear jeans with confidence. I am also so much more energetic – I used to feel lazy to leave the house. My life used to be so dull, but now I am bubbling with energy. Now that I have lost the weight my osteoporosis is also under control and my whole life has changed.

All I have to say is that if a hopeless case like me could stay on the programme and change her life, anyone can!

● ● ●

THE LIVE WELL DIET DAILY RECORD

	Day :	Date :	Weight:

FOOD AND BEVERAGE INTAKE

Time	Quantity	Food/Beverage	Comments

ESSENTIAL DAILY INTAKE

Food	Beverages	Miscellaneous
3 whole fruits	2-3 litres water	2-3 teaspoons oil
1 bowl (1½ katori)/ 300 ml vegetable soup	1 litre lime water	3-4 pieces dried fruit or nuts
1 bowl (1½ katori) or 1 plate salad	2 – 2 ½ cups milk	Vitamins
1 bowl (1½ katori) cooked vegetables	1 glass coconut water	Folic Acid
1 bowl (1½ katori) cooked leafy vegetables	3-4 cups green tea	Calcium
1 bowl (1½ katori) cooked dal/chicken/fish	1 glass vegetable juice	Vitamin B12
½ - 1 katori yoghurt	1 glass buttermilk	Vitamin C/E

DAILY EXERCISE

Type	Time	Duration	Comments
Walk			
Pranayam			
Suryanamaskar/ Stretching			
Other			

I JUST STARTED LOVING THE DIFFERENCE

To start with I had developed a complete wrong eating pattern during my college days due to late night studying and by staying outdoors most of the day. I used to eat anything and everything available at my dinner table. The word 'exercise' at that time, was like Greek and Latin to me. I just used to sit, eat and sleep the whole day. And hence over a period of time, I gained 25 kg. I could not even afford to wear any kind of western clothes because I looked like a disaster in those outfits. I had to switch to wearing only Indian salwar kameez that fit me and made me not look quite awful.

I decided to join Dr Davare the day I realised that it was high time I did something about my weight, because I had already started looking like a 35 year old lady at the age of 20. People often mistook me to be my mother. That was extremely embarrassing.

I had tried a couple of diets earlier, but they didn't really help me. I lost and again regained weight within 6 months, as soon as I returned to my old routine eating habits. And by losing and gaining and losing again the cycle just went on reducing my immunity. My hair became thin and with every passing day my frustration kept on increasing. I had reached a point wherein I just felt giving up on weight loss.

The Live Well Diet on paper looked extremely difficult and impossible at first glance but with each passing day it just made me feel better and better. I initially felt that I was being made to starve but then I realised that it's not starvation but my craving for wrong food items that was making me long for food. Initially walking was a task for me, but gradually I got accustomed to it as I realised that it just helped me and my body look better. The diet made sure that I carry my food wherever I go so that I am not tempted to cheat on my diet. It just made me more conscious and vigilant about myself and my health.

The diet I feel just turned my eating habits... I started becoming more and more sensible about putting food in my stomach. I realised that we have a stomach and not a garbage bin where you can dump any trash. 1½ hours of walks and 4 litres of water a day and the diet are now like a bible to me. The diet is so healthy and so filling that I don't even feel hungry or a craving to eat anything else. The diet has made me so weight conscious and I think 10 times before putting any rubbish in my mouth. Unhealthy food is just not on my list.

I didn't experience any kind of hair loss. My skin with each passing day was glowing more and more. From within, I used to feel so clean and healthy that I felt like I should continue eating this diet food lifelong. My energy levels have increased incredibly. Earlier I could not even walk for 45 minutes and today I can walk for 2 hours at a stretch. Earlier I couldn't even drink 2 glasses of water in a day and today I have 4 litres of water daily! I have started loving this difference in my lifestyle, my looks and above all my confidence. My confidence has increased incredibly with this weight loss and better looks.

Live Well Diet Recipes

Cooking done with care is an act of love.
– Craig Claiborne

Ban the bland and boycott the boring

This section is chock-a-block with great food recipes to help you produce the best and tastiest food within the guidelines of the Live Well Diet.

There is no dearth of variety here, rather, there are many delicious options for you to create in your kitchen so that you can enjoy the food that your diet prescribes. No more bland and boring diet food but a banquet of mouth-watering dishes from all over India and abroad that will have you wondering whether you are on a diet at all!

There are indications at the end of each recipe about the diet that it is most appropriate for: Diet A- The All Foods Diet, Diet B – The Basic Diet, Diet C – The Control Diet.

While each recipe serves 4 persons, the recommended portion sizes have been mentioned so you know exactly what and how much you are expected to eat.

Happy Cooking!

Sanjeev Kapoor

BEVERAGES

AAM KA ABSHOLA

INGREDIENTS

500 grams unripe green mangoes

3-4 sprigs fresh mint leaves

1 lemon

8 level teaspoons sugar substitute (sucralose)

½ level teaspoon rock salt

4-5 black peppercorns, crushed

1 teaspoon roasted cumin powder

Chilled club soda for serving

METHOD

Chill serving glasses in a refrigerator.

Wash, boil, peel mangoes and extract the pulp.

Reserve a few mint leaves for garnishing and purée the rest. Cut the lemons into round slices.

Combine mango pulp, sugar substitute, rock salt and two cups of water in a non-stick pan.

Cook on high heat for one minute. Add crushed peppercorns, roasted cumin powder and puréed mint leaves. Stir and cook for two to three minutes.

Remove from heat and pass the mixture through a sieve. Cool.

Pour some of the mango mixture into the glasses.

Top up with club soda. Garnish with mint leaves and a slice of lemon and serve chilled.

{ Diet Plans: **A B C**
Portion: **1 glass**

ALOE VERA JUICE

INGREDIENTS

2 cups aloe vera juice

A few basil leaves

1 inch ginger

METHOD

Combine aloe vera juice, basil leaves and ginger in a blender jar. Add two cups water and blend well. Strain and serve chilled.

Recipe courtesy Dr Sarita Davare

Diet Plans: **A B C**
Portion: **1 glass**

AMLA JUICE

INGREDIENTS

8 Indian gooseberries (amla)

2 inches ginger

4 teaspoons cumin seeds

METHOD

Combine Indian gooseberries, ginger and cumin seeds in a blender jar. Add five cups water and blend well. Strain and serve chilled.

Recipe courtesy Dr Sarita Davare

Diet Plans: **A B C**
Portion: **1 glass**

BEET JUICE

2 beetroots, roughly chopped

6-8 fresh mint leaves

2 teaspoons cumin seeds

METHOD

Combine beetroots, mint leaves, cumin seeds in a blender jar. Add four cups water and blend well. Strain and serve chilled.

Recipe courtesy Dr Sarita Davare

Diet Plans: **A B C**
Portion: **¾ glass**

DOODHI JUICE

INGREDIENTS

2 cups chopped bottle gourd (doodhi)

10-12 fresh mint leaves

6-8 basil leaves

2 inches ginger

8 drops lemon juice

¼ teaspoon black pepper powder

2 teaspoons cumin seeds

METHOD

Combine bottle gourd, mint leaves, basil leaves, ginger, lemon juice, pepper powder and cumin seeds in a blender jar. Add five cups of water and blend well. Strain and serve chilled.

Recipe courtesy Dr Sarita Davare

Diet Plans: **A B C**
Portion: **1 glass**

CARROT JUICE

INGREDIENTS

4 large red carrots (gajar),
roughly chopped

METHOD

Place the carrots in a blender jar and add five cups water. Blend well. Strain and serve chilled.

Recipe courtesy Dr Sarita Davare

{ Diet Plans: **A B C**
Portion: **1 glass**

CUCUMBER JUICE

INGREDIENTS

8 medium cucumbers (kakdi), roughly chopped
¼ teaspoon black pepper powder
2 teaspoons cumin seeds

METHOD

Combine cucumbers, pepper powder and cumin seeds in a blender jar. Add five cups water and blend well.

Strain and serve chilled.

Recipe courtesy Dr Sarita Davare

***Note:** Avoid if you suffer from flatulence.*

{ Diet Plans: **A B C**
Portion: **1 glass**

MASALA CHAAS

INGREDIENTS

2 cups skimmed milk yogurt (dahi)

1 green chilli, chopped

1 teaspoon roasted cumin powder

4 teaspoons chopped fresh coriander

½ level teaspoon black salt

Fresh mint leaves, to garnish

METHOD

Whisk the yogurt well, and gradually whisk in about two cups water. Add the green chilli, roasted cumin powder, chopped fresh coriander and black salt. Mix thoroughly.

Serve chilled, garnished with mint leaves.

Diet Plans: **A B C**
Portion: **1 glass**

MELON MAGIC

INGREDIENTS

½ medium ripe musk melon, cubed

2 cups fresh orange juice

2 tablespoons lemon juice

2 teaspoons sugar substitute (sucralose)

12-16 ice cubes, crushed

METHOD

Place crushed ice cubes in a blender jar and add the melon. Pour in the orange juice, lemon juice and sugar substitute. Blend till slushy. Pour into individual chilled glasses.

Serve immediately.

Diet Plans: **A B C**
Portion: **1 glass**

MIXED VEGETABLE JUICE

INGREDIENTS

4 small tomatoes, chopped
4 small carrots, chopped
4 small beetroots, chopped

2 inches ginger
4 teaspoons lemon juice
½ level teaspoon table salt

METHOD

Combine tomatoes, carrots, beetroots, ginger, lemon juice and salt in a blender jar. Add five cups of water and blend well.

Strain and serve chilled.

Recipe courtesy Dr Sarita Davare

{ Diet Plans: **A B C**
Portion: **1 glass**

ADRAK NIMBU PANI

INGREDIENTS

1 tablespoon ginger juice
4 tablespoons lemon juice
1 medium lemon, sliced
1 teaspoon roasted cumin powder

¼ level teaspoon black salt
¼ level teaspoon table salt
8 level teaspoons sugar substitute (sucralose)
Ice cubes, as required

METHOD

Mix together ginger juice, lemon juice, roasted cumin powder, black salt, salt, and sugar substitute in a large jug.

Add six cups of water and stir.

Place ice cubes in individual glasses and pour in the ginger-lemon mixture.

Serve, garnished with a slice of lemon fixed on the rim.

{ Diet Plans: **A B C**
  Portion: **1 glass**

PALAK JUICE

INGREDIENTS

30-35 fresh spinach leaves (palak)

1½ cups chopped fresh coriander

1 small green capsicum, chopped

10-12 fresh mint leaves

2 inches ginger

4 teaspoons lemon juice

½ level teaspoon table salt

METHOD

Combine spinach leaves, chopped coriander, capsicum, fresh mint, ginger, lemon juice and salt in a blender jar. Add one cup water and blend well.

Strain and serve chilled.

Recipe courtesy Dr Sarita Davare

{ Diet Plans: **A B C**
  Portion: **1 glass**

PANI PURI PANI

INGREDIENTS

4 cups chopped
fresh coriander

1 cup chopped fresh
mint leaves

8 drops of lemon juice

2 inches ginger

4 teaspoons pani puri masala

4 teaspoons coriander-
cumin powder

½ level teaspoon table salt

4 green chillies, chopped

METHOD

Combine chopped coriander, mint leaves, lemon juice, ginger, pani puri masala, coriander-cumin powder, salt and green chillies in a blender jar. Add four cups water and blend well.

Strain and serve chilled.

Recipe courtesy Dr Sarita Davare

{ Diet Plans: **A B C**
  Portion: **1 glass**

TOMATO JUICE

INGREDIENTS

8 medium tomatoes, roughly chopped

¼ teaspoon black pepper powder

2 teaspoons cumin seeds

METHOD

Combine tomatoes, pepper powder, and cumin seeds in a blender jar.

Add five cups of water and blend well.

Strain and serve chilled.

Recipe courtesy Dr Sarita Davare

{ Diet Plans: **A B C**
Portion: **1 glass**

VAGHARELI CHAAS

INGREDIENTS

1¼ cups skimmed milk yogurt

¼ teaspoon oil

¼ teaspoon cumin seeds

2 inches ginger, chopped

2-3 green chillies, chopped

8-10 curry leaves

1 tablespoon chopped fresh coriander

1 tablespoon chopped fresh mint leaves

½ level teaspoon table salt

METHOD

Whisk yogurt with three cups of water till smooth.

Heat oil in a non-stick pan and add cumin seeds. When they change colour, add ginger, green chillies and curry leaves and sauté.

Add the fried spices to the yogurt and mix.

Add chopped coriander, mint leaves and salt. Mix well and serve at room temperature.

{ Diet Plans: **A B C**
Portion: **1 glass**

CARROT AND TOMATO SMOOTHIE

INGREDIENTS

8 medium carrots, cut into 1-inch cubes
12 medium tomatoes, quartered
1 celery stalk, chopped
½ level teaspoon table salt
1 teaspoon black pepper powder
4 tablespoons lemon juice
Ice cubes, as required

METHOD

Place the carrots and tomatoes in the freezer till completely frozen. Place the frozen tomatoes in a blender jar and blend for a few seconds.

Add frozen carrot cubes and blend again. Add celery, salt and pepper powder and blend till smooth. Add ice cubes and lemon juice and blend for a few seconds.

Serve chilled in individual stemmed glasses.

Diet Plans: **A B C**
Portion: **1 glass**

ICED PAPAYA TEA

INGREDIENTS

900 ml freshly brewed hot tea
16 tablespoons chopped ripe papaya cubes
Crushed ice, as required

METHOD

Pour tea into serving jug and add papaya cubes. Chill thoroughly. Pour over crushed ice in glasses.

Serve immediately.

Diet Plans: **A B C**
Portion: **1 glass**

BREAKFAST

BHAJNEE THALIPEETH

INGREDIENTS

3 cups Bhajnee Flour
(recipe below)
1 level teaspoon table salt

½ teaspoon turmeric powder
1 medium onion, chopped
6 teaspoons oil

METHOD

Place bhajnee flour in a bowl with the salt, turmeric powder, chopped onion and two teaspoons of oil. Add water, a little at a time, and make a soft dough.

Divide the dough into eight equal portions. Flatten each portion into a quarter-inch thick, four to five-inch round on a dampened banana leaf, or thick polythene sheet. Make a hole in the centre of each thalipeeth.

Heat a non-stick tawa, and spread one-fourth teaspoon of oil over it. Transfer thalipeeth carefully onto the tawa. Drizzle one-fourth teaspoon of oil around the sides and cook on low heat for one minute.

Turn the thalipeeth over and cook the other side for one minute, or till crisp and golden brown. Make more in a similar manner. Serve hot with yogurt.

Note: *To make bhajnee flour, dry-roast separately 1 cup wholewheat flour, 1 cup rice, 2 cups sorghum (jowar), 2 cups pearl millet (bajra), ¾ cup split Bengal gram (chana dal), ¾ cup skinless split black gram (dhuli urad dal), and ½ cup coriander seeds. Cool, mix and grind to a fine powder. Bhajnee flour can be stored for up to one month.*

Diet Plans: **A B**
Portion: **1½**
thalipeeth

EGG WHITE OMELETTE WITH MUSHROOMS AND CAPSICUM

INGREDIENTS

8 eggs

8 medium fresh button mushrooms, chopped

1 small green capsicum, seeded and chopped

4 teaspoons oil

2 small onions, chopped

½ teaspoon table salt

½ teaspoon white pepper powder

METHOD

To make one omelette, break two eggs and separate the yolks from the whites.

Heat one teaspoon oil in a shallow non-stick pan. Add one-fourth portion of chopped onions, mushrooms and capsicums and sauté.

Place the egg whites in a bowl, add one-fourth teaspoon salt and whisk.

Add this to the pan and rotate the pan to spread the eggs. Sprinkle a little white pepper powder.

Flip the omelette over and cook the other side too.

Serve immediately. Make more omelettes in a similar manner.

VARIATIONS:

1. **Spinach Omelette: Omit the mushrooms and capsicums and add chopped spinach.**

2. **Masala Omelette: Add chopped tomatoes, onion and coriander.**

{ Diet Plans: **A B C**
Portion: **1 omelette using 2 egg whites**

ENERGY DOSA

INGREDIENTS

¼ cup rice flour

¼ cup wholewheat flour (atta)

¼ cup soya flour

¼ cup finger millet (nachni) flour

Buttermilk, as required

½ level teaspoon table salt

2 tablespoons chopped fresh coriander

2 green chillies, chopped

4 teaspoons oil

METHOD

Mix together the rice, wheat, soya and millet flour with the buttermilk to make a smooth batter.

Add the salt, chopped coriander and green chillies, and mix well. Let the batter rest for about fifteen minutes.

Heat a thick non-stick tawa or frying pan. Add two drops of oil and wipe the tawa clean with a piece of wet muslin.

Add one-fourth teaspoon of oil to the tawa; pour half a ladleful of batter and spread it to a thin three-inch round. Drizzle one-fourth teaspoon oil all around. When the underside is cooked, flip the dosa and cook the other side.

Make more dosa in a similar manner.

Note: If you do not have soya flour, you can replace it with gram flour or sorghum flour.

Makes 4 dosai

Diet Plans: **A B**
Portion: **2 dosai**

GREEN PEA AND CARROT DALIA

INGREDIENTS

½ cup shelled green peas

2 small carrots, diced

1 cup broken wheat (dalia)

1½ teaspoons rice bran oil

1 teaspoon cumin seeds

1 small onion, chopped

1 medium tomato, seeded and chopped

¾ level teaspoon table salt

2 tablespoons chopped fresh coriander

METHOD

Soak dalia in two cups of water for thirty minutes. Drain.

Heat the oil in a pressure cooker and add the cumin seeds. As they begin to change colour, add the onion and sauté till lightly coloured.

Add the green peas, carrots and tomato and sauté for one minute. Add the dalia and three cups of water; add salt.

Bring the mixture to a boil, seal the pressure cooker with the lid and cook till the pressure is released twice (two whistles).

Sprinkle with chopped coriander and serve at once

{ Diet Plan: **A**
Portion: **1 bowl**
(1½ katori)

FRUITY YOGURT WITH CEREAL TOPPING

INGREDIENTS

2 medium apples, cubed

8-10 cherries, stoned

1 cup skimmed milk
yogurt, whisked

1 teaspoon raisins (kishmish)

3-4 walnut kernels or
almonds, chopped

4 tablespoons muesli, toasted

METHOD

Combine apples and cherries and refrigerate until ready to serve.

Just before serving, mix chilled fruit, yogurt, raisins and nuts.

Spoon into individual bowls, sprinkle toasted muesli over and
serve at once.

Note: *You can use any fruits permitted by the diet.*

Diet Plans: **A B, without
muesli A B C**
Portion: **1 bowl (1½ katori)**

HOT AND SOUR IDLI

INGREDIENTS

1 cup split pigeon peas (arhar dal/toovar dal)

1 cup rice

6 dried red chillies, broken

2 tablespoons Tamarind Pulp (page 334)

1 tablespoon grated jaggery

A generous pinch of asafoetida (hing)

½ teaspoon turmeric powder

½ level teaspoon table salt

1 tablespoon rice bran oil, for greasing

2 small onions, chopped

METHOD

Soak the split pigeon peas and the rice separately in three cups of water for four to six hours.

Drain and set aside. Do not mix. Grind the red chillies and tamarind to a fine paste. Grind dal smooth and rice coarsely separately. Mix them thoroughly.

Add the red chilli-tamarind paste, grated jaggery, asafoetida, turmeric powder and salt and mix well. Set aside for four to five hours to ferment.

Lightly grease the idli moulds. Heat a little water in a steamer. Pour the batter into the moulds, sprinkle the onions on top and steam for about fifteen to twenty minutes or till done.

Serve hot with coriander chutney.

{ Diet Plans: **A B C**
Portion: **2-3 idli**

MOONG DAL UTTAPAM

INGREDIENTS

1 cup skinless split green gram (dhuli moong dal), soaked

¾ level teaspoon table salt

¼ teaspoon baking powder

¼ teaspoon turmeric powder

4 teaspoons oil

Topping

1 large green capsicum, seeded and diced

1 small tomato, seeded and diced

1 small onion, diced

4-5 green chillies, chopped

Tomato ketchup, to serve

METHOD

Drain the split gram and grind it to a coarse paste.

Transfer into a bowl and add salt, baking powder and turmeric powder. Mix well and set aside.

In a separate bowl, mix the capsicum, tomato, onion and green chillies.

Heat a non-stick tawa and pour a small ladleful of the dal batter and spread it evenly into a round, taking care that it is not too thin.

Drizzle one-fourth teaspoon oil around the sides.

Spread some of the topping over it. Cook for a minute and turn the dosa over.

Drizzle one-fourth teaspoon oil around the sides and allow the other side to cook till golden. Serve hot with tomato ketchup.

{ Diet Plans: **A B C**
Portion: **1 medium or 2 small uttapam**

PROTEIN RICH POHA

INGREDIENTS

2 cups brown
beaten rice (poha)
½ cup sprouted brown gram
(matki/moth), blanched
1 tablespoon oil
½ teaspoon cumin seeds
1 inch ginger, grated
3 green chillies, halved

6-8 curry leaves
2 medium onions, chopped
½ teaspoon turmeric powder
¾ level teaspoon table salt
1 tablespoon lemon juice
2 tablespoons chopped
fresh coriander

METHOD

Place the beaten rice in a colander and pour three to four cups of water over to moisten them. Drain and set aside.

Heat the oil in a non-stick pan and add cumin seeds. When they begin to change colour, add the ginger, green chillies, curry leaves, onions, turmeric powder and sprouted gram and sauté for five to seven minutes, till the onions soften.

Add the beaten rice and toss over medium heat till heated through. Add salt and lemon juice and toss well to mix.

Serve at once, garnished with chopped coriander.

{ Diet Plan: **A**
Portion: **1 bowl**
(1½ katori)

MOONG TOAST

INGREDIENTS

1 cup whole green gram (sabut moong), soaked
8 slices wholewheat or multigrain bread
¾ level teaspoon table salt
5 teaspoons olive oil
1 bay leaf
3-4 cloves
½ teaspoon cumin seeds
12 curry leaves
½ teaspoon turmeric powder
½ teaspoon red chilli powder
1 tablespoon chopped fresh coriander
Tomato ketchup, to serve

METHOD

Place the gram, five cups of water and salt in a deep non-stick pan. When the water begins to boil, lower the heat and simmer until the gram is completely cooked and soft. You can also pressure-cook the gram till the pressure is released four times (four whistles). Drain and reserve the stock for use in some other recipe.

Heat one teaspoon oil in a non-stick pan; add the bay leaf and cloves and sauté for ten seconds. Add the cumin seeds, and when they begin to change colour, add the curry leaves and sauté for ten to fifteen seconds.

Add the turmeric powder and chilli powder, and stir again. Add the boiled green gram and salt, if required, and cook for two minutes. Add the chopped coriander and mix well.

Place four slices of bread on the worktop and spread the green gram mixture evenly on them. Cover each topped slice with another slice.

Spread a little olive oil on the outer surfaces of the sandwiches and grill or toast them in a sandwich toaster till crisp and golden on both sides. Serve immediately with tomato ketchup.

Chef's tip: You can use the reserved moong stock in a soup, or to knead wholewheat flour to make roti. Healthy and tasty!

Diet Plan: **B**

Portion: **1 whole sandwich or 2 triangles**

RAYALSEEMA PESARETTU
Spicy Green Gram Pancakes

INGREDIENTS

1 cup whole green gram (sabut moong), soaked

1 medium onion, chopped

1 inch ginger, chopped

4 green chillies, chopped

4 dried red chillies

5-6 black peppercorns, crushed

½ teaspoon cumin seeds, crushed

¼ cup chopped fresh coriander

10-12 curry leaves, chopped

1 tablespoon rice flour

1 level teaspoon table salt

4 teaspoons oil

Chutney or Sambhar (page 322), to serve

METHOD

Drain and grind the gram along with onion, ginger, green and dried chillies.

Mix in crushed peppercorns, cumin seeds, chopped coriander; curry leaves, rice flour and salt.

Heat a non-stick tawa or a dosa griddle; brush with two drops of oil. Pour a ladleful of batter on to the tawa and spread with the back of the ladle, to make a six inch round thin dosa.

Pour one-fourth teaspoon oil around the edges, cover with a deep lid and cook for two to three minutes on medium heat. Turn the dosa over, drizzle one-fourth teaspoon oil around and cook the other side for a few minutes or till golden and crisp.

Serve hot with chutney or sambhar.

Chef's Tip: Traditionally pesarettu is very spicy, but you can reduce the number of chillies to suit your taste.

{ Diet Plan: **A**
Portion: **2 pesarettu**

VEGETABLE RAWA UPMA

INGREDIENTS

1½ cups semolina (rawa/sooji)

1 medium carrot, cut into small cubes

6-8 French beans, cut into small pieces

¼ cup shelled green peas

1 green capsicum, cut into small pieces

2 tablespoons oil

½ teaspoon mustard seeds

2 dried red chillies

2 teaspoons split black gram (dhuli urad dal)

10-12 curry leaves

4 green chillies, chopped

1 medium onion, chopped

1 inch ginger, chopped

1 level teaspoon table salt

¼ teaspoon asafoetida (hing)

1 tablespoon lemon juice

METHOD

Roast the semolina in a dry non-stick kadai without browning, remove and cool.

Heat oil in a non-stick kadai; add mustard seeds, stir-fry till they splutter. Add dried chillies, black gram, curry leaves and green chillies. Add onion and sauté for a few seconds.

Add carrot, French beans and green peas and cook on low heat till the vegetables are tender. Sprinkle water to avoid scorching. Add the capsicum and cook for two minutes. Add the ginger, salt and asafoetida. Mix well.

Pour four cups of hot water into the non-stick kadai and bring to a boil. Add roasted semolina, stirring continuously, to prevent lump forming.

Cook for three to four minutes on medium heat, stirring continuously. Stir in lemon juice. Remove from heat and leave covered for 5 minutes. Serve hot.

Diet Plans: **A, with Oat Sooji Plan B**
Portion: **1 bowl (1½ katori)**

WHOLEMEAL, OAT AND CINNAMON PANCAKES

INGREDIENTS

1 cup wholewheat flour

¼ cup oatmeal

½ teaspoon cinnamon powder

2 tablespoons sugar substitute (sucralose)

¼ teaspoon baking powder

¼ teaspoon soda bicarbonate

1½ cups buttermilk

Maple syrup or honey, optional

METHOD

Place wholewheat flour in a bowl. Add oats, sucralose and mix. Add baking powder, soda bicarbonate, cinnamon powder and mix.

Add buttermilk gradually and whisk continuously so that there are no lumps. The consistency should not be too thin.

Heat a non-stick frying pan on low heat. Pour a ladleful of batter into the pan and swirl to let it spread around the pan. Cook till the underside is done.

Flip over and cook till the other side is done. Similarly make the rest of the pancakes.

Serve hot with maple syrup or with honey if desired.

Diet Plans: **A B**
Portion: **1½ pancakes**

OAT AND MIXED FLOUR ONION CHEELA

INGREDIENTS

½ cup rolled oats

2 cups finger millet (nachni) flour

¼ cup wholewheat flour (atta)

2-3 spring onions, chopped

6-7 spring onion green stalks, chopped

¾ teaspoon ginger paste

2 green chillies, chopped

¾ teaspoon cumin seeds

Salt to taste

4 teaspoons oil for shallow-frying

METHOD

Mix together the oats, finger millet and wholewheat flour in a bowl. Add sufficient water to make a smooth batter of pouring consistency. Cover and set aside to rest for half an hour.

Add the spring onions, spring onion greens, ginger paste, green chillies, cumin seeds and salt to taste and mix well.

Heat a non-stick tawa and lightly grease it. When moderately hot, wipe it clean with a cloth.

Pour one ladleful of batter on the tawa and spread it with the back of the ladle as thinly as possible into a round.

Cook for a while and flip it over. Drizzle few drops of oil around and cook on both sides till golden brown.

Serve hot with chutney.

{ Diet Plans: **A B**
Portion: **2 small cheele**

KANDE POHE WITH OATS

INGREDIENTS

4 medium onions, chopped
2 cups brown beaten rice (poha), thick variety
1 cup rolled oats
Salt to taste
½ teaspoon sugar
2 tablespoons oil
1 tablespoon roasted split Bengal gram
1 teaspoon mustard seeds
1 teaspoon cumin seeds
A pinch of asafoetida (hing)
6-7 curry leaves
4 green chillies, chopped
½ teaspoon turmeric powder
¼ teaspoon red chilli powder
½ medium potato, cut into ½-inch cubes
2 tablespoons boiled green peas
1 teaspoon lemon juice
2 tablespoons chopped fresh coriander

METHOD

Place oats and beaten rice in a colander and wash under running water. The flakes should be moist but not mashed. Drain well, add salt and sugar and toss lightly and set aside. Heat the oil in a non-stick kadai; add roasted gram and sauté till they are lightly browned. Drain on absorbent paper.

Add mustard seeds to the oil remaining in the kadai, and when they begin to splutter add cumin seeds, asafoetida and curry leaves and sauté for a few seconds.

Add onions and continue to sauté till onions turn light brown. Add green chillies and sauté for half a minute. Add the turmeric powder and chilli powder and stir well. Add potato, stir and continue to cook till potato is tender. Add the roasted gram and green peas and stir. Add oats and poha and stir lightly. Reduce heat, cover the pan and cook till the oats and poha are heated through. Add lemon juice and stir lightly.

Transfer the mixture into a serving bowl, garnish with chopped coriander and serve hot.

{ Diet Plans: **A B**
Portion: **1 bowl**
(**1½ katori**)

PALAK DHOKLA

INGREDIENTS

1 large bunch fresh spinach leaves, trimmed, blanched and puréed

1 cup split pigeon peas (arhar dal/toovar dal), soaked for 4 hours

2 cups skimmed milk yogurt

3 green chillies, chopped

¾ level teaspoon table salt

1 teaspoon sugar

¼ teaspoon asafoetida (hing)

1 teaspoon fruit salt

1 tablespoon lemon juice

2 teaspoons oil + for greasing

METHOD

Drain the split pigeon peas and place in a blender with the yogurt. Blend together to smooth paste. Transfer into a deep bowl.

Add the green chillies, spinach purée, salt, sugar and asafoetida and mix well.

Grease the dhokla plates lightly. Heat sufficient water in the steamer pot.

Mix the fruit salt and the lemon juice and add to the batter and mix. Add two teaspoons of oil and mix.

Pour the batter into the dhokla plates, place on a stand in the steamer. Cover with a lid and steam for fifteen minutes or till the point of a knife inserted into the dhokla comes out clean.

Cool slightly, cut into pieces and serve with chutney.

{ Diet Plans: **A B C**
Portion: **3 dhokla**

SCRAMBLED EGGS ON TOAST

INGREDIENTS

6 egg whites

1 tablespoon oil

1 loaf multigrain bread

¾ level teaspoon table salt

¼ teaspoon black pepper powder

2 tablespoons skimmed milk

Chopped spring onion greens, for garnishing

METHOD

Pour the egg whites into a deep non-stick pan. Add oil and place on heat and stir lightly. Cook, taking the pan off the heat once in a while.

Cut the loaf into slices and toast on a hot non-stick tawa till well browned on both sides.

Add salt and pepper powder to the egg whites and mix well. Add milk and stir to mix. Cook till egg whites are done, ensuring that the eggs do not get overcooked.

Serve hot on toasted slices garnished with spring onion greens.

{
Diet Plans: **A B**
Portion: **2 slices of toast with 1-2 egg whites**

STEAMED EGG KATORI

INGREDIENTS

8 eggs

¾ level teaspoon table salt

1 teaspoon crushed red chillies

1 small onion, chopped

½ medium green capsicum, seeded and thinly sliced

4 teaspoons grated processed cheese

METHOD

Take four microwave-proof bowls (katori). Break two eggs into each bowl.

Remove the yolks carefully. Sprinkle salt, half of crushed red chillies, onion, green capsicum and grated cheese equally on all.

Sprinkle remaining crushed red chillies and place the bowls in a microwave oven and cook, uncovered, on MEDIUM (60%) for two minutes.

Serve hot.

Note: *You can steam the eggs by placing the eggs in stainless steel katori and steaming them in a steamer or a pressure cooker.*

{ Diet Plans: **A B C**
Portion: **1 katori**

TOMATO EGG CUPS

INGREDIENTS

4 large firm red tomatoes	1 level teaspoon table salt
4 eggs	2 teaspoons olive oil
1 medium green capsicum, chopped	5-6 black peppercorns

METHOD

Preheat the oven to 180°C/350°F/Gas Mark 4.

Cut a thin slice off the bottom of the tomatoes so that they can stand firmly. Cut off a slice off the top and scoop out the flesh and seeds. These can be used in some other dish.

Retain the top slices.

Place a few capsicum pieces at the base of four ramekins. Sprinkle a little salt and olive oil. Place the tomatoes on top of the capsicum.

Break each egg into a bowl and carefully remove the yolk. Pour the egg white into a tomato cup.

Sprinkle salt and crushed peppercorns. Place the tops of the tomatoes at the side and cook in the preheated oven till the egg whites are cooked and well set.

Serve hot.

{ Diet Plans: **A B C**
Portion: **2 tomato egg cups**

SOUPS

BEAN AND VEGETABLE SOUP

INGREDIENTS

⅓ cup red kidney beans (rajma)

1 medium onion

4 garlic cloves

2 medium tomatoes, puréed

1 medium carrot, diced into ¼-inch cubes

10-15 French beans, cut into small pieces

3 cups Vegetable Stock (page 334)

½ cup fresh button mushrooms, diced

¾ level teaspoon table salt

½ teaspoons red chilli powder

1 medium capsicum, cut into ¼-inch pieces

1 medium cucumber, peeled, seeded and cut into ¼-inch pieces

2 tablespoons chopped fresh coriander

METHOD

Soak the kidney beans in sufficient water overnight. Pressure-cook along with the onion and garlic, until the kidney beans are soft. Drain, and reserve the cooking liquid. Mash the kidney beans lightly and set aside.

In a deep non-stick pan, mix together lightly, the mashed kidney beans and the cooking liquid. Stir in the puréed tomatoes and bring to a boil.

Add the carrot, French beans and vegetable stock, and continue to simmer on low heat, till the vegetables are cooked. Stir in the mushrooms, salt, chilli powder and capsicum. Simmer for five minutes and add the cucumber. Serve hot, garnished with chopped coriander.

Diet Plans: **A B C**
Portion: **1 bowl**
(1½ katori)

CHICKEN NOODLE SOUP

INGREDIENTS

300 grams wholewheat noodles

2 fresh red chillies, seeded and sliced

1 tablespoons soy sauce

1¼ cups bean sprouts, blanched

1 medium onion, sliced

White pepper powder to taste

2 tablespoons chopped fresh coriander

10-12 fresh basil leaves

1 lemon, cut into wedges

Broth

10 cups Chicken Stock (page 334)

500 grams boneless chicken, skinned and cubed

1 inch cinnamon

4 spring onions, sliced

1 inch ginger, crushed

1 tablespoons fish sauce

METHOD

Place the sliced red chillies in a bowl and add the soy sauce. Set aside.

For the broth, bring the chicken stock, chicken, cinnamon, spring onions, and ginger to a boil over high heat in a deep non-stick pan. Reduce heat and simmer for forty-five minutes, skimming off the scum as it rises to the surface.

Add the fish sauce and remove from heat. Remove the chicken and set aside to cool. Strain the mixture and keep the clear broth warm over very low heat. Slice the chicken into thin strips when cool.

Boil plenty of water in a deep non-stick pan; add the noodles and blanch for about five minutes or until they soften. Drain and rinse in cold water. Drain thoroughly and set aside.

Place the noodles in individual serving bowls; top with the bean sprouts, chicken strips and onion. Pour the hot broth over. Sprinkle the white pepper powder and serve piping hot, garnished with chopped coriander and basil leaves along with lemon wedges and the bowl of red chillies in soy sauce.

{
Diet Plan: **A**
Portion: **1 bowl (1½ katori)
with 5-6 pieces of chicken**
}

CHILLED CUCUMBER
AND BUTTERMILK SOUP

INGREDIENTS

2 medium cucumbers, peeled, seeded and roughly chopped

2 cups buttermilk

½ inch ginger, roughly chopped

1 green chilli, seeded and chopped

2 teaspoons lemon juice

A few sprigs of mint

½ level teaspoon table salt

½ teaspoon black pepper powder

METHOD

Place the cucumbers, ginger, green chilli and lemon juice in a blender and process till smooth.

Reserve a few sprigs of mint leaves for garnishing, and finely chop the rest.

Stir in the buttermilk and the chopped mint. Season with the salt and pepper powder.

Garnish with the reserved sprigs of mint and serve chilled.

Chef's Tip: Buttermilk should not have lumps. If you do not have buttermilk, you can mix equal quantities of yogurt and water, and whisk till smooth.

Diet Plans: **A B C**
Portion: **1 bowl**
(1½ katori)

MASOOR DAL SOUP

INGREDIENTS

⅓ cup split red lentils (masoor dal)

1 medium onion, roughly chopped

2 garlic cloves, chopped

½ teaspoon red chilli powder

2 large tomatoes, roughly chopped

2 teaspoons lemon juice

¾ level teaspoon table salt

A coriander sprig for garnishing

METHOD

Heat a non-stick kadai. Add onion and garlic and sauté for one minute.

Add washed split lentils, chilli powder, three cups water and tomatoes. Mix well and cook for a minute.

Transfer into a pressure cooker and cook till pressure is released three times (three whistles). Cool and purée in a blender.

Pour back into a non-stick pan and add lemon juice and salt. Stir well and bring to a boil.

Garnish with a coriander sprig and serve piping hot.

Recipe courtesy Dr Sarita Davare

{ Diet Plans: **A B C**
Portion: **1 bowl**
(1½ katori)

PALAK SOUP

INGREDIENTS

12 spinach leaves
1 medium onion
2 medium tomatoes
1 teaspoon cumin seeds
2 garlic cloves
½ inch ginger

1 green chilli
2 teaspoons skimmed milk
1 teaspoon garam masala powder
¾ level teaspoon table salt
Black pepper powder to taste

METHOD

Pressure-cook spinach, onion, tomatoes, cumin seeds, garlic, ginger and green chilli with one cup water till pressure is released once (one whistle). Cool and transfer into a blender jar and blend well.

Transfer into a non-stick pan and place on heat. Add milk, garam masala powder, salt and pepper powder and cook till it comes to a boil.

Serve piping hot.

Serves 2

Recipe courtesy Dr Sarita Davare

{ Diet Plans: **A B C**
Portion: **1 bowl**
(1½ katori)

RED PUMPKIN SOUP

INGREDIENTS

½ cup roughly chopped red pumpkin, boiled

2 garlic cloves, roughly chopped

1 medium onion, roughly chopped

½ small potato, boiled, peeled and roughly chopped

1 cup skimmed milk

Black pepper powder to taste

¾ level teaspoon table salt

A few chopped mint leaves

METHOD

Heat a non-stick kadai. Add garlic and onion and sauté for one minute.

Add pumpkin, potato, milk and one cup of water. Stir to mix and bring it to a boil. Remove from heat and set aside to cool.

Transfer to a blender jar and blend well.

Transfer into a non-stick pan. Add pepper powder, salt and mint leaves. Stir to mix and bring to a boil.

Serve piping hot.

Recipe courtesy Dr Sarita Davare

{ Diet Plans: **A B C**
Portion: **1 bowl**
(1½ katori)

SOUR AND SPICY CHICKEN SOUP

INGREDIENTS

2 tablespoons white vinegar

1 tablespoons green chilli sauce

½ tablespoon chilli oil

¼ cup boiled and chopped boneless chicken

1 canned bamboo shoot slice

3 tablespoons cornflour

2 teaspoons oil

1 small onion, chopped

2-3 garlic cloves, chopped

1 inch ginger, grated

2 inches celery stalk, chopped

½ medium carrot, grated

1 tablespoon chopped cabbage

2 fresh button mushrooms, chopped

½ medium green capsicum, chopped

2 French beans, chopped

½ teaspoon white pepper powder

¾ level teaspoon table salt

½ teaspoon sugar

1 tablespoons soy sauce

4-5 cups Chicken Stock (page 334)

1 spring onion green stalk, chopped

METHOD

Boil bamboo shoot in one cup of water for two to three minutes; drain, cool and chop.

Mix cornflour and half a cup water.

Heat oil in a non-stick wok; add onion, garlic and ginger and stir-fry for a few seconds.

Add bamboo shoot, celery, carrot, cabbage, mushrooms, capsicum and French beans; sauté for two to three minutes or until vegetables are almost cooked, stirring continuously. Add chicken and sauté for one minute.

Add white pepper powder, salt, sugar, soy sauce and green chilli sauce; mix well.

Stir in chicken stock and bring to a boil. Stir in cornflour mixture and continue to cook for one minute, or until the soup thickens, stirring continuously.

Stir in the vinegar, drizzle chilli oil over the soup and serve piping hot, garnished with spring onion greens.

{ Diet Plans: **A C**
Portion: **1 bowl**
(1½ katori)

MASOOR, GAJAR AUR PUMPKIN SOUP

INGREDIENTS

½ cup split red lentils (masoor dal), soaked

2 medium carrots, sliced

250 grams red pumpkin, chopped

2 teaspoons oil

3 garlic cloves

1 large onion, chopped

7-8 black peppercorns, freshly crushed

¾ cup skimmed milk

¾ level teaspoon table salt

METHOD

Heat the oil in a non-stick pan. Add the garlic, onion, carrots and pumpkin, and sauté for a few minutes. Add one and a half cups of water and the crushed peppercorns and stir.

Add the lentils and mix well. Cover and cook on medium heat till completely cooked and soft.

Cool and process in a blender to make a smooth purée. Transfer the purée to a non-stick pan and add the milk. Bring to a boil and stir in the salt. Serve hot.

{ Diet Plans: **A B C**
Portion: **1 bowl**
(1½ katori)

MIXED VEGETABLE SOUP

INGREDIENTS

1 medium carrot, finely chopped

6-8 fresh button mushrooms, finely chopped

¼ medium green cabbage, finely chopped

6-8 French beans, finely chopped

4-5 small cauliflower florets, grated

1 medium capsicum, finely chopped

1 medium onion, finely chopped

1 tablespoon oil

2 bay leaves

2 teaspoons wholewheat flour

¾ level teaspoon table salt

White pepper powder to taste

2 cups Vegetable Stock (page 334)

2 cups skimmed milk

METHOD

Heat the oil in a thick-bottomed non-stick pan; add the bay leaves and chopped onion, and sauté for two minutes over medium heat.

Add the chopped carrot, mushrooms, cabbage, French beans and grated cauliflower. Stir and cook on high heat, for three to four minutes.

Sprinkle the flour and cook over medium heat, stirring continuously, for two minutes, or till fragrant. Add the salt and white pepper powder.

Stir in the vegetable stock and bring to a boil. Add the chopped capsicum, lower the heat and simmer till the vegetables are cooked and the soup thickens.

Gradually stir in the milk and simmer for three to four minutes.

Remove the bay leaves, adjust the seasoning and serve piping hot.

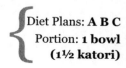

Diet Plans: **A B C**
Portion: **1 bowl**
(1½ katori)

MUSHROOM SOUP WITH LIGHT SOY

INGREDIENTS

4-5 medium fresh button mushrooms

1 teaspoon light soy sauce

3 cups Vegetable Stock (page 334)

150 grams silken bean curd (tofu), finely diced

½ level teaspoon table salt

½ teaspoon black pepper powder

4 teaspoons sliced spring onions

METHOD

Bring the vegetable stock and soy sauce to a boil in a deep non-stick pan.

Add the mushrooms and tofu, and cook on low heat for three to four minutes, but do not allow the mixture to boil.

Add the salt and pepper powder. Stir to mix well.

Ladle into individual soup bowls, sprinkle a teaspoon of chopped spring onions on each one and serve piping hot.

{ Diet Plans: **A B C**
Portion: **1 bowl**
(1½ katori)

THAI HOT AND SOUR VEGETABLE SOUP

INGREDIENTS

8-10 snow peas, sliced diagonally

8-10 fresh button mushrooms

1 inch bamboo shoot

¼ small cabbage, cut into ½-inch cubes

2 lemon grass stalks, sliced

4 Kaffir lime leaves

1 tablespoon Thai red curry paste

½ level teaspoon table salt

4 fresh red chillies, sliced diagonally

2 tablespoons lemon juice

2 fresh coriander sprigs, roughly torn

METHOD

Add the snow peas, button mushrooms, bamboo shoot, lemon grass and lime leaves in a pan along with 5 cups water.

Stir in the red curry paste. Bring the mixture to a boil; add the cabbage and salt. Stir again and add the fresh red chillies.

Remove from the heat and add the lemon juice.

Add the fresh coriander, stir and serve piping hot.

Chef's Tip: We have used tinned bamboo shoot slices, which are preserved in brine, hence they have to be boiled in water before use.

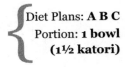
Diet Plans: **A B C**
Portion: **1 bowl**
(1½ katori)

TOMATO EGG DROP SOUP

INGREDIENTS

4 medium tomatoes, finely chopped	½ medium onion, finely chopped
2 egg whites	4 tablespoons tomato sauce
2 tablespoons cornflour	½ level teaspoon table salt
4 cups Vegetable Stock (page 334)	1 teaspoon sugar
1 tablespoons oil	½ teaspoon white pepper powder
1 inch ginger, finely chopped	2 tablespoons vinegar
2-3 garlic cloves, finely chopped	1 tablespoon chopped fresh coriander

METHOD

Place the egg whites in a bowl and whisk lightly. Set aside. Mix the cornflour in a cup of vegetable stock.

Heat the oil in a non-stick wok or pan; add ginger and garlic and stir-fry for half a minute. Add onion and continue to stir-fry for a minute longer.

Add the tomato sauce and chopped tomatoes and cook on high heat for about two to three minutes.

Stir in the remaining vegetable stock and bring it to a boil. Add the salt, sugar and white pepper powder.

Stir in the cornflour mixture and cook for a minute or until the soup thickens, stirring continuously.

Add the vinegar and pour the whisked egg whites in a steady stream, stirring gently to form egg threads. Allow the egg to coagulate and come to the top.

Serve hot, garnished with the chopped coriander.

Diet Plans: **A B C**
Portion: **1 bowl
(1½ katori)**

TOMATO SOUP

INGREDIENTS

2 tomatoes

4 teaspoons skinless split green gram (moong dal)

1 onion, chopped

4 teaspoons skimmed milk

Black pepper powder to taste

Salt to taste

METHOD

Pressure-cook tomatoes and split green gram in two cups of water till soft or pressure is released two times (two whistles).

Remove from heat and cool.

Transfer into a blender jar and blend well. Strain the mixture.

Heat a non-stick kadai. Add onion and sauté well.

Add the strained mixture and bring to a boil.

Add milk, pepper powder and salt and bring to a boil.

Serve piping hot.

Recipe courtesy Dr Sarita Davare

Diet Plans: **A B C**
Portion: **1 bowl**
(1½ katori)

TOMATO, BEET AND CARROT SOUP

INGREDIENTS

3 tomatoes, roughly chopped

1 small beetroot, peeled and roughly chopped

1 small carrot, roughly chopped

1 onion

½ teaspoon cumin seeds

1 teaspoon garam masala powder

Salt to taste

Black pepper powder to taste

METHOD

Pressure-cook tomato, beetroot, carrot, onion, cumin seeds, with one cup water till the pressure is released once (one whistle). Remove from heat and cool.

Transfer into a blender jar and blend well.

Transfer back into a deep non-stick pan and place on heat.

Add garam masala powder, salt and pepper powder and cook till it comes to a boil.

Serve piping hot.

Recipe courtesy Dr Sarita Davare

Diet Plans: **A B C**
Portion: **1 bowl
(1½ katori)**

CLEAR VEGETABLE SOUP

INGREDIENTS

6-8 fresh button mushrooms, sliced

½ medium carrot, thinly sliced

4-6 Chinese cabbage leaves, cut into 1-inch pieces

1 inch celery stalk, sliced diagonally

1 spring onion, sliced

1 red capsicum, cut into 1-inch pieces

8-10 snow peas, halved

12-16 spinach leaves, chopped

4-5 cups Vegetable Stock (page 334)

2-3 garlic cloves, crushed

¼ teaspoon peppercorns, crushed

¾ level teaspoon table salt

½ cup bean sprouts

½ teaspoon lemon juice (optional)

METHOD

Heat the vegetable stock in a non-stick pan or wok; add the crushed garlic and bring to a boil.

Add the mushrooms, carrot, Chinese cabbage, celery, spring onion, capsicum, snow peas, and spinach, and cook for two to three minutes.

Add the crushed peppercorns, salt and bean sprouts.

Stir in the lemon juice and serve piping hot.

{ Diet Plans: **A B C**
Portion: **1 bowl**
(1½ katori)

SPINACH AND TOFU SOUP

INGREDIENTS

250 grams spinach, roughly shredded

100 grams bean curd (tofu)

1 teaspoon oil

½ inch ginger, chopped

2 garlic cloves, chopped

3 cups Vegetable Stock (page 334)

1 tablespoon light soy sauce

Salt to taste

Black pepper powder to taste

METHOD

Cut the tofu into one-fourth-inch thick slices and then into one-inch triangles.

In a non-stick wok or frying pan, heat the oil on high heat and sauté chopped ginger and garlic.

Add the vegetable stock and bring to a boil.

Add the tofu and light soy sauce, and bring to a boil; lower the heat and simmer for about two minutes.

Add the shredded spinach leaves and simmer for a minute, stirring gently. Remove the scum to clarify the soup.

Add the salt and pepper powder to taste and serve hot.

{ Diet Plans: **A B C**
Portion: **1 bowl**
(1½ katori) — 4-6
pieces tofu

SALADS

CHILLED MELON BALL SALAD

INGREDIENTS

¼ watermelon
1 medium muskmelon

Dressing

1½ teaspoons lemon juice
2 tablespoons fresh orange juice

3-4 black peppercorns, crushed

1 tablespoon roughly torn fresh mint leaves

¼ level teaspoon black salt

METHOD

Using a Parisienne scoop (melon baller) scoop out small balls from the watermelon. Discard all seeds.

Cut the muskmelon in half. Scoop out small balls from the centre, leaving a thick shell. Discard all the seeds. Reserve the melon shells.

Place melon balls in a refrigerator to chill thoroughly.

Mix together all the ingredients for the dressing. Pour over the melon balls and toss gently once or twice to mix. Spoon into the melon shells and serve immediately.

Chef's Tip: The melon shells can be given a decorative zigzag edge using a small sharp knife.

{ Diet Plan: **C**
Portion: **1 bowl**
(**1½ katori**)

CITRUS CUCUMBER SALAD

INGREDIENTS

1 medium sweet lime, segments removed, halved

5-6 orange segments, halved

1 medium cucumber, peeled, cut into 1-inch strips

4 lettuce leaves

1 tablespoon lemon juice

1½ teaspoons extra-virgin olive oil

A generous pinch of red chilli flakes

4-5 fresh mint leaves

¼ level teaspoon table salt

½ medium carrot, cut into thin strips

1 small tomato, quartered and sliced

METHOD

Trim the lettuce leaves, wash under running water and soak in chilled water, to keep them fresh and crisp.

Mix the lemon juice, oil, red chilli flakes and mint leaves. Add salt and whisk well.

Drain the lettuce leaves and tear them into bite-sized pieces. Arrange a bed of lettuce leaves on a serving dish. Drizzle one-fourth of the dressing over the leaves.

Combine the sweet lime, orange segments, cucumber, carrot and tomato in a bowl.

Add the remaining dressing, toss to mix and spoon onto the bed of lettuce.

Serve immediately.

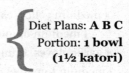

Diet Plans: **A B C**
Portion: **1 bowl**
(1½ katori)

KAKDI RAITA

INGREDIENTS

4 medium cucumbers (kakdi)

8 teaspoons skimmed milk yogurt, whisked

½ level teaspoon table salt

2 green chillies, chopped

½ level teaspoon chaat masala

METHOD

Peel and finely chop the cucumbers. Transfer into a deep bowl. Add yogurt, salt, green chillies and chaat masala. Mix well. Serve chilled.

Recipe courtesy Dr Sarita Davare

{ Diet Plans: **A B C**
Portion: **1 bowl**
(1½ katori)

LAPSI AUR SHIMLA MIRCH SALAD

INGREDIENTS

200 grams broken wheat (lapsi/dalia)

2 medium red capsicums

1 medium yellow capsicum

1 medium onion, sliced

4 garlic cloves, thinly sliced

2 medium tomatoes, seeded and diced

1 tablespoon chopped fresh coriander

½ level teaspoon table salt

½ teaspoon white pepper powder

A pinch of sugar

1 tablespoon lemon juice

4 tablespoons chopped fresh mint leaves

A few iceberg lettuce leaves

METHOD

Soak the broken wheat in water for fifteen to twenty minutes. Drain.

Pierce each capsicum with a fork. Roast the capsicums on an open flame till lightly charred. Dip in a bowl of water and peel off the charred skin. Remove the seeds and cut into small pieces. Place the soaked wheat in a salad bowl, and stir in the onion and garlic.

Stir in the chopped capsicum, tomatoes and chopped coriander; add the salt, white pepper powder and sugar and mix. Add the lemon juice and chopped mint leaves.

Tear the iceberg lettuce and add to the salad. Toss well and serve.

{ Diet Plan: **A**
Portion: **1 bowl**
(1½ katori)

RED PUMPKIN RAITA

INGREDIENTS

3 cups roughly chopped red pumpkin (kaddu), boiled and strained

8 teaspoons skimmed yogurt

1 teaspoon roasted cumin powder

½ level teaspoon table salt

2 green chillies, chopped

METHOD

Combine the pumpkin, yogurt, cumin powder, salt and green chillies in a bowl. Mix well. Serve chilled.

Recipe courtesy Dr Sarita Davare

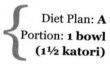

{ Diet Plans: **A B C**
Portion: **1 bowl**
(1½ katori)

SLIMMERS' SALAD
WITH NO-OIL DRESSING

INGREDIENTS

1 bunch (150 grams) iceberg lettuce

2 oranges

A few sprigs of fresh mint leaves

10-12 black peppercorns

1 teaspoon mustard seeds

4 garlic cloves

3 tablespoons lemon juice

2 teaspoons malt vinegar

1 medium onion, quartered and layers separated

¼ small watermelon, seeded and cubed

1 medium cucumber, seeded and cubed

2 medium tomatoes, seeded and cubed

1 celery stalk, chopped

1 medium green capsicum, diced

2 spring onions, cut into 1-inch pieces

½ level teaspoon table salt

METHOD

Tear the lettuce into bite-sized pieces and place in ice-cold water so that the leaves remain crisp.

Peel the oranges, separate segments and remove the seeds. Cut them in half.

Reserve some mint leaves for garnishing and chop the rest.

Crush the peppercorns, mustard seeds and garlic with lemon juice with a mortar and pestle. Mix in malt vinegar.

In a bowl, mix all the fruits, vegetables and chopped mint leaves.

Add the dressing and toss well. Add salt and toss again.

Serve the salad on a bed of crisp lettuce, garnished with reserved mint leaves.

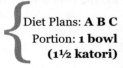
Diet Plans: **A B C**
Portion: **1 bowl**
(1½ katori)

LETTUCE AND EGG SALAD

INGREDIENTS

1 medium (150 grams) bunch lettuce

8 eggs

Dressing

½ level teaspoon table salt

½ teaspoon white pepper powder

7-8 black peppercorns, crushed

6 tablespoons vinegar

1 teaspoon mustard powder

METHOD

Cook eggs in boiling water for twelve minutes. When cool, peel and place in cold water.

Trim the lettuce and wash the leaves under running water and then place in a bowlful of chilled water.

Cut egg whites into bite-sized pieces and discard the yolk.

Drain lettuce leaves and tear roughly. Gently combine with the eggs in a bowl.

Prepare the dressing by mixing all the ingredients.

Mix the dressing gently into the lettuce and eggs. Serve chilled.

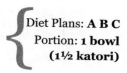

Diet Plans: **A B C**
Portion: **1 bowl
(1½ katori)**

MOTH AND MOONG SPROUT SALAD

INGREDIENTS

¾ cup sprouted brown gram (moth)

¾ cup sprouted green gram (moong)

1 medium onion, chopped

1 medium green capsicum, chopped

1 medium tomato, seeded and chopped

2 green chillies, chopped

2 teaspoons lemon juice

1½ teaspoons chaat masala

¼ level teaspoon table salt

2 tablespoons chopped fresh coriander

METHOD

Mix the sprouted brown gram and sprouted green gram, onion, capsicum, tomato and green chillies in a bowl.

Cover with cling film and refrigerate for half an hour.

For the dressing, mix together the lemon juice, chaat masala and salt.

Add the dressing to the chilled salad just before serving.

Garnish with chopped coriander and serve at once.

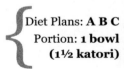

Diet Plans: **A B C**
Portion: **1 bowl**
(1½ katori)

POACHED FISH AND DILL SALAD

INGREDIENTS

250 grams fish fillets, cut into 1-inch pieces

A few fresh dill leaves (suva), finely chopped

4-5 black peppercorns

1 bay leaf

2 inches celery stalk, sliced

1 tablespoon lemon juice

½ level teaspoon table salt

¼ teaspoon crushed black peppercorns

½ tablespoon olive oil

1 medium green capsicum, cut into ½-inch pieces

METHOD

Heat sufficient water in a shallow non-stick pan; add peppercorns, bay leaf and celery and bring to a boil.

Add the fish pieces and cook uncovered for two minutes or till the fish is done. Do not overcook. Remove from the water carefully and cool.

Prepare dressing using lemon juice, salt, crushed peppercorns and olive oil. Add the dill leaves, reserving some for garnishing.

In a bowl, arrange poached fish cubes carefully. Add capsicum and sprinkle with the dressing.

Gently mix and serve chilled, garnished with remaining dill leaves.

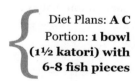

Diet Plans: **A C**
Portion: **1 bowl
(1½ katori) with
6-8 fish pieces**

SOM TAM

Thai Papaya Salad

INGREDIENTS

2 cups shredded green papaya

4 garlic cloves

1/4 level teaspoon table salt

1 fresh red chilli, roughly chopped

4 cherry tomatoes, quartered

2 tablespoons lemon juice

1 tablespoon grated jaggery

1/2 tablespoon dark soy sauce

1/2 tablespoon Tamarind Pulp (page 334)

1-2 tablespoons crushed roasted peanuts (optional)

METHOD

Place the shredded papaya in a large bowl and crush lightly with a pestle.

Crush the garlic cloves and salt with a mortar and pestle. Add the red chilli and cherry tomatoes and continue to crush lightly.

Add the crushed garlic mixture to the papaya with the lemon juice and mix well.

Crush the jaggery with the mortar and pestle and add the soy sauce and tamarind pulp.

Add the mixture to the papaya and mix.

Add the crushed roasted peanuts, if using, and toss well.

Serve immediately.

{ Diet Plans: **A B C**
Portion: **1 bowl
(1½ katori)**

SPRING ONION-TOMATO KOSHIMBIR

INGREDIENTS

4 tomatoes, chopped
8 spring onions, chopped
8 drops lemon juice

8 teaspoons skimmed milk yogurt
½ level teaspoon table salt

METHOD

Combine tomatoes, spring onions, lemon juice, yogurt and salt in a bowl. Mix well. Serve chilled.

Recipe courtesy Dr Sarita Davare

{ Diet Plans: **A B C**
Portion: **1 bowl**
(1½ katori)

VEGETABLE RAITA

INGREDIENTS

2 medium onions, chopped
2 medium carrots, chopped
1 small green capsicum, chopped
6 teaspoons grated cauliflower

8 teaspoons skimmed milk yogurt
½ level teaspoon chaat masala
½ level teaspoon table salt

METHOD

Combine onions, carrots, capsicum, cauliflower, yogurt, chaat masala and salt in a bowl. Mix well. Serve chilled.

Recipe courtesy Dr Sarita Davare

{ Diet Plans: **A B C**
Portion: **1 bowl**
(1½ katori)

TZATZIKI

INGREDIENTS

4 medium cucumbers

3 tablespoons chopped fresh mint leaves + 1 sprig to garnish

1 garlic clove, crushed

1 teaspoon caster sugar

1 cup drained skimmed milk yogurt

½ level teaspoon table salt

½ teaspoon paprika

METHOD

Peel the cucumber and cut in half lengthways.

Remove the seeds and slice as thinly as possible.

Combine the chopped mint, garlic, caster sugar and yogurt in a bowl.

Mix the cucumbers with the yogurt. Add the salt.

Serve chilled, garnished with a sprinkling of paprika and the sprig of mint.

{ Diet Plans: **A B C**
Portion: **1 bowl**
(1½ katori)

TANDOORI MURGH CHAAT

INGREDIENTS

2 (300 grams) boneless chicken breasts, skinned

1 teaspoon Kashmiri red chilli powder

1 teaspoon ginger paste

1 teaspoon garlic paste

½ cup drained skimmed milk yogurt

¾ level teaspoon table salt

1 tablespoon lemon juice

½ teaspoon garam masala powder

3 teaspoons olive oil

1 small green capsicum, seeded and cut into thin strips

½ small red capsicum, seeded and cut into thin strips

½ small yellow capsicum, seeded and cut into thin strips

1 medium onion, sliced

2 green chillies, chopped

2 tablespoons chopped fresh coriander

1 tablespoon lemon juice

1 teaspoon chaat masala

½ small green unripe mango, chopped (optional)

METHOD

Make incisions with a sharp knife on the chicken breasts and set aside.

Combine chilli powder, ginger paste, garlic paste, drained yogurt, salt, lemon juice, garam masala powder and two teaspoons oil well. Apply this mixture to the chicken pieces and leave to marinate for three to four hours, preferably in a refrigerator.

Preheat oven to 200°C/400°F/Gas Mark 6.

Thread the chicken pieces onto skewers and cook in the preheated oven or in a moderately hot tandoor for ten to twelve minutes or until almost done. Baste with the remaining oil and cook for another four minutes. When cool, shred chicken pieces and set aside.

In a large bowl combine shredded chicken, green, red and yellow capsicum strips, onion, green chillies, half the chopped coriander, lemon juice, chaat masala, mango and salt and toss to mix well.

Transfer onto a serving plate and serve, garnished with the remaining chopped coriander.

{ Diet Plans: **A C**
Portion: **1 bowl**
(1½ katori)
with 6 pieces
of chicken

SNACKS

BAKED VEGETABLE SAMOSA

INGREDIENTS

Covering

1 cup wholewheat flour (atta)

½ teaspoon carom seeds (ajwain)

¼ level teaspoon table salt

Filling

1 teaspoon cumin seeds

½ inch ginger, chopped

2 green chillies, chopped

1 cup chopped mixed vegetables (carrots, beans, cauliflower)

2 tablespoons fresh green peas

½ teaspoon red chilli powder

½ teaspoon dried mango powder (amchur)

½ teaspoon garam masala powder

½ level teaspoon table salt

2 tablespoons chopped fresh coriander

METHOD

Mix together all the ingredients for the covering. Add water and knead to a smooth, stiff dough. Rest the dough, covered with a damp cloth, for ten to fifteen minutes.

For the filling, heat a non-stick pan and lightly roast the cumin seeds. Add the ginger, green chillies, mixed vegetables and green peas and stir.

Add the chilli powder, dried mango powder, garam masala powder and salt, and stir well.

Sprinkle over a little water and cook, covered, for ten to twelve minutes. Add the chopped coriander and mix. Remove from heat and leave to cool. Divide into eight equal portions.

Preheat an oven to 200°C/400°F/Gas Mark 6.

Divide the dough into four equal portions and roll them into balls. Roll out the balls into oval puri.

Cut each one in half and moisten the edges with water. Shape each half into a cone and stuff it with the filling. Press the edges well to seal.

Arrange the samose on a baking tray and bake in the oven at 180°C/350°F/Gas Mark 4 for twenty to twenty-five minutes, turning them every five minutes. Serve hot.

> Diet Plan: **A**
> Portion: **2 samose**

HEALTHY CORNFLAKES BHEL

INGREDIENTS

2 cups cornflakes	¼ level teaspoon table salt
1 medium onion, chopped	1 teaspoon chaat masala
1 large cucumber, seeded and diced	2 tablespoons green unripe mango, chopped
1 large tomato, seeded and diced	2 tablespoons chopped fresh coriander
1 cup pomegranate kernels	2 teaspoons lemon juice

METHOD

In a large bowl, combine onion, cucumber, tomato, pomegranate kernels, salt, chaat masala and mango and toss well.

Add cornflakes, chopped coriander and lemon juice and toss again. Transfer the bhel into a serving bowl.

Serve immediately.

> Diet Plan: **A**
> Portion: **1 bowl**
> **(1½ katori)**

EGG CHAAT

INGREDIENTS

Whites of 6 hard-boiled eggs

½ medium onion, finely chopped

½ medium cucumber, peeled and sliced vertically

2 green chillies, finely chopped

15-20 fresh mint leaves, finely chopped

2 tablespoons chopped fresh coriander

¼ level teaspoon table salt

Chaat masala to taste

¾ teaspoon roasted cumin seeds, crushed

2 teaspoons Mint Chutney (page 334)

¼ medium red capsicum, cut into thin strips and halved

A few lettuce leaves

METHOD

Place the onion, cucumber, green chillies, chopped mint and coriander in a large bowl.

Cut each egg half into four slices lengthways.

Add the salt, chaat masala, crushed cumin seeds, mint chutney to the bowl and mix.

Add the eggs to the onion mixture. Reserve some of the red capsicum for garnishing and add the rest. Mix gently.

Make a bed of lettuce on a serving platter; spoon the egg chaat over the leaves. Garnish with the reserved red capsicum and serve immediately.

Diet Plans: **A B C**
Portion: **1 bowl
(1½ katori)**

GREEN CHANA CHAAT

INGREDIENTS

1½ cups dried green Bengal gram (hare chane), soaked overnight

2 medium onions, chopped

2 medium tomatoes, chopped

2-3 green chillies, chopped

2 tablespoons chopped fresh coriander

½ level teaspoon black salt

1 teaspoon roasted cumin powder

1 teaspoon chaat masala

½ teaspoon red chilli powder

2 tablespoons lemon juice

METHOD

Pressure-cook the soaked Bengal gram in three cups of water till the pressure is released two or three times (two to three whistles), or till cooked.

Transfer the gram to a non-stick kadai and cook on low heat till all the water evaporates.

Place the hot green Bengal gram in a bowl.

Add the onions, tomatoes, green chillies, chopped coriander, black salt, roasted cumin powder, chaat masala, chilli powder and lemon juice and mix well.

Serve immediately.

{ Diet Plans: **A B C**
Portion: **1 bowl**
(1½ katori)

GRILLED FISH FINGERS

INGREDIENTS

400 grams fish fillets
3 tablespoons lemon juice
4 tablespoons orange juice
½ teaspoon mustard paste
White pepper powder to taste
A pinch of dried thyme

1 tablespoon Worcestershire sauce
½ cup wholewheat flour (atta)
¼ level teaspoon table salt
1 tablespoon oil

METHOD

Clean, wash and cut fish fillets into finger-sized pieces. Pat dry with a clean and absorbent kitchen towel.

Combine lemon juice, orange juice, mustard paste, white pepper powder, dried thyme and Worcestershire sauce thoroughly.

Mix the fish fingers in the marinade. Refrigerate the marinated fish fingers for about fifteen to twenty minutes.

Season wholewheat flour with salt and white pepper powder.

Roll marinated fish fingers in seasoned flour. Shake the excess flour off.

Heat a non-stick tawa; grease lightly with a few drops of oil.

Place the fish fingers on it and cook on medium heat, turning occasionally for uniform cooking and colour.

Cook till golden brown.

Chef's Tip: Alternatively, cook fish fingers in a preheated oven or a grill.

{ Diet Plans: **A C**
Portion: **4 fish fingers**

METHI KHAKRA

INGREDIENTS

1 teaspoon dried
fenugreek leaves

2 cups wholewheat
flour (atta)

¾ level teaspoon table salt

¼ teaspoon turmeric powder

1 teaspoon cumin powder

1 teaspoon ginger-green
chilli paste

METHOD

Mix the flour and salt together in a bowl.

Add the turmeric powder, cumin powder, ginger-green chilli paste and dried fenugreek leaves, and mix well. Add enough water and knead into a medium soft dough.

Divide the dough into twelve equal balls. Roll out each ball into very thin, round chapati.

Heat a non-stick tawa; place each chapati on it and roast on low heat.

Turn and press the chapati with a wooden khakra press. Continue pressing and turning till the khakra is evenly cooked on both sides, light brown and crisp.

Take off the heat and allow to cool. Store in an airtight container, handling the khakra carefully as they are very crisp and may break.

{ Diet Plans: **A B**
(see note)
Portion: **2 khakra**

Note: *Plan B if made of sorghum flour (jowar ka atta).*

MIXED SPROUT USSAL

INGREDIENTS

1 cup mixed sprouts (such as moong, moth/matki and chana)

½ teaspoon mustard seeds

6-8 curry leaves

2 medium onions, chopped

½ teaspoon turmeric powder

½ teaspoon red chilli powder

1 teaspoon goda masala

1 teaspoon grated jaggery

½ level teaspoon table salt

Masala Paste

6-7 garlic cloves

3-4 green chillies, chopped

1 teaspoon cumin seeds, roasted

1 tablespoon grated fresh coconut

METHOD

For the masala paste, grind together the garlic, green chillies, cumin seeds and grated coconut to make a smooth paste. Set aside.

Heat a non-stick pan and add the mustard seeds. When they splutter, add the curry leaves and onions, and dry-roast, stirring continuously, till the onions turn light golden.

Stir in the paste and cook on medium heat for three to four minutes.

Add the turmeric powder, chilli powder, goda masala, jaggery and salt, and stir well.

Add the sprouts, mix well, and add just enough water to cover. Bring to a boil and cook on medium heat, stirring occasionally, until the sprouts are tender. Serve hot.

{ Diet Plans: **A B C**
Portion: **1 bowl**
(**1½ katori**)

MOONG KE CHEELE

INGREDIENTS

1 cup skinless split green gram (dhuli moong dal)

1 teaspoon cumin seeds

2 green chillies

A pinch of asafoetida (hing)

¾ level teaspoon table salt

2 medium onions, chopped

2 medium tomatoes, chopped

2 tablespoons chopped fresh coriander

½ teaspoon red chilli powder

METHOD

Soak the split green gram in two cups of water for two hours. Grind it with the cumin seeds and green chillies. Add the asafoetida and half a teaspoon salt to the batter, and mix well.

Mix together the onions, tomatoes, chopped coriander, remaining salt and chilli powder.

Heat a heavy-bottomed non-stick frying pan. Pour a ladleful of the batter onto the frying pan and spread it to make a four to five-inch pancake. Cook for half a minute.

Sprinkle two tablespoons of the topping over the cheela. Cook for fifteen seconds on medium heat.

Turn the cheela over and let it cook on the other side for two minutes on low to medium heat.

Turn it over again and cook for another minute on high heat. Make more cheela in a similar manner.

Serve hot with Mint Chutney (page 334).

{ Diet Plans: **A B C**
Portion: **2 cheele**

NUTRITIOUS SOYA KABABS

INGREDIENTS

2 cups soya chunks (nuggets), soaked and drained

1 large onion, finely chopped

2 green chillies, finely chopped

1 teaspoon coriander powder

¾ level teaspoon table salt

1 teaspoon cumin powder

½ teaspoon red chilli powder

1 inch ginger, grated

¼ teaspoon dried mango powder (amchur)

150 grams bean curd (tofu), grated

½ cup beaten brown rice, soaked and mashed

1 teaspoon garam masala powder

1 tablespoon chopped fresh coriander

4 teaspoons oil

METHOD

Blend together the soya chunks, onion, green chillies, coriander powder, salt, cumin powder, chilli powder, ginger and dried mango powder in a blender. Add the bean curd and continue to blend for two more minutes.

Transfer the mixture to a bowl; add the mashed beaten rice, garam masala powder and chopped coriander, and mix well.

Preheat the oven to 180°C/350°F/Gas Mark 4.

Divide the mixture into sixteen equal portions and shape them into flat round kababs.

Grease a baking tray with some oil. Gently place the kababs on the tray and lightly brush with oil.

Bake for fifteen minutes, turn over the kababs and bake on the other side for seven to eight minutes. Serve hot.

Diet Plans: **A B C**
Portion: **4 kababs**

PAV BHAJI

INGREDIENTS

8 wholewheat pav
1 medium potato, boiled and grated
4 medium tomatoes, finely chopped
1 medium green capsicum, chopped
¼ cup shelled green peas, boiled and mashed lightly
¼ small cauliflower, grated
1 tablespoon olive or rice bran oil

2 medium onions, finely chopped
3-4 green chillies, finely chopped
2 teaspoons ginger paste
2 teaspoons garlic paste
1½ tablespoons pav bhaji masala
¾ level teaspoon table salt
2 tablespoons finely chopped fresh coriander
2 lemons, cut into wedges

METHOD

Heat the oil in a non-stick pan; add three-fourth of the onions and sauté till light brown. Add the green chillies, ginger paste and garlic paste and stir-fry for half a minute.

Add half the tomatoes and cook over medium heat, stirring continuously, for three to four minutes, or till the oil separates.

Add the capsicum, peas, cauliflower, potatoes and one and a half cups of water. Bring to a boil, lower heat and simmer for ten minutes, mashing the vegetables with the back of the spoon a few times, till all the vegetables are completely mashed. Add the pav bhaji masala, salt and the remaining tomatoes. Cook over medium heat for two minutes, stirring continuously.

Heat a non-stick tawa. Cut the pav horizontally into two and fry, pressing down two or three times, for half a minute, or till the pav is crisp and light brown. Garnish the bhaji with the chopped coriander. Serve hot with pav, the remaining chopped onions and lemon wedges.

{ Diet Plan: **A (see notes)**
Portion: **2 pav and 1 bowl (1½ katori) bhaji**

Notes: *Plan C if the pav is omitted and only the bhaji is consumed.*
Plan B if the pav is made from sorghum flour (jowar ka atta).

SAUNFIA PANEER TIKKA

INGREDIENTS

½ teaspoon Lucknowi fennel (saunf) powder

500 grams skimmed milk cottage cheese (paneer)

2 tablespoons gram flour (besan)

¼ teaspoon turmeric powder

½ tablespoon ginger paste

½ tablespoon garlic paste

½ teaspoon white pepper powder

½ level teaspoon table salt

2 tablespoons lemon juice

½ teaspoon green cardamom powder

A few saffron threads

1 cup skimmed milk yogurt, drained

2 medium green capsicums, cut into 1½-inch squares

1½ teaspoons chaat masala

METHOD

Cut the cottage cheese into one-and-a-half-inch squares of half-inch thickness.

Heat a non-stick pan. Add the gram flour and roast on medium heat till fragrant. Remove from the heat and add the turmeric powder. Cool and transfer to a bowl.

Add the ginger paste, garlic paste, white pepper powder, salt, one tablespoon of lemon juice, cardamom powder, fennel powder, saffron and yogurt. Whisk well to make a batter.

Add the cottage cheese cubes to the batter and marinate for at least an hour. Thread the cottage cheese cubes and capsicum squares alternately onto skewers. Roast in a tandoor/charcoal grill for five minutes till the tikka are golden in colour.

Alternatively, cook the tikka in a convection oven or on a grill. Preheat the oven to 220°C/425°F/Gas Mark 7 and cook for three minutes on either side.

Remove and sprinkle with chaat masala and the remaining lemon juice. Serve with chutney of your choice.

Note: *Consume paneer only once a week.*

{ Diet Plans: **A B C**
Portion: **5 pieces paneer tikka**

STEAMED MOMOS

INGREDIENTS

½ cup refined flour (maida)

½ cup wholewheat flour (atta)

10 French beans, finely chopped

1 medium carrot, finely chopped

4-5 fresh button mushrooms, finely chopped

2 spring onions, finely chopped

¼ cup bean sprouts

1 inch ginger, finely chopped

1 green chilli, finely chopped

8-10 black peppercorns, crushed

½ tablespoon light soy sauce

1 teaspoon sesame oil

½ level teaspoon table salt

1 spring onion green stalk, chopped

METHOD

Mix together the refined flour and wholewheat flour. Add five tablespoons of water and knead into a stiff dough. Cover with a damp cloth and set aside for fifteen minutes.

In a large bowl, combine the French beans, carrot, mushrooms, spring onions, bean sprouts, ginger, green chilli, peppercorns, soy sauce, sesame oil and salt.

Divide the dough into sixteen equal portions and roll out into thin 4-inch discs.

Place a spoonful of the vegetable filling in the centre of each disc and bring the sides together in the centre, pinching firmly together to form a dumpling.

Line a steamer with a clean, damp piece of muslin and arrange the momos in it. Cover and steam for eight to ten minutes, until the momos are cooked through.

Transfer to a serving plate. Garnish with spring onion greens and serve hot.

{ Diet Plans: **A B C**
Portion: **4 momos**

THEPLA

INGREDIENTS

2 cups wholewheat flour (atta)

½ cup gram flour (besan)

1 cup chopped fresh fenugreek leaves (methi)

¼ teaspoon turmeric powder

½ teaspoon red chilli powder

1 teaspoon ginger-green chilli paste

¾ level teaspoon table salt

Yogurt, as required

8 teaspoons olive oil to shallow-fry

METHOD

Mix wholewheat flour, gram flour, fenugreek leaves, turmeric powder, chilli powder, ginger-green chilli paste, salt and mix well.

Add sufficient yogurt and knead into a semi-soft dough. Cover with a damp cloth and set aside for fifteen minutes.

Divide into sixteen equal balls and roll out into thin thepla.

Heat a non-stick tawa and roast the thepla, applying a little oil on either side, till both sides are evenly golden.

Thepla can be eaten hot or cold.

{ Diet Plans: **A B**
(see note)
Portion: **2 thepla**

Note: Plan B if using sorghum flour (jowar ka atta).

VEGETABLE CUTLETS

INGREDIENTS

2 potatoes (300 grams), boiled, peeled and mashed

3 tablespoons blanched and chopped French beans

3 tablespoons grated cauliflower

3 tablespoons chopped carrot

3 tablespoons boiled and crushed green peas

2 teaspoons ginger-garlic-green chilli paste

1 teaspoon salt

4 tablespoons wholewheat breadcrumbs

2 teaspoons oil

METHOD

Mix potato, French beans, cauliflower, carrot, green peas, ginger-garlic-green chilli paste, and salt in a bowl.

Divide the mixture into twelve equal parts and shape the mixture into twelve cutlets.

Spread the breadcrumbs on a plate and roll the cutlets in the crumbs.

Brush a non-stick pan with a little oil. Place the prepared cutlets on it. Cook on medium heat till golden brown on both sides.

Drain on absorbent paper.

Serve hot with ketchup or chutney.

{ Diet Plans: **A B**
Portion: **3 cutlets**

VEGETABLE SEEKH KABABS

INGREDIENTS

1 medium potato, boiled and mashed

1 medium carrot, grated

½ cup green peas, crushed

5-6 French beans, finely chopped

1 teaspoon ginger paste

1 teaspoon dried mango powder (amchur)

2 teaspoons chaat masala

3-4 green chillies, chopped

3 tablespoons roasted chana powder

75 grams skimmed milk cottage cheese, grated

Salt to taste

METHOD

Heat a non-stick kadai. Add ginger paste and cook for half a minute. Add mashed potato, carrot, green peas and French beans and roast till a nice aroma is given out.

Add amchur, chaat masala, green chillies, roasted chana powder and continue to cook for two to three minutes.

Add cottage cheese and mix well. Add salt and mix again.

Divide into eight equal portions. Take each portion and spread it around a skewer in a cylindrical shape.

Heat a non-stick tawa and place the skewers on it.

Cook on medium heat, rotating the skewers from time to time so that the kababs get cooked evenly on all sides, to a golden brown.

Serve hot with chutney.

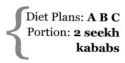

Diet Plans: **A B C**
Portion: **2 seekh kababs**

MAIN MEALS CHICKEN

QUICK JEERA CHICKEN

INGREDIENTS

800 grams chicken, cut into medium pieces

½ teaspoon cumin seeds

1 tablespoon lemon juice

1 tablespoon oil

4 green chillies, stemmed and broken into large bits

½ cup skimmed milk yogurt

1 tablespoon chopped fresh coriander

1 level teaspoon table salt

½ cup fresh mint leaves, roughly torn

METHOD

Apply lemon juice to chicken and mix well.

Heat oil in a non-stick pan and add cumin seeds. When they begin to change colour, add green chillies and sauté for a minute.

Add chicken pieces and roast for a while. Add yogurt and chopped coriander.

Cover and cook till the chicken is almost tender. Add salt and continue to cook.

Add mint leaves, stir and serve hot.

{ Diet Plans: **A C**
Portion: **1 bowl**
(1½ katori) - 6-8
pieces of chicken

CHICKEN STEW

INGREDIENTS

400 grams chicken pieces

1 medium carrot, cut into ¾-inch pieces

1 medium turnip, peeled and cut into ¾-inch pieces

6-8 French beans, cut into 1-inch pieces

3-4 medium cauliflower florets, separated into tiny florets

6-8 shallots, peeled

2 bay leaves

6-8 fresh parsley sprigs

2 inches celery stalk, lightly crushed

½ teaspoon dried thyme

6-8 black peppercorns, lightly crushed

2 tablespoons olive oil

6-8 garlic cloves, crushed

4 tablespoons wholewheat flour (atta)

1 level teaspoon table salt

METHOD

Tie bay leaf, fresh parsley, celery, dried thyme and crushed peppercorns in a small piece of muslin to make a bundle (potli).

Heat oil in a thick-bottomed non-stick pan; add crushed garlic and stir-fry for a few seconds. Gradually add the wholewheat flour, and cook, stirring continuously, over medium heat for one minute.

Add the chicken and cook on high heat for three to four minutes, stirring continuously.

Lower the heat, and add the carrot, turnip, French beans, cauliflower and whole shallots. Mix well and add four cups of water.Add the spice potli and salt to taste. Bring to a boil, stirring frequently.

Lower the heat, cover with a tight-fitting lid and simmer for ten to twelve minutes, or until the chicken is completely cooked and the stew has thickened slightly.

Remove the potli, adjust seasoning and serve steaming hot.

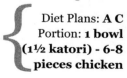

Diet Plans: **A C**
Portion: **1 bowl**
(1½ katori) - 6-8
pieces chicken

KAIRI MURGH

INGREDIENTS

800 grams chicken, cut into 1½-inch pieces

2 small green unripe mangoes

½ tablespoon ginger paste

½ tablespoon garlic paste

1 level teaspoon table salt

1 teaspoon garam masala powder

1 teaspoon green chilli paste

4 cloves

3 teaspoons oil

2 medium onions, sliced

¼ teaspoon turmeric powder

1 teaspoon red chilli powder

2 teaspoons coriander powder

METHOD

Peel and chop mangoes into small pieces. Purée half the pieces in a blender.

In a bowl, marinate the chicken with half the ginger paste, half the garlic paste, salt, half the garam masala powder, half the green chilli paste and puréed mango for about an hour.

Place a piece of coal over a gas flame and when it is red hot place it in a katori in the centre of the marinated chicken. Place a few cloves on the coal and sprinkle one-fourth teaspoon of oil on it and immediately cover it with a lid. Leave covered for a few minutes.

Heat the remaining oil in a non-stick kadai; add the sliced onions and sauté till translucent. Add the remaining ginger paste, garlic paste and green chilli paste and sauté for two minutes.

Add marinated chicken, turmeric powder, chilli powder, coriander powder, remaining garam masala powder and chopped mango. Stir so that the masala coats the chicken evenly.

Cook on high heat for a few minutes. Sprinkle a little water, and cover and cook till done. Serve hot.

Diet Plans: **A C**
Portion: **1 bowl
(1½ katori) - 6-8
pieces of chicken**

SESAME SOY CHICKEN

INGREDIENTS

4 boneless chicken breasts, skinned, cut into 1-inch pieces

2 teaspoons white sesame seeds (til), roasted

1 teaspoon sesame oil

2 tablespoons dark soy sauce

1 teaspoon oil

5-6 garlic cloves, finely chopped

1 medium spring onion, chopped

2 dried red chillies, thinly sliced

1 tablespoon cornflour

½ level teaspoon table salt

1 tablespoon white vinegar

1 stalk spring onion greens, chopped

METHOD

Heat oil in a non-stick pan; add garlic and spring onion and stir-fry briefly. Stir in soy sauce and red chillies.

Immediately add chicken pieces and continue cooking on high heat, tossing continuously. Stir in one cup of water, and bring to a boil. Cook for one minute, stirring frequently.

Stir in cornflour mixed in one-fourth cup water. Mix well. Simmer for two to three minutes. Add salt, vinegar and sesame oil. Mix well.

Serve hot, sprinkled with roasted sesame seeds and garnished with spring onion greens.

{ Diet Plans: **A C**
Portion: **1 bowl**
(1½ katori) - 6-8
pieces of chicken

SPICY SALSA CHICKEN

4 boneless chicken breasts, cut into 1½-inch cubes

Salsa

1½ cups Tomato Concassé (page 334)

1 medium onion, chopped

4 garlic cloves, chopped

2-3 jalapeño chillies, chopped

½ teaspoon dried oregano

1 level teaspoon table salt

½ teaspoon freshly crushed black peppercorns

1 tablespoon lemon juice

1 teaspoon chopped fresh parsley

6 olives, chopped

Garnish

2 tablespoons chopped fresh coriander

1 lemon, sliced

METHOD

Mix tomato concassé, onion, garlic, jalapeños, oregano, salt, peppercorns, lemon juice, parsley and olives together.

Marinate chicken cubes in this mixture for about fifteen minutes.

Heat a deep non-stick pan and cook the marinated chicken cubes till tender, stirring occasionally.

Serve hot, garnished with chopped coriander and lemon slices.

Diet Plans: **A C**
Portion: **1 bowl (1½ katori) - 6-8 pieces of chicken**

CHICKEN HALEEM

INGREDIENTS

4 boneless chicken breasts (400 grams), cut into ½-inch cubes

1 tablespoons oil

2-3 green cardamoms

5-6 cloves

1 inch stick cinnamon

2 bay leaves

1 teaspoon cumin seeds

3 medium onions, sliced

1 tablespoon ginger paste

1 tablespoon garlic paste

2 tablespoons split green gram (moong dal), soaked

2 tablespoons split Bengal gram (chana dal), soaked

3 tablespoons broken wheat (dalia), soaked

½ teaspoon turmeric powder

¾ teaspoon red chilli powder

1 level teaspoon table salt

½ teaspoon garam masala powder

2 tablespoons chopped fresh coriander

10-12 fresh mint leaves, roughly torn

1 tablespoon lemon juice

METHOD

Heat the oil in a deep non-stick pan. Add the green cardamoms, cloves, cinnamon, bay leaves, cumin seeds and onions. Sauté till light brown.

Add the ginger paste and garlic paste and continue to sauté. Add the green gram, Bengal gram and the broken wheat and stir well. Add the turmeric powder and chilli powder and mix well. Add half a cup of water and sauté for two to three minutes.

Add the chicken and salt and mix well. Add four cups water and bring the mixture to a boil. Add the garam masala powder, chopped coriander, mint leaves and lemon juice. Stir and cover the pan. Cook on medium heat till the chicken is tender.

Remove the bay leaves. Purée the chicken and gravy preferably with a hand blender and serve hot.

Diet Plans: **A C**
Portion: **1 bowl**
(1½ katori) - 6-8
pieces of chicken

CHICKEN DHANSAK

INGREDIENTS

500 grams boneless chicken cubes

¼ cup split pigeon peas (arhar dal/toovar dal), soaked

¼ cup split red lentils (masoor dal), soaked

1 tablespoon oil

2 medium onions, sliced

1 inch ginger, chopped

5-6 garlic cloves, chopped

10 black peppercorns

2 green chillies, chopped

½ teaspoon turmeric powder

1 teaspoon red chilli powder

100 grams pumpkin, chopped

3 medium brinjals, chopped

1 small potato

1 level teaspoon table salt

¼ medium bunch (5 tablespoons) fresh fenugreek leaves, chopped

¼ medium bunch (1 cup) fresh mint leaves, chopped

2 medium tomatoes, chopped

2 tablespoons dhansak masala

3 tablespoons Tamarind Pulp (page 334)

½ medium bunch fresh coriander, chopped

METHOD

Heat the oil in a deep non-stick pan; add sliced onions and sauté.

Add chopped ginger and garlic and sauté for three to four minutes. Add chicken pieces and continue to sauté for five to six minutes or till lightly browned.

Add peppercorns, green chillies, turmeric powder and chilli powder and mix.

Drain and add split pigeon peas and split red lentils and mix.

Add pumpkin, brinjals, potato, salt and three cups of water. Bring to a boil, lower heat and cook for ten minutes.

Add the fenugreek and mint leaves and mix. Add chopped tomatoes, cover pan with a lid and cook till the chicken is tender.

Remove from heat and remove the chicken pieces.

Add dhansak masala and tamarind pulp to the pan and mix. Mash the mixture with a hand blender.

Transfer into another deep non-stick pan and add chicken pieces. Adjust consistency by adding water.

Sprinkle chopped coriander and cook for a further five minutes. Serve.

{ Diet Plans: **A C**
Portion: **1 bowl**
(1½ katori) - 6-8
pieces of chicken

MAIN MEALS FISH

HOT AND FRAGRANT FISH

INGREDIENTS

2 whole (450 grams) pomfrets

4 large green chillies, seeded and chopped

10 shallots

10 garlic cloves

4 tablespoons lemon juice

1 tablespoon fish sauce

1 teaspoon soy sauce

1 teaspoon tablespoons brown sugar

½ teaspoon sugar substitute (sucralose)

8 kaffir lime leaves, finely shredded

½ level teaspoon table salt

1 tablespoon oil

2 stalks spring onion greens, chopped

Clean the fish well and make a few slits on both sides.

Wrap the chillies, shallots and garlic in aluminum foil and place under a hot grill for ten minutes.

When the package is cool enough to handle, pound the contents with a mortar and pestle, or grind coarsely in a food processor.

Add the lemon juice, fish sauce, soy sauce, brown sugar, sugar substitute, lime leaves, salt and oil; mix well.

Stuff the paste into the slits in the fish. Smear a little paste on the skin as well.

Grill the fish for about five minutes on each side, until just cooked through.

Place the grilled fish on a platter, garnish with spring onion greens and serve hot.

{ Diet Plans: **A C**
Portion: **½ pomfret**

METHIWALI MACHCHI

INGREDIENTS

1 medium bunch (250 grams) fresh fenugreek leaves, chopped

4 (800 grams) fish fillets, cut into 1-inch pieces

1 tablespoon lemon juice

½ level teaspoon table salt

2 teaspoons oil

½ teaspoon mustard seeds

1 inch ginger, chopped

3-4 garlic cloves, chopped

3-4 spring onions, chopped

3-4 green chillies, chopped

1 medium tomato, chopped

1 medium green unripe mango, chopped

Marinate the fish in lemon juice and salt.

Heat the oil in a non-stick pan; add the mustard seeds. When they begin to splutter, add the ginger and the garlic, and sauté for a minute.

Add the onions and cook on high heat till translucent. Add the chopped fenugreek and green chillies and cook for two minutes, stirring continuously.

Add the tomato and mango, and mix well. Add one cup of water and continue to cook over high heat for six to eight minutes, stirring frequently.

Add the marinated fish. Cover the pan, lower the heat and simmer for three to four minutes, or until fish is cooked.

Stir gently, adjust the seasoning and serve hot.

{ Diet Plans: **A C**
Portion: **1 bowl**
(1½ katori)
with 1 fish fillet

PUDINA KALI MIRCH RAWAS TIKKA

INGREDIENTS

20-25 fresh mint leaves, coarsely chopped

4-5 tablespoons crushed black peppercorns

500 grams Indian salmon (rawas) fillets, cut into 1½-inch cubes

2 teaspoons oil

3 tablespoons gram flour (besan)

2 tablespoons lemon juice

½ level teaspoon table salt

¼ teaspoon turmeric powder

¼ cup skimmed milk yogurt

1 teaspoon carom seeds (ajwain)

A pinch of garam masala powder

1 teaspoon garlic paste

1 teaspoon ginger paste

Brush a non-stick pan with a little oil. Add the gram flour and roast for three to four minutes. Set aside.

Add the lemon juice, salt and turmeric powder to the fish cubes and marinate for about fifteen minutes.

Mix together mint leaves, yogurt, roasted gram flour, carom seeds, garam masala powder, garlic paste and ginger paste. Add the fish cubes and mix. Set aside to marinate for half an hour.

Thread the fish cubes onto skewers and gently press them close together. This will help retain moisture.

Roll them in crushed black peppercorns and cook on the barbecue, rotating the skewers and basting with remaining oil a few times, till the fish is completely cooked.

Serve hot.

{ Diet Plans: **A C**
Portion: **6-8 cubes of fish**

STEAMED FISH

2 medium (750 grams) king fish (surmai) fillets

1 inch ginger, sliced

6-8 garlic cloves, crushed

2-3 green chillies, slit

½ level teaspoon table salt

2 tablespoons lemon juice

2-3 lemons, cut into round slices

¼ small (1 cup) bunch fresh coriander leaves

1 medium carrot, cut into thin strips

¼ medium cabbage, shredded

Cut each fillet into two pieces.

Place fish pieces in a heatproof clay or earthenware pot. Add ginger, garlic, green chillies, salt, lemon juice and mix.

Add lemon slices and half a cup of water.

Put the lid on and bring to a boil. Reduce heat and cook for about four minutes.

Chop the fresh coriander along with their stems and add them together with carrot and cabbage to the boiling fish. Cover once again and cook for one minute.

Serve hot.

Diet Plans: **A C**
Portion: **1 bowl
(1½ katori)
with 2 pieces**

MASALA POMFRET

INGREDIENTS

2 fresh pomfrets
(600 grams each)

¾ level teaspoon table salt

Crushed black
peppercorns to taste

1 teaspoon red chilli powder

½ teaspoon turmeric powder

1½ tablespoons olive oil

1 tablespoon garlic paste

1 tablespoon red chilli paste

1 tablespoon fresh
coriander leaf paste

1 tablespoon Tamarind
Pulp (page 334)

½ teaspoon clove powder

½ cup rice flour

1 tablespoon chopped
fresh coriander

1 medium onion,
cut into rings

1 lemon, cut
into wedges

Make half-inch deep slits on either side of the pomfrets. Apply salt, crushed peppercorns, chilli powder and turmeric powder and set aside to marinate for fifteen minutes.

Prepare another marinade with two teaspoons olive oil, garlic paste, red chilli paste, fresh coriander leaf paste, tamarind pulp, clove powder and a pinch of salt. Apply this on the pomfrets on all sides. Set aside for another fifteen minutes.

Heat a non-stick tawa. Roll each pomfret in rice flour and place on the tawa. Drizzle some olive oil all round the fish and cook for two to three minutes. When the underside is golden turn over, drizzle some more olive oil all round and cook till the other side is evenly golden.

Garnish with chopped coriander and serve hot with onion rings and lemon wedges.

Diet Plans: **A C**
Portion: **½ pomfret**

MAIN MEALS VEG

BAINGAN BHARTA

1 kilogram large brinjals (baingan)

1½ tablespoons olive oil/rice bran oil

1 teaspoon cumin seeds

3 medium onions, chopped

1½ inches ginger, chopped

2 green chillies, chopped

2 teaspoons red chilli powder

1 level teaspoon table salt

4 large tomatoes, chopped

2 tablespoons chopped fresh coriander

Wash and wipe the brinjals dry. Prick each one with a fork and roast over an open flame, in a tandoor or preheated oven, until the skin begins to blister and brinjals begin to shrivel. Set aside to cool. (When in a hurry, cool brinjals by dipping them in cold water). Peel off the skin and mash the flesh till smooth.

Heat the oil in a non-stick kadai; add the cumin seeds and sauté till they change colour. Add the onions and sauté till translucent. Add the ginger and green chillies and sauté for one minute.

Add the chilli powder and mashed brinjal and sauté for seven to eight minutes over moderate heat, stirring continuously. Add salt.

Stir in the tomatoes and cook on moderate heat for seven to eight minutes till the oil separates.

Garnish with chopped coriander and serve hot.

Chef's Tip: Add garlic to enhance the flavour of the bharta.

{ Diet Plans: **A B C**
Portion: **1 bowl**
(1½ katori)

EIGHT JEWEL VEGETABLES

INGREDIENTS

¼ small head broccoli, separated into florets, blanched

1 small carrot, cut into ½-inch cubes, blanched

1 small red capsicum, cut into ½-inch pieces

1 small yellow capsicum, cut into ½-inch pieces

1 small green capsicum, cut into ½-inch pieces

1 small zucchini, cut into ½-inch pieces

5-6 fresh button mushrooms, halved

½ tablespoon oil

3 spring onions, sliced

3-4 garlic cloves, chopped	1 teaspoon jaggery
1 inch ginger, chopped	2 teaspoons cornflour
2 fresh red chillies, sliced	1 teaspoon sesame oil (optional)
½ tablespoon black bean sauce	½ level teaspoon table salt (optional)
½ tablespoon dark soy sauce	

METHOD

Heat the oil in a non-stick wok until almost smoking. Add spring onions, garlic and ginger and sauté on medium heat for half a minute.

Add sliced red chillies, red, yellow and green capsicums, zucchini and mushrooms and stir-fry for two minutes.

Add broccoli, carrot, black bean sauce, soy sauce and jaggery together with two tablespoons of water; continue to stir-fry for another two minutes. Stir in the cornflour mixed with four teaspoons of water.

Add the sesame oil, if using; adjust seasoning and toss to mix well. Serve hot.

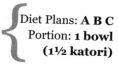

Diet Plans: **A B C**
Portion: **1 bowl**
(1½ katori)

BEAN CURD WITH FRENCH BEANS AND HOT HOISIN SAUCE

INGREDIENTS

200 grams firm bean curd (tofu)	1 inch ginger, sliced
250 grams French beans, halved	10 garlic cloves, chopped
	1 medium onion, sliced
2 tablespoons hoisin sauce	1 tablespoon red chilli sauce
½ tablespoon rice bran oil	1 tablespoon soy sauce
	½ level teaspoon table salt

Cut the bean curd into half-inch thick fingers.

Heat the oil in a non-stick wok. Add the ginger and garlic and sauté for two minutes.

Add the onion and sauté for another two minutes. Add the hoisin sauce and red chilli sauce and mix. Add the French beans and mix again. Add the bean curd, soy sauce and salt and toss gently till heated through. Serve hot.

{ Diet Plans: **A B C**
Portion: **1 bowl**
(**1½ katori**)

MAATHACHI BHAJI

INGREDIENTS

1 bunch amaranth leaves (lal maath), finely shredded	4-5 green chillies, finely chopped
1 tablespoon oil	¼ teaspoon turmeric powder
5-6 garlic cloves, finely chopped	1 tablespoon gram flour or green gram flour (moong ka atta)
1 medium onion, finely chopped	½ level teaspoon table salt

METHOD

Heat the oil in a non-stick pan; add the garlic and sauté for a few seconds. Add chopped onion and sauté till light brown.

Add the green chillies, turmeric powder and shredded amaranth leaves; sprinkle a little water and cook for a few minutes.

Mix together the gram flour and a little water and add to the pan. Add salt, and mix well. Cook for another five to six minutes, stirring frequently. Serve hot.

{ Diet Plans: **A B C**
Portion: **1 bowl**
(**1½ katori**)

MICROWAVED CELERY-CORN MEDLEY

INGREDIENTS

2 celery stalks, cut into 1-inch pieces

1 cup fresh corn kernels

4 medium tomatoes, quartered

1 medium onion, chopped

4-5 garlic cloves, crushed

1 medium green capsicum, seeded, diced

2 teaspoons oil

2 teaspoons grated jaggery

2 tablespoons tomato ketchup

½ level teaspoon table salt

5-6 black peppercorns, crushed

8-10 fresh button mushrooms, chopped

1 tablespoon chopped fresh parsley

METHOD

Put the tomatoes into a large microwave-safe bowl with the onion and garlic. Cover and cook in a microwave oven on HIGH (100%) for five minutes, till you get a thick and pulpy sauce, stirring twice in between.

Combine the celery, capsicum, corn and oil in a medium-sized microwave-safe bowl. Cover and cook in a microwave oven on HIGH (100%) for three minutes, or till the vegetables are just tender. Stir.

Mix the jaggery, tomato ketchup, salt, peppercorns, mushrooms and celery-capsicum-corn mixture into the tomato sauce.

Cover and cook on HIGH (100%) for three minutes, stirring once. Sprinkle the chopped parsley and serve hot.

{ Diet Plans: **A B C**
Portion: **1 bowl
(1½ katori)**

CHAKVATACHI BHAJI

INGREDIENTS

1 bunch wild spinach (chakvat/bathua), finely shredded

¼ cup split Bengal gram (chana dal)

½ tablespoon oil

1 teaspoon cumin seeds

¼ teaspoon asafoetida (hing)

4 green chillies, finely chopped

A pinch of sugar

¾ level teaspoon table salt

1 tablespoon gram flour (besan)

½ cup buttermilk

1 tablespoon chopped fresh coriander

METHOD

Wash and soak the split Bengal gram in half a cup of water for an hour. Drain.

Heat the oil in a non-stick pan; add the cumin seeds and sauté till they change colour.

Add the asafoetida, green chillies and wild spinach and stir-fry for a few minutes.

Add the Bengal gram, sugar and salt; mix well and cook till the gram is soft but firm.

Mix together the gram flour and buttermilk till smooth and add to the pan.

Cook for another five to six minutes, stirring frequently.

Serve hot, garnished with chopped fresh coriander.

Diet Plans: **A B C**
Portion: **1 bowl**
(1½ katori)

DHINGRI MATAR

INGREDIENTS

400 grams fresh button mushrooms (dhingri/khumb), quartered

1 cup green peas

½ tablespoon oil

½ tablespoon ginger paste

½ tablespoon garlic paste

1 medium onion, chopped

2 medium tomatoes, chopped

2 teaspoons red chilli powder

1 teaspoon turmeric powder

1 tablespoon coriander powder

1 teaspoon cumin powder

1 level teaspoon table salt

2 tablespoons skimmed milk

1 tablespoon chopped fresh coriander

METHOD

Heat oil in a non-stick kadai. Add ginger paste, garlic paste and sauté for two minutes.

Add onions and sauté for another two minutes or until the onions are golden brown.

Add the tomatoes and cook on high heat for four to five minutes or until the tomatoes are completely cooked.

Add chilli powder, turmeric powder, coriander powder, cumin powder, salt and cook for another two minutes.

Add the mushrooms and green peas and cook for five to seven minutes or until the vegetables are cooked.

Add the milk and cook for another minute. Remove from heat and serve hot, garnished with chopped coriander.

{ Diet Plans: **A B C**
Portion: **1 bowl**
(1½ katori)

LAUKI CHANA DAL

INGREDIENTS

½ small bottle gourd (doodhi/lauki), cut into 1-inch pieces

½ cup split Bengal gram (chana dal)

¾ level teaspoon table salt

½ teaspoon turmeric powder

1 tablespoon oil

½ teaspoon cumin seeds

2 green chillies, chopped

A pinch of asafoetida (hing)

½ teaspoon red chilli powder

2 teaspoons coriander powder

2 medium tomatoes, chopped

½ teaspoon garam masala powder

¼ teaspoon jaggery

2 teaspoons lemon juice

2 tablespoons chopped fresh coriander

METHOD

Soak the split Bengal gram in one and half cups of water for one hour. Drain.

Cook the split Bengal gram and bottle gourd with salt, turmeric powder and one cup of water till soft. Mash lightly with the back of ladle and mix well.

Heat the oil in a separate non-stick pan. Add the cumin seeds, green chillies and asafoetida and cook for one minute. Add the chilli powder and coriander powder and cook till fragrant.

Add the tomatoes and cook till they soften.

Add the cooked chana dal and bottle gourd and stir to mix. Add the garam masala powder and jaggery. Lower the heat and cook for two minutes.

Stir in the lemon juice, garnish with chopped coriander and serve hot.

{ Diet Plans: **A B C**
Portion: **1 bowl**
(1½ katori)

MAKAI PALAK

INGREDIENTS

½ cup fresh corn kernels, boiled

400 grams fresh spinach leaves, chopped

2 medium onions, chopped

1 inch ginger, grated

2 green chillies, chopped

A pinch of turmeric powder

½ teaspoon red chilli powder

½ teaspoon dried mango powder

¼ cup skimmed milk yogurt

¾ level teaspoon table salt

½ teaspoon garam masala powder

¼ teaspoon dried fenugreek leaves, powdered

1 inch ginger, cut into thin strips

METHOD

Blanch the spinach, drain and purée in a blender.

Heat a non-stick pan and roast the onions, ginger and green chillies for two to three minutes.

Add the turmeric powder, chilli powder and dried mango powder. Stir in one-fourth cup of water, lower heat and simmer for one to two minutes.

Add the yogurt and mix well. Add the spinach purée, boiled corn and salt, and cook for two minutes.

Add the garam masala powder, powdered dried fenugreek leaves and remove from heat.

Garnish with the ginger strips and serve hot with roti.

{ Diet Plans: **A B C**
Portion: **1 bowl**
(1½ katori)

MASALA KHUMB

INGREDIENTS

600 grams fresh button mushrooms (khumb/ dhingri), quartered

8 dried red chillies

3 teaspoons coriander seeds

1 tablespoon oil

1 teaspoon cumin seeds

2 medium onions, sliced

3 teaspoons garlic paste

4 large tomatoes, puréed

½ level teaspoon table salt

4 green chillies, chopped

2 inches ginger, chopped

2 teaspoons garam masala powder

½ cup chopped fresh coriander

METHOD

Roast and pound the dried red chillies and coriander seeds with a mortar and pestle to a coarse powder.

Heat one tablespoon of oil in a non-stick kadai.

Add the cumin seeds, onions and garlic paste and sauté for one minute over medium heat. Add the powdered spices and sauté for half a minute.

Add the tomato purée and salt and sauté till the oil separates. Add the green chillies and ginger and continue to sauté for one minute. Add the mushrooms and cook, stirring gently, for seven to eight minutes. Stir in the garam masala powder.

Garnish with fresh coriander and serve hot.

{ Diet Plans: **A B C**
Portion: **1 bowl**
(1½ katori)

MASALEDAR KADDU

INGREDIENTS

400 grams red pumpkin (kaddu)

½ teaspoon fenugreek seeds (methi dana)

A pinch of asafoetida (hing)

2 green chillies, chopped

¾ level teaspoon table salt

½ teaspoon turmeric powder

1 tablespoon coriander powder

1 inch ginger, cut into thin strips

1½ teaspoons red chilli powder

A pinch of jaggery

1½ tablespoons lemon juice

METHOD

Peel the pumpkin and cut into one-inch pieces.

Heat a non-stick pan and add the fenugreek seeds, asafoetida, green chillies and pumpkin pieces and mix.

Add the salt, turmeric powder, coriander powder, ginger and chilli powder and mix.

Add a little water, cover and cook on medium heat for ten to fifteen minutes.

Add jaggery and lemon juice.

Cover and cook on medium heat for ten minutes till the pumpkin is very soft.

Mash the pumpkin gently with the back of a spoon. Serve hot.

{ Diet Plans: **A B C**
Portion: **1 bowl**
(1½ katori)

MIDDLE-EASTERN VEGETABLE STEW

INGREDIENTS

1 small potato, cut into 1-inch pieces

2 medium carrots, cut into 1-inch pieces

1 celery stalk, cut into 1-inch pieces

1 medium green capsicum, cut into 1-inch pieces

2 medium zucchini, cut into 1-inch pieces

125 grams fresh spinach leaves, chopped

½ cup chickpeas (kabuli chana)

3 cups Vegetable Stock (page 334)

1 inch ginger, sliced

3-4 cloves

8-10 black peppercorns

1 teaspoon cumin powder

A pinch of red chilli powder

¾ level teaspoon table salt

½ teaspoon black pepper powder

A few sprigs of fresh mint leaves, chopped

METHOD

Soak the chickpeas overnight in sufficient water. Pressure-cook till tender and set aside.

Bring the vegetable stock to a boil in a non-stick pan.

Tie the ginger slices, cloves and peppercorns in a piece of muslin (potli) and add it to the boiling stock.

Add the potato, chickpeas, carrots, celery, cumin powder and chilli powder. Mix well and cook on medium heat till the mixture begins to boil.

Cover and simmer on low heat till all the vegetables are tender. Add the capsicum, zucchini and spinach, and cook for two minutes. Remove the potli and discard.

Season with salt and pepper powder, and serve hot, garnished with chopped fresh mint.

{ Diet Plans: **A B C**
Portion: **1 bowl**
(1½ katori)

RATATOUILLE

INGREDIENTS

2 medium long brinjals

2 medium zucchini

¾ level teaspoon table salt

1 tablespoon olive oil

2 medium onions, sliced into rings

4 tablespoons tomato purée

4 garlic cloves, chopped

2 medium green capsicums, cut into thin strips

3 medium tomatoes, blanched, peeled, seeded and chopped

¼ teaspoon coriander powder

A pinch of cinnamon powder

A few fresh basil leaves, shredded

White pepper powder to taste

METHOD

Halve the brinjals and zucchini lengthways. Cut them again into thick slices.

Place the brinjals in a colander and sprinkle with half the salt. Top with a heavy plate and leave to drain for one hour.

Heat the olive oil in a non-stick pan; add the onions and sauté over low heat until translucent.

Stir in the tomato purée and cook over medium heat for three to four minutes, stirring occasionally.

Rinse the salted brinjals and drain well. Add the drained brinjal and the zucchini to the pan.

Add the garlic and capsicums, and simmer for about five minutes.

Add the tomatoes, coriander powder, cinnamon powder, basil, remaining salt and white pepper powder.

Stir once or twice and cook over medium heat for about ten minutes, stirring frequently. Adjust the seasoning and serve hot.

{ Diet Plans: **A B C**
Portion: **1 bowl**
(1½ katori)

MOOLI SAAG

4 medium white radishes with leaves

½ level teaspoon table salt

1 teaspoon oil

½ teaspoon mustard seeds

½ teaspoon cumin seeds

A pinch of asafoetida (hing)

½ teaspoon turmeric powder

1 teaspoon red chilli powder

A pinch of sugar

1 teaspoon dried mango powder (amchur)

METHOD

Chop the radishes into small pieces. Shred the leaves. Sprinkle a little salt on the radishes and set aside for twenty minutes. Drain the liquid.

Heat the oil in a non-stick kadai and add the mustard seeds. When they begin to splutter add the cumin seeds and asafoetida, and sauté for half a minute.

Add the turmeric powder and chilli powder, and sauté for ten seconds.

Add the radishes with the leaves, and sauté for a minute. Sprinkle a little water to prevent scorching.

Cover and cook on medium heat for ten minutes or till the radishes are soft and tender.

Sprinkle the sugar and dried mango powder, and mix well. Adjust salt.

Serve hot.

{ Diet Plans: **A B C**
Portion: **1 bowl**
(1½ katori)

PESHAWARI CHANA

INGREDIENTS

1 cup chickpeas (Kabuli chana), soaked overnight

2 teaspoons tea leaves

¾ level teaspoon table salt

1 medium onion, finely sliced

2 tablespoons ginger-garlic-green chilli paste

1 cup tomato purée

1½ tablespoons chana masala

2 tablespoons chopped fresh coriander

4 green chillies, slit

METHOD

Tie the tea leaves in a small piece of muslin (potli).

Drain and boil chickpeas with three cups of water, tea leaves and salt in a pressure cooker till soft. Drain and remove the potli. Reserve the cooking liquid.

Heat a non-stick kadai. Add onion and roast till golden brown.

Add ginger-garlic-green chilli paste and continue to cook for two more minutes.

Add tomato purée and cook for five minutes.

Add boiled chickpeas, reserved cooking liquid and cook for five minutes.

Take the pan off the heat and sprinkle chana masala. Mix well.

Garnish with chopped coriander and green chillies and serve hot.

Diet Plans: **A B C**
Portion: **1 bowl**
(1½ katori)

SARSON DA SAAG

INGREDIENTS

4 cups fresh mustard leaves, chopped

2 cups spinach leaves (optional), chopped

1 cup chopped wild spinach (bathua) (optional)

½ tablespoon oil

2 medium onions, chopped

2 inches ginger, chopped

6-8 garlic cloves, chopped

4-6 green chillies, chopped

1 teaspoon red chilli powder

¾ level teaspoon table salt

2 tablespoons maize flour (makai ka atta)

½ teaspoon cow's milk ghee

METHOD

Heat the oil in a non-stick pan; add the onions and sauté till light brown. Add the ginger, garlic and green chillies, and sauté for a few minutes longer.

Add the chilli powder, mustard leaves, spinach leaves and wild spinach leaves, and continue to sauté for a couple of minutes.

Add the salt and cook on medium heat for ten minutes. Add the maize flour and a little water, and cook till the greens are soft.

Cool slightly and transfer the mixture to a blender and process to a slightly coarse mixture.

Transfer back into the same pan. Cook for five to ten minutes. Add the ghee.

Serve hot with makki di roti.

Diet Plans: **A B C**
Portion: **1 bowl**
(1½ katori)

SHANGHAI STIR-FRIED VEGETABLES

INGREDIENTS

¼ small cauliflower, separated into florets

6-8 tender baby corn cobs

1 medium carrot, thinly sliced lengthways

8-10 fresh button mushrooms, quartered

1 medium onion, quartered and separated

2 spring onions with greens, sliced

1 medium green capsicum, cut into 1-inch pieces

3-4 water chestnuts (singhara), sliced (optional)

½ medium Chinese cabbage, cut into 1-inch pieces

1 tablespoon cornflour

1 teaspoon oil

6-8 garlic cloves, crushed

1 tablespoon light soy sauce

4 teaspoons white pepper powder

¼ level teaspoon table salt

METHOD

Slice the cauliflower florets into two through the stem.

Slice the baby corn into three to four pieces diagonally. Mix the cornflour with half a cup of water. Set aside.

Heat the oil in a non-stick wok; add the garlic, stir and add the cauliflower, baby corn, carrot and mushrooms. Toss well and sprinkle a little water on the vegetables. Cook on high heat, stirring frequently, for two to three minutes.

Add the onion, spring onions, capsicum, water chestnuts and the Chinese cabbage. Stir-fry on high heat for two minutes. Add the soy sauce, white pepper powder and salt and toss well.

Add the cornflour mixture to the vegetables and cook for a minute longer, stirring continuously. Serve immediately.

{ Diet Plans: **A B C**
Portion: **1 bowl**
(1½ katori)

VEGETABLE SHASHLIK

INGREDIENTS

1 medium yellow zucchini

1 medium green zucchini

1 medium onion

1 medium tomato

1 medium green capsicum

½ cup fresh coriander leaves

¼ cup fresh mint leaves

½ level teaspoon table salt

1 green chilli

Juice of a lemon

1 tablespoon skimmed milk yogurt

2 teaspoons mustard sauce

1 tablespoon olive oil

METHOD

Halve the yellow zucchini lengthways and slice thickly. Cut the green zucchini into thick round slices. Quarter onion, separate layers keeping two layers per piece. Quarter tomato and halve each quarter. Cut the capsicum into one-inch pieces.

Place all the vegetables in a bowl.

For the marinade, grind together coriander leaves, mint leaves, salt, green chilli, lemon juice, yogurt, mustard sauce and half tablespoon olive oil. Add this to the vegetables and mix well.

Heat the remaining olive oil in a non-stick grill pan.

Thread the vegetables onto satay sticks in the following order: yellow zucchini, tomato, capsicum, onion, green zucchini, tomato. Place the skewers on the hot grill pan, drizzle some of the remaining marinade over them and cook, rotating the skewers to ensure even cooking.

When the vegetables are lightly charred take off the heat.

Drizzle some of the remaining marinade over them and serve immediately.

{ Diet Plans: **A B C**
Portion: **1 bowl**
(1½ katori)

RICE, ROTI, PASTA AND NOODLES

CHAR DAL NI KHICHDI

INGREDIENTS

1½ tablespoons split pigeon peas (arhar dal/ toovar dal), soaked

1½ tablespoons split field beans (vaal ki dal), soaked

1½ tablespoons skinless split green gram (dhuli moong dal), soaked

1½ tablespoons split red lentils (masoor dal), soaked

¾ cup brown rice, soaked for 20 minutes in 3 cups water

1 teaspoon rice bran oil

6- 8 cloves

2 inches cinnamon

3-4 black cardamoms

2 medium onions, sliced

A pinch of asafoetida (hing)

1 inch ginger, chopped

1 teaspoon turmeric powder

¾ level teaspoon table salt

METHOD

Heat the oil in a non-stick pan; add the cloves, cinnamon, black cardamoms and onions and sauté till onions turn brown.

Add asafoetida, ginger and turmeric powder and mix well.

Drain and add brown rice and all the dal and sauté for three to four minutes.

Add the salt and five cups of water. When the mixture comes to a boil, lower the heat, cover and cook till done.

If the khichdi looks too dry, sprinkle a little water, cover and cook for five more minutes. Serve hot.

{ Diet Plan: **A**
Portion: **1 bowl**
(1½ katori)

CLAY POT RICE

INGREDIENTS

1 cup/katori long grained brown Basmati rice

2½ cups Chicken Stock (page 334)

½ level teaspoon table salt

600 grams boneless chicken, cut into ½-inch cubes

1 chicken sausage, sliced

5 dried black mushrooms, soaked and quartered

1 inch ginger, sliced

1 spring onion, sliced

Marinade

½ tablespoon olive oil

½ tablespoon oyster sauce

2 teaspoons soy sauce

½ teaspoon sesame oil

⅓ teaspoon sugar substitute (sucralose)

½ teaspoon white pepper powder

METHOD

Put the rice with stock and salt in a clay pot, cover and cook over low heat for about twenty minutes.

Combine the ingredients for the marinade in a bowl, add the chicken cubes and mix.

Once the rice has cooked for twenty minutes, place the marinated chicken, sausage slices, mushrooms and ginger on top. Cover and cook for another ten minutes.

Sprinkle spring onion and serve hot.

{ Diet Plan: **A**
Portion: **1 bowl (1½ katori)**
with total of 3-4 pieces
chicken and 3-4 pieces
chicken sausage

GREEN FRIED RICE

INGREDIENTS

3 cups cooked brown rice

8-10 small broccoli florets, blanched

5-6 French beans, cut into diamonds and blanched

3 tablespoons green chilli sauce

1 medium green capsicum, cut into diamonds

½ cup bean sprouts

10 fresh spinach leaves, chopped

2 spring onion greens, chopped

1 tablespoon olive oil

2 medium onions, sliced

½ level teaspoon table salt

METHOD

Heat the oil in a non-stick pan. Add the onions and sauté.

Add the broccoli, French beans, and green chilli sauce. Stir and add the capsicum and salt.

Sauté for a minute and add the bean sprouts and spinach.

Add the rice and mix well and sauté till heated through.

Add the spring onion greens and mix again. Serve hot.

{ Diet Plan: **A**
Portion: **1 bowl**
(1½ katori)

ANDA PARANTHA

INGREDIENTS

5 egg whites

2 cups wholewheat flour (atta) + for dusting

1 level teaspoon table salt

2 green chillies, finely chopped

½ teaspoon carom seeds (ajwain)

3 teaspoons oil

2 tablespoons chopped fresh coriander

METHOD

Sift wholewheat flour and half teaspoon salt.

Whisk four egg whites with remaining salt.

Make a soft dough with the flour, green chillies, carom seeds, the remaining egg white and water (approximately three-fourth cup). Cover with a damp cloth and set aside for an hour.

Divide the dough into four equal parts. Roll out each one into a four-inch disc. Brush one-fourth teaspoon oil on each disc, sprinkle a little flour and fold into four.

Roll out again on floured surface into a six-inch round parantha.

Place over a heated non-stick tawa. When one side is half done, turn over and spread some egg and fresh coriander on the top. Pour one-fourth teaspoon oil around the edges and turn over.

Apply some egg and chopped coriander on the other side and drizzle one-fourth teaspoon oil and cook till both sides are evenly golden brown.

Serve hot.

{ Diet Plans: **A B**
Portion: **1-1½**
paranthe

DHANIA PUDINA PARANTHA

INGREDIENTS

¼ cup chopped fresh coriander

¼ cup chopped fresh mint leaves

2 cups wholewheat flour (atta) or sorghum flour (jowar ka atta)

½ level teaspoon table salt

½ cup skimmed milk yogurt

2 teaspoons chaat masala

METHOD

Place the flour and salt in a bowl. Add chopped coriander, mint leaves and knead into a soft dough using water. Cover and rest the dough for twenty to twenty-five minutes.

Divide the dough into eight equal portions. Shape them into balls.

Blend yogurt and chaat masala.

Roll out each ball into a medium-sized chapati. Spread a tablespoon of the yogurt mixture.

Fold the chapati like a fan and twist it back into the form of a ball. Set aside for five minutes.

Roll out each portion into a parantha of seven-inch diameter. Cook on a hot non-stick tawa till both sides are light golden brown.

Before serving, crush the parantha lightly between your palms to open out the layers.

Chef's Tip: If you are cooking the parantha in a tandoor, apply a little water on the side that you are going to stick to the tandoor wall.

Diet Plans: **A if using wholewheat flour (atta)**

B if using sorghum flour (jowar ka atta)

Portion: **1½ paranthe**

303

SPINACH AND CABBAGE PARANTHA

INGREDIENTS

1 bunch (200 grams) fresh spinach leaves, stems removed and finely chopped

1/4 medium cabbage, grated

1/2 cup green gram flour (moong ka atta)

2 cups wholewheat flour (atta)

3/4 level teaspoon table salt

1/2 teaspoon carom seeds (ajwain)

1 teaspoon red chilli powder

A pinch of asafoetida (hing)

2-3 green chillies, seeded and chopped

1/2 cup skimmed milk

4 teaspoons oil

METHOD

Mix green gram flour and wholewheat flour along with salt in a bowl. Add carom seeds, chilli powder and asafoetida.

Add spinach, cabbage, green chillies and milk. Make a medium soft dough, using water as required.

Cover the dough with a damp cloth and set aside for fifteen minutes. Divide the dough into eight equal portions and shape into balls.

Using a little flour, roll out each ball into a six-inch diameter parantha. Heat a non-stick tawa on medium heat. Place the rolled out parantha on the tawa and cook on one side for half a minute.

Flip it over and cook the other side. Brush one-fourth teaspoon oil to the first cooked side, increase heat and sprinkle a little water.

Cook the oiled side pressing it all round with a flat spoon, turn over and brush one-fourth teaspoon of oil on this side as well. Cook on medium to low heat for a minute, turning once more. Serve hot.

{ Diet Plans: **A B**
(see note)
Portion: **1½**
paranthe

Note: *Plan B if using sorghum flour (jowar ka atta)*

MIXED FLOUR-METHI CHAPATI

INGREDIENTS

½ cup wholewheat flour (atta)

½ cup barley flour (jau ka atta)

2 tablespoons green gram flour (moong ka atta) or gram flour (besan)

1 cup fresh fenugreek leaves (methi), finely chopped

¾ level teaspoon table salt

¼ small cabbage, finely grated

½ cup skimmed milk yogurt

1 teaspoon red chilli powder

METHOD

Mix the wholewheat flour, barley flour and green gram flour along with the salt.

Mix the fenugreek and cabbage into the flour mixture. Add the yogurt, chilli powder and water, a little at a time, to make a moderately soft dough. Knead well.

Cover with a damp cloth and set aside for about fifteen minutes.

Divide the dough into eight equal portions, and shape into balls.

Roll out each ball into a six-inch chapati.

Heat a non-stick tawa till moderately hot. Place the chapati on the tawa and cook on one side for about half a minute.

Flip it over and cook the other side. Lower the heat and cook on both sides till light brown.

Serve hot.

{ Diet Plans: **A B**
Portion: **1½-2 chapati**

MOOLI-BAJRA ROTI

INGREDIENTS

3 medium radishes, grated

2 cups pearl millet flour
(bajra ka atta) + for dusting

½ level teaspoon table salt

1 small onion, finely chopped

2 green chillies,
finely chopped

1 teaspoon red chilli powder

1 teaspoon ginger paste

1 teaspoon dried mango
powder (amchur)

½ teaspoon garam
masala powder

2 tablespoons chopped
fresh coriander

4 teaspoons oil

METHOD

Sprinkle half the salt on the grated radish and set aside for half an hour. Squeeze well to remove excess moisture.

In a deep bowl, mix together the radish, millet flour, onion, green chillies, chilli powder, ginger paste, dried mango powder, garam masala powder, chopped coriander and remaining salt. Add sufficient warm water and knead into a dough.

Divide the dough into eight equal portions and roll into balls. Lightly dust each ball with flour, place on a plastic sheet and pat with your fingers into a thick roti.

Heat a non-stick tawa and place the roti on it. Cook for a while, then flip the roti over and drizzle one-fourth teaspoon oil all around. Flip the roti over again and drizzle one-fourth teaspoon oil all around and cook till both sides are cooked and golden brown. Serve hot.

Chef's Tip: Do not rest the dough as the radish will release water and make the dough sticky.

{ Diet Plans: **A (see note below) B**
Portion: **2 roti**

Note: *Can be part of Diet Plan A if made with wholewheat flour (atta).*

PAUSHTIK BAJRE KI ROTI

INGREDIENTS

1 cup pearl millet flour
(bajra ka atta)

¼ cup wholewheat
flour (atta)

¾ level teaspoon table salt

1 medium onion, grated

1 medium carrot, grated

2 green chillies, chopped

1 teaspoon carom seeds
(ajwain)

METHOD

Sift the millet flour, wholewheat flour and salt together. Mix the flour mixture with the grated onion, grated carrot, chopped green chillies and carom seeds.

Add water, a little at a time, and knead the mixture into a moderately soft dough. Do not over handle the dough.

Divide the dough into eight equal portions and shape into balls. Wet your palms with water, and pat each portion of dough between your palms to make five-inch roti.

Heat a non-stick tawa and place the roti on it. Cook one side for about half a minute over medium heat; flip the roti over and cook the other side.

Lower heat and cook both sides till the bajra roti is slightly browned. Serve hot.

Chef's Tip: It takes some practice, but you must try to make the roti as thin as possible.

Diet Plan: **B**
Portion: **2 roti**

JAWARI BHAKRI

2 cups sorghum flour
(jawari atta)

½ level teaspoon
table salt

Mix together the flour and salt. Add enough water to make a soft dough; knead well.

Divide dough into eight equal portions. Shape each portion into a round ball.

Roll out each portion of dough into a thin circle.

Heat a non-stick tawa till moderately hot. Cook each bhakri on the tawa until one side is cooked.

Sprinkle a little water on the bhakri, turn over and cook the other side till done.

{ Diet Plan: **B**
Portion: **2 bhakri**

RAJGIRE KA THEPLA

INGREDIENTS

1 cup amaranth seed flour (rajgira ka atta)

1 cup wholewheat flour (atta)

½ level teaspoon table salt

1 inch ginger, grated

½ teaspoon sesame seeds

2 green chillies, finely chopped

2 tablespoons chopped fresh coriander

2 tablespoons skimmed milk yogurt

6 teaspoons oil

METHOD

Place both the flours in a bowl. Mix in the salt, ginger, sesame seeds, green chillies and chopped coriander.

Knead into a semi-soft dough with the yogurt and a little water. Cover with a damp cloth and set aside for half an hour.

Divide into twelve equal portions and shape into balls. Dust with flour and pat each ball into a thepla. If you can, roll it out with a rolling pin.

Heat a non-stick tawa. Cook each thepla on both sides using half a teaspoon of oil till light brown and crisp.

Serve hot.

{ Diet Plan: **A**
Portion: **1½**
thepla

CHICKEN TETRAZINI

250 grams boneless chicken breasts, cut into 1-inch pieces

100 grams wholewheat spaghetti

¾ level teaspoon table salt

5 teaspoons olive oil

4 medium tomatoes

5-6 basil leaves, roughly torn

1 large onion, peeled and finely chopped

5-6 garlic cloves, peeled and finely chopped

½ teaspoon black pepper powder

4-5 fresh button mushrooms, thickly sliced

1 small green capsicum, seeded and cut into 1-inch pieces

1 small red capsicum, seeded and cut into 1-inch pieces

1 small yellow capsicum, seeded and cut into 1-inch pieces

⅓ cup/katori grated cheese (optional)

METHOD

Preheat the oven to 200°C/400°F/Gas Mark 6.

Boil spaghetti in five cups of water with one-fourth teaspoon salt till just done (al dente).

Drain, refresh in cold water, add one teaspoon of olive oil and mix gently. Each strand of pasta should remain separate.

Purée tomatoes in a blender. Reserve a few basil leaves for garnishing.

Heat three teaspoons of olive oil in a non-stick pan. Add onion, garlic and basil, and sauté for two or three minutes.

Add tomato purée, remaining salt and pepper powder and cook on medium heat for five minutes.

Heat remaining olive oil in another non-stick pan; add chicken, mushrooms and capsicums. Sauté for five minutes.

Spread the tomato sauce in an ovenproof dish. Spread a layer of spaghetti over the sauce, topped with a layer of the chicken and vegetable mixture.

Sprinkle basil leaves and grated cheese over the top. Bake uncovered, for five minutes or till the cheese turns golden brown and bubbly.

Serve hot.

Note: *Cheese should be consumed only once in 10 days*

{
Diet Plan: **A**
Portion: **1 bowl**
(1½ katori)
with 5-6 pieces
of chicken

OODLES OF NOODLES

INGREDIENTS

200 grams wholewheat flour noodles

½ tablespoon oil

2 spring onions, sliced

1 small yellow capsicum, sliced

1 small red capsicum, sliced

4-5 French beans, sliced diagonally and blanched

½ cup sweet corn kernels, boiled

1 teaspoon dark soy sauce

¼ level teaspoon table salt

2 tablespoons hot and sweet tomato ketchup

½ tablespoon sweet chilli sauce

¼ cup bean sprouts

2 spring onion green stalks, sliced

METHOD

Boil the noodles in plenty of water. Drain, refresh in cold water and set aside.

Heat the oil in a non-stick pan; add the spring onions and stir-fry for fifteen seconds.

Add the capsicums and French beans and stir-fry for one or two minutes.

Add the sweet corn and soy sauce and mix well. Add the noodles and salt and toss well to mix.

Add the hot and sweet tomato ketchup and sweet chilli sauce and mix gently.

Add the bean sprouts and spring onion greens and mix well. Serve hot.

{ Diet Plan: **A**
Portion: **1 bowl**
(1½ katori)

DAL AND KADHI

DAL DHOKLI

INGREDIENTS

¾ cup split pigeon peas (arhar dal/toovar dal), boiled

¾ cup wholewheat flour (atta)

1½ teaspoons grated jaggery

6-8 curry leaves

3 kokum rinds

¾ teaspoon turmeric powder

¾ teaspoon red chilli powder

¾ level teaspoon table salt

2 teaspoons oil

1 teaspoon cow's milk ghee

½ teaspoon mustard seeds

1 dried red chilli, broken into large bits

¾ teaspoon cumin seeds

3 cloves

1 inch cinnamon

2 pinches asafoetida (hing)

1½ teaspoons lemon juice

METHOD

Put the boiled dal in a deep non-stick pan; add sufficient water so that the consistency is thin. Bring to a boil.

Add jaggery, curry leaves, kokum, half teaspoon turmeric powder, half teaspoon chilli powder and half teaspoon salt. Mix and let it simmer on medium heat, stirring occasionally.

For dhokli, mix wholewheat flour, two teaspoons oil, one-fourth teaspoon salt, remaining chilli powder and remaining turmeric powder and mix.

Add sufficient water and knead into a stiff dough.

Heat ghee in a small non-stick pan. Add mustard seeds, red chilli, cumin seeds, cloves, cinnamon and asafoetida and sauté for a few seconds. Pour the spices into the dal and stir.

Roll out portions of the dough as thinly as possible. Cut into strips and then diagonally in diamond shapes.

Slide these pieces into the boiling dal and stir just once.

Simmer till the dhokli are cooked. Drizzle lemon juice and serve hot.

Diet Plans: **A B (see note below)**
Portion: **1 bowl (1½ katori)**

Note: *Can be eaten as part of Plan B if dhokli are made from sorghum flour (jowar ka atta)*

KAIRI KI DAL

INGREDIENTS

1 small green unripe mango, peeled and chopped

¾ cup split pigeon peas (arhar dal/toovar dal), soaked

2 teaspoons oil

8 shallots, peeled

½ teaspoon mustard seeds

½ teaspoon cumin seeds

5 garlic cloves, sliced

4 dried red chillies, broken into large bits and seeded

15 curry leaves

¾ level teaspoon table salt

METHOD

Bring the split pigeon peas and three cups of water to a boil in a non-stick pan.

Heat one teaspoon oil in a non-stick pan. Add shallots and sauté till golden. Add to the boiling dal and continue to cook.

Heat the remaining oil in another non-stick pan. Add mustard seeds, cumin seeds and garlic and sauté.

Add red chillies and curry leaves and sauté for a few seconds. Add the mango cubes and continue to sauté.

Sprinkle salt and let the mango pieces soften. Add to the dal and mix well.

Cover and cook for about ten minutes on medium heat. Serve hot.

{ Diet Plans: **A B C**
Portion: **1 bowl (1½ katori)**

KEOTI DAL

INGREDIENTS

¼ cup split pigeon peas (arhar dal/toovar dal), soaked

½ cup split Bengal gram (chana dal), soaked

¼ cup split red lentils (masoor dal), soaked

¾ level teaspoon table salt

¼ teaspoon turmeric powder

½ tablespoon oil

½ teaspoon mustard seeds

½ teaspoon cumin seeds

7-8 curry leaves

4 dried red chillies, chopped, seeded

2 medium onions, chopped

5-6 garlic cloves, chopped

METHOD

Drain and put split pigeon peas, split Bengal gram, split red lentils, salt, turmeric powder and three cups water in a pressure cooker and cook under pressure till the pressure is released three times (three whistles).

Heat the oil in a small non-stick pan; add mustard seeds and let them splutter.

Add cumin seeds, curry leaves, red chillies, onions and garlic and sauté till fragrant.

Remove the lid of the cooker when the pressure has reduced completely, add the spices and mix well.

Serve hot with roti.

Diet Plans: **A B C**
Portion: **1 bowl
(1½ katori)**

PALAKWALI DAL

INGREDIENTS

15-20 fresh spinach leaves, roughly shredded

¾ cup skinless split green gram (dhuli moong dal)

½ level teaspoon table salt

1 teaspoon turmeric powder

½ tablespoon oil

A pinch of asafoetida (hing)

1 teaspoon cumin seeds

2 medium onions, chopped

2 green chillies, seeded and chopped

1 inch ginger, chopped

6-8 garlic cloves, chopped

1 teaspoon lemon juice

METHOD

Cook the split green gram with the salt, turmeric powder and five cups of water in a pressure cooker till the pressure is released twice (two whistles).

Heat the oil in a non-stick kadai; add the asafoetida and cumin seeds. When the cumin seeds begin to change colour, add the onions and green chillies.

Cook till the onions are soft and translucent.

Add the ginger and garlic, and cook for half a minute.

Add the dal, bring to a boil, and stir in the spinach and lemon juice. Simmer for two minutes and serve hot.

Diet Plans: **A B C**
Portion: **1 bowl
(1½ katori)**

BHINDA NI KADHI

INGREDIENTS

15 ladies' fingers (bhindi), cut into ½-inch pieces

1 tablespoon oil

2 cups sour skimmed milk yogurt

4 tablespoons green gram flour (moong ka atta)

½ teaspoon turmeric powder

1 teaspoon red chilli powder

½ level teaspoon table salt

¾ teaspoon mustard seeds

½ teaspoon fenugreek seeds (methi dana)

1 inch ginger, cut into thin strips

2 green chillies, chopped

¼ teaspoon asafoetida (hing)

2 tablespoons chopped fresh coriander

METHOD

Heat one tablespoon oil in a non-stick pan; add the ladies' fingers and sauté till lightly browned.

Whisk together the yogurt, green gram flour, turmeric powder, chilli powder and salt till smooth. Add four cups of water and whisk again.

Heat the remaining oil in a non-stick kadai; add the mustard seeds and fenugreek seeds.

When they begin to splutter, add the ginger, green chillies and asafoetida, and sauté for half a minute.

Add the yogurt mixture and bring to a boil. Lower heat and cook, stirring continuously, till quite thick.

Add the fried ladies' fingers and simmer for two or three minutes. Garnish with chopped coriander and serve hot.

Diet Plans: **A B C**
Portion: **1 bowl**
(1½ katori)

LEELI TUVAR NI KADHI

INGREDIENTS

½ cup fresh green pigeon peas (leeli tuvar), boiled and drained

4 tablespoons green gram flour (moong ka atta)

2 cups skimmed milk yogurt

½ tablespoon oil

1 teaspoon carom seeds (ajwain)

4 dried red button chillies

1 inch ginger, chopped

2 teaspoons garlic paste

3 green chillies, chopped

8-10 curry leaves

A pinch of asafoetida (hing)

2 medium brinjals, diced

¾ level teaspoon table salt

⅔ teaspoon sugar substitute (sucralose)

1 tablespoon chopped fresh coriander

METHOD

Whisk the green gram flour and yogurt together. Add four cups of water and whisk till smooth.

Heat the oil in a deep non-stick pan.

Add carom seeds, button chillies, ginger, garlic, green chillies and curry leaves and sauté for two minutes. Add asafoetida and brinjals and sauté for two minutes.

Add boiled pigeon peas and sauté for a minute. Add yogurt mixture and bring to a boil.

Add salt and sugar substitute and simmer, stirring gently, for ten to fifteen minutes or till thickened to the desired consistency.

Add chopped coriander and serve hot.

Diet Plans: **A B C**
Portion: **1 bowl (1½ katori)**

CHOLE DHANIA MASALA

INGREDIENTS

¾ cup chickpeas (Kabuli chana)

1 cup chopped fresh coriander

¼ cup split Bengal gram (chana dal)

½ level teaspoon table salt

½ inch cinnamon

1½ teaspoons cumin seeds

1½ teaspoons coriander seeds

1 black cardamom

4-5 cloves

2 green chillies

1 tablespoon oil

1 medium onion, sliced

1 teaspoon garlic paste

1 teaspoon ginger paste

½ tablespoon dried mango powder (amchur)

½ teaspoon garam masala powder

½ level teaspoon black salt

¼ teaspoon red chilli powder

METHOD

Soak the chickpeas and split Bengal gram separately for four to six hours.

Drain, mix, add three cups of water and salt, and pressure-cook till the pressure is released five to six times (five to six whistles).

Lightly roast and powder the cinnamon, cumin seeds, coriander seeds, black cardamom and cloves.

Grind together the fresh coriander and green chillies to a smooth paste.

Heat half tablespoon oil in a non-stick kadai; add the onion and sauté for three to four minutes till golden brown.

Add the garlic paste and ginger paste, and continue to sauté for another minute.

Add the spice powder, dried mango powder, garam masala powder, black salt and coriander paste, and sauté for two to three minutes or till the oil separates from the masala.

Add the chickpeas and split Bengal gram, and mix. Add half a cup of water if the mixture is too dry.

Let the mixture come to a boil. Lower the heat and simmer for four to five minutes.

Heat the remaining oil in a small non-stick pan; take it off the heat and add the chilli powder and immediately pour over the chickpeas.

Cover immediately and leave to stand for five minutes.

Serve hot with roti.

{ Diet Plans: **A B C**
Portion: **1 bowl**
(1½ katori)

SAMBHAR

INGREDIENTS

½ cup split pigeon peas, soaked

¼ teaspoon turmeric powder

2 teaspoons olive oil/ rice bran oil

1 lemon-sized ball tamarind

½ teaspoon mustard seeds

4 dried red chillies, halved

½ teaspoon fenugreek seeds, optional

¼ teaspoon asafoetida (hing)

4 green chillies, slit

10-12 curry leaves

2 drumsticks, cut into 2½-inch pieces

1½ teaspoons sambhar powder

Salt to taste

¼ cup chopped fresh coriander

METHOD

Pressure-cook the dal in two and half cups of water with turmeric powder and one teaspoon oil till pressure is released three times (three whistles).

Remove lid once the pressure has reduced. Mash the cooked dal lightly with a round ladle

Soak the tamarind in one cup warm water, squeeze out the pulp, strain and set aside.

Heat the remaining oil in a thick-bottomed non-stick pan. Add the mustard seeds.

When they splutter add the red chillies, fenugreek seeds and asafoetida.

Stir and add the green chillies, curry leaves and drumsticks and cook for one minute on medium heat, stirring occasionally.

Add the tamarind pulp, sambhar powder, salt and one cup water.

Reduce heat and simmer for six to eight minutes or till drumsticks are cooked.

Add the boiled dal and simmer for two to three minutes.

Sprinkle the chopped coriander and serve hot.

Chef's Tip: You can use different vegetables like white radish, ladies' fingers, pumpkin, brinjal, shallots, etc., either individually or in any combination. In south India, each family has their own style of making sambhar.

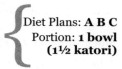
Diet Plans: **A B C**
Portion: **1 bowl**
(1½ katori)

KHATTE MOONG

INGREDIENTS

½ cup whole green gram (sabut moong)

2 tablespoons green gram flour (moong ka atta)

1½ cups skimmed milk yogurt

¼ teaspoon turmeric powder

1 teaspoon ginger paste

1 teaspoon green chilli paste

⅓ teaspoon sugar substitute (sucralose)

¾ level teaspoon table salt

½ teaspoon mustard seeds

¼ teaspoon fenugreek seeds (methi dana)

½ teaspoon cumin seeds

8-10 curry leaves

2 dried red chillies

3-4 cloves

1 inch cinnamon

A pinch of asafoetida (hing)

2 tablespoons chopped fresh coriander

METHOD

Soak green gram in two cups of water for about an hour. Drain, add two cups of water and boil till soft.

Whisk together green gram flour and yogurt to make a smooth mixture.

Add turmeric powder, ginger paste, green chilli paste, sugar substitute and three cups of water and mix well.

Transfer the mixture to a non-stick pan and cook, stirring continuously, till the kadhi is moderately thick. Add salt.

Heat a small non-stick pan and add mustard seeds, fenugreek seeds, cumin seeds, curry leaves, red chillies, cloves, cinnamon and asafoetida. Roast on medium heat till fragrant.

Add the roasted spices to the kadhi and mix well.

Stir in the boiled moong and adjust seasoning. Simmer for two minutes. Serve hot, garnished with chopped coriander.

Diet Plans: **A B C**
Portion: **1 bowl**
(1½ katori)

SWEETS AND DESSERTS

APPLE CRUMBLE

INGREDIENTS

5 medium apples

1 cup wholewheat flour (atta)

½ cup porridge oats

7 teaspoons sugar substitute (sucralose)

2 tablespoons soft low-calorie butter

½ cup skimmed milk

3 tablespoons skimmed milk powder

10-12 almonds, flaked

¼ teaspoon cinnamon powder

METHOD

Preheat the oven to 180°C/350°F/Gas Mark 4.

For the topping, place flour in a deep bowl. Add the oats, half the sugar substitute and rub in the soft butter with your fingertips so that it resembles breadcrumbs.

Add the milk and mix. Add the milk powder and almonds and mix.

Quarter the apples, core and cut into half-inch pieces. Place them in a single layer in a deep baking dish. Mix the cinnamon powder with the remaining sugar substitute and sprinkle over the apples evenly.

Spread the topping evenly over the apples and bake in the preheated oven for thirty-five to forty minutes.

Serve hot or warm.

{ Diet Plans: **A B**
Portion: **1 katori**

CHOCOLATE YOGURT

INGREDIENTS

2 tablespoons unsweetened cocoa powder

2 tablespoons fresh cream mixed with 3 tablespoons skimmed milk

2 cups drained skimmed milk yogurt

8 teaspoons sugar substitute (sucralose)

12 walnut kernels, toasted and crushed

METHOD

Whisk cocoa powder and cream together. Set aside a little of this mixture for garnishing.

Add the sugar substitute to the yogurt and mix well. Add cocoa-cream mixture and stir with a fork to get a marbled effect.

Set aside a tablespoon of walnuts and add the rest to the yogurt mixture and mix lightly.

Transfer into a serving bowl, sprinkle the remaining walnuts on top.

Drizzle the remaining cocoa-cream mixture on top and serve.

{ Diet Plans: **A B C**
Portion: **1 small katori (100 ml)**

DOODHI HALWA

INGREDIENTS

1 medium (approximately 500 grams) bottle gourd (doodhi/lauki)

3 cups skimmed milk

1½ tablespoons cow's milk ghee

4 teaspoons sugar substitute (sucralose)

½ teaspoon green cardamom powder

6-8 almonds, chopped

6-8 raisins

6-8 pistachios, chopped

METHOD

Peel the gourd, scrape out the seeds and grate it finely.

Heat the milk and reduce to around two cups.

Heat the ghee in a non-stick pan; add the grated gourd and sauté for five to seven minutes.

Add reduced milk and cook, stirring continuously, till all the liquid has evaporated. Add the sugar substitute and cardamom powder. Mix thoroughly.

Serve hot or cold, decorated with almonds, raisins and pistachios.

Diet Plans: **A B C**
Portion: ¾ **katori**
(150 ml)

FRUIT SORBET

INGREDIENTS

½ cup strawberries, cubed

1 apple, peeled and cubed

1 inch ginger, chopped

5-6 fresh mint leaves

1 tablespoon lemon juice

3 teaspoons sugar substitute (sucralose)

Crushed ice as required

METHOD

Chill the fruit in the freezer for two hours.

Put them in a blender. Add the ginger, mint leaves, lemon juice and sugar substitute and blend till pulpy.

Add crushed ice and blend some more.

Pour into small individual glasses and serve immediately.

Diet Plans: **A B C**
Portion: **1 katori (200 ml)**

MIXED FRUIT CUSTARD

INGREDIENTS

3 tablespoons vanilla custard powder

2 cups skimmed milk

2 teaspoons sugar substitute (sucralose)

4 bananas, peeled and cut into pieces

½ small musk melon, cubed

4 plums, stoned and cubed

10-12 strawberries, halved

4 tablespoons pomegranate kernels

METHOD

Whisk the custard powder and milk well and heat in a non-stick pan. Add the sugar substitute and cook till thick. Set aside to cool. Chill in the refrigerator.

Mix the bananas, musk melon and plums. Place a portion of the mixed fruit in a stemmed glass. Pour some chilled custard on top.

Arrange the strawberries decoratively along the rim of the glass. Place some pomegranate kernels in the centre.

Serve chilled.

Diet Plans: **A B C**
Portion: ¾ **katori**
(150 ml)

OAT AND NUT COOKIES

INGREDIENTS

¾ cup oats

½ cup chopped nuts
(walnuts and almonds)

¾ cup butter

¼ cup + ⅔ tablespoon sugar
substitute (sucralose)

2 egg whites

1 cup + 2 tablespoons
wholewheat flour (maida)

1½ teaspoons baking powder

METHOD

Preheat the oven to 180°C/350°F/Gas Mark 4.

Line a seven-inch by five-inch baking tray with butter paper.

Place the butter and sugar substitute (sucralose) in a glass bowl and cream them till light and fluffy. Add the egg and mix well.

Sift the flour and baking powder together. Add the oats and nuts and mix.

Add the flour mixture to the butter mixture and mix well.

Divide the dough into sixteen equal portions. Make small balls and flatten each lightly on your palm. Place them on the tray, a little distance apart from each other.

Place the tray in the preheated oven and bake for twenty to twenty-five minutes.

Remove tray from oven and place the cookies on wire rack to cool.

Serve when cool or store in an airtight container.

{ Diet Plans: **A B**
Portion: **2-3 cookies**

OATS WITH DRIED FRUIT

INGREDIENTS

85 grams porridge oats

3 cups skimmed milk

4-5 almonds, slivered

4-5 dried apricots, chopped

4-5 prunes, chopped

METHOD

Put the oats in a non-stick pan and roast for two minutes.

Add the milk and bring to the boil. Stir in the almonds and cook for about ten minutes, or until the oat mixture thickens.

Add the apricots and prunes, mix well, and serve hot.

> Diet Plan: **B**
> Portion: **1 katori**
> **(200 ml)**

PINEAPPLE YOGURT FOOL

INGREDIENTS

½ medium (300 grams) pineapple, cut into small pieces

1 inch cinnamon

¾ cup drained skimmed milk yogurt

METHOD

Place the pineapple and cinnamon in a non-stick pan and stew over low heat for thirty minutes. Set aside to cool.

Remove the pineapple pieces from the pan and mix into the yogurt. Blend together in a mixer. Chill in a refrigerator and serve chilled.

> Diet Plans: **A B C**
> Portion: **1 medium katori (150 ml)**

SAEB AUR SOOJI HALWA

INGREDIENTS

2 large apples thinly sliced +
1 large apple, puréed

½ cup semolina (rawa/sooji)

1 cup skimmed milk

5 teaspoons sugar
substitute (sucralose)

½ teaspoon green
cardamom powder

A generous pinch of saffron

5-6 pistachios, blanched
and slivered

METHOD

Dry-roast the semolina taking care that it does not change colour.

Boil the milk with one cup of water in a deep non-stick pan. Add the sugar substitute, cardamom powder and half the saffron.

Slowly add the semolina and cook, stirring continuously, till almost dry.

Add the puréed apple and cook for two to three minutes.

Divide into four portions. Pack each portion tightly into a bowl, turn it upside down onto a serving plate and unmould.

Decorate with apple slices, pistachios and remaining saffron.

{ Diet Plans: **A B**
Portion: **1 small
katori (100 ml)**

WATERMELON AND STRAWBERRY GRANITA

INGREDIENTS

1 small watermelon, cubed and frozen overnight

5-6 fresh strawberries

1 inch ginger, roughly chopped

2 teaspoons sugar substitute (sucralose)

½ teaspoon chaat masala

4 sprigs fresh mint

METHOD

Put the watermelon cubes in a blender.

Add the strawberries, ginger, sugar substitute and chaat masala and blend till smooth.

Pour into stemmed glasses, garnish with fresh mint sprigs and serve immediately.

{ Diet Plans: **A B C**
Portion: **1 katori
(200 ml)**

BASIC RECIPES

Chicken Stock

Boil 200 grams chicken bones in water for 5 minutes. Drain and discard water. Boil blanched bones with a roughly chopped carrot, celery stalk, leek, 2-3 parsley stalks, 6-7 black peppercorns, 5-6 cloves, 1 bay leaf and 10 cups of water. Remove any scum which rises to the surface and replace it with more cold water. Simmer for at least 1 hour. Remove from heat, strain, cool and store in a refrigerator till further use.

Mint Chutney

Grind 5 cups mint leaves, 3 cups coriander leaves, 10 green chillies, 3 onions and 3 inches of ginger to a fine paste, adding a little water if required. Stir in 1 tablespoon lemon juice, salt and pomegranate seed powder.

Tamarind Pulp

Soak 75 grams tamarind in 100 ml warm water for 10-15 minutes. Grind to a smooth paste and strain to remove any fibres. Store in an airtight container in the refrigerator.

Tomato Concassé

To make 1 cup of tomato concassé, blanch 5 medium tomatoes in plenty of boiling water for two minutes. Drain and refresh in cold water; peel, cut in half, remove seeds and chop roughly.

Vegetable Stock

Peel, wash and chop 1 onion, ½ medium carrot, 2-3 inch celery stalk and 2-3 garlic cloves. Place in a pan with 1 bay leaf, 5-6 peppercorns, 2-3 cloves and 5 cups of water and bring to a boil. Lower heat and simmer for 15 minutes and strain. Cool and store in a refrigerator till further use.

GLOSSARY

English	Hindi
Almonds	Badam
Aloe vera	Dritkumari
Amaranth	Rajgire
Apricots	Khubani
Asafoetida	Hing
Bamboo	Bans
Barley	Jau
Basil leaves	Tulsi ke patte
Bay leaf	Tej patta
Bean sprouts	Ankurit moong
Beaten rice	Poha
Beetroot	Chukandar
Black salt	Kala namak
Bottle gourd	Doodhi
Buttermilk	Chhaas
Capsicum	Shimla mirch
Cardamoms, black	Badi elaichi
Cardamoms, green	Chhoti elaichi
Carom seeds	Ajwain
Carrots	Gajar
Cauliflower	Phool gobhi
Celery	Ajmud
Chestnuts	Singhara
Chickpeas	Kabuli chana
Cinnamon	Dalchini

English	Hindi
Cloves	Laung
Coriander seeds	Sabut dhania
Coriander, fresh	Hara dhania
Cottage cheese	Paneer
Cucumber	Kakdi
Cumin seeds	Jeera
Curry leaves	Kadhi patta
Dill leaves	Suva bhaji
Dried mango powder	Amchur
Drum sticks	Saijan ki phalli
Egg white	Ande ki safedi
Fennel	Saunf
Fenugreek leaves, dried	Kasuri methi
Fenugreek seeds	Methidana
Field beans, split	Sem ki dal
Ginger	Adrak
Gram, Bengal, green	Hare chane
Gram, Bengal, split roasted	Daalia
Gram, black skinless split	Dhuli udad dal
Gram, brown	Matki/moth
Gram, green skinless split	Dhuli moong dal

English	Hindi	English	Hindi
Gram, green whole	Sabut moong	Pineapple	Ananas
Jaggery	Gur	Pistachios	Pista
Kidney beans, red	Rajma	Plum	Aloo bukhara
Ladies' fingers	Bhindi	Pomegranate kernels	Anar ke dane
Lemon	Nimboo	Prunes	Sukhe aloo bukhare
Lentils, red split	Masoor dal		
Maize	Makai	Pumpkin	Kaddu
Milk, skimmed	Malai rahit doodh	Radish, white	Mooli
		Raisins	Kishmish
Millet, finger	Ragi	Refined flour	Maida
Millet, pearl	Bajra	Rock salt	Sendha namak
Mint, fresh	Pudina ke taaze patte		
		Saffron	Kesar
Mushroom	Khumb/ dhingri	Semolina	Rawa/sooji
		Sesame	Til
Musk melon	Kharbooj	Sorghum	Jowar
Mustard	Sarson/rai	Spinach	Palak
Oat	Jai	Tamarind	Imli
Oatmeal	Jai ka dalia	Turmeric powder	Haldi
Olive	Jaitun		
Orange	Santara	Turnip	Shalgam
Papaya	Papita	Unripe green mango	Keri
Peanuts	Moongphali		
Peas, green	Taaze matar	Vinegar	Sirka
Peppercorns	Kali mirch	Walnut	Akhrot
Pigeon peas, fresh green	Taaze hare toovar	Watermelon	Tarbooj
		Yogurt	Dahi
Pigeon peas, split	Toovar dal/ arhar dal		